William Hazlitt, John Webster

**Dramatic Works**

Edited by William Hazlitt - Vol. 2

William Hazlitt, John Webster

**Dramatic Works**
*Edited by William Hazlitt - Vol. 2*

ISBN/EAN: 9783337303143

Printed in Europe, USA, Canada, Australia, Japan

Cover: Foto ©Andreas Hilbeck / pixelio.de

More available books at **www.hansebooks.com**

THE

# DRAMATIC WORKS OF

## JOHN WEBSTER.

EDITED BY WILLIAM HAZLITT,

OF THE MIDDLE TEMPLE.

IN FOUR VOLUMES.

VOL. II.

.

LONDON.

REEVES & TURNER,

1897.

# CONTENTS

|  | Page |
|---|---|
| THE WHITE DEVIL ; OR, VITTORIA COROMBONA | 1 |
| THE DUCHESS OF MALFI | 145 |

# THE
# WHITE DIVEL,

## OR

The Tragedy of *Paulo Giordano*
*Vrſini*, Duke of *Brachiano*,

### With

The Life and Death of Vittoria
Corombona the famous
*Venetian* Curtizan.

*Aɛted by the Queenes Majeſties Seruants.*

Written by JOHN WEBSTER.

*Non inferiora ſecutus.*

LONDON,
Printed by N. O. for *Thomas Archer*, and are to
be ſold at his Shop in Popeshead Pallace
neere the Royall Exchange 1612.

# WHITE DEVIL.

**B**ESIDES the edition of this Tragedy set forth on the title-page, there appeared, at intervals, the following :—

1. The White Devil, or, the Tragedy of Paulo Giordano Vrsini, Duke of Brachiano, With the Life, and Death of Vittoria Corombona, the famous Venetian Curtizan. As it hath bin diuers times Acted, by the Queenes Maiesties seruants, at the Phœnix, in Drury-lane. Written by John Webster. Non inferiora secutus. London, Printed by I. N. for Hugh Perry, and are to be sold at his shop at the signe of the Harrow in Brittainsburse. 1631. 4to.

2. The White Devil, or Vittoria Corombona, a Lady of Venice. A Tragedy, by John Webster. Acted formerly by her Majesties servants at the Phœnix in Drury-lane; and at this present (by his now Majesties) at the Theatre Royal. *Non inferiora secutus.* London, printed by G. Miller, for John Playfere, at the White Lion, in the Upper Walk of the New Exchange, and William Crooke at the Three Bibles on Fleet Bridge 1665.

3. Vittoria Corombona, or the White Devil. A Tragedy, by J. Webster. As it is acted at the Theatre Royal, by his Majesties servants. London, printed for

William Crooke, at the Green Dragon without Temple Bar. 1672.

Further, writes Mr. Collier: "Upon looking into the play of *Injured Love, or the Cruel Husband*, which the title page says was *written* by Mr. N. Tate, *author* of the Tragedy of King Lear, I found it to be no other than our author's play of the White Devil, with a different name. It appears never to have been acted, though designed for representation at the Theatre Royal."

The plot of the Tragedy is thus outlined by Mr. Genest in his Account of the English Stage :—" The Duke of Brachiano is married to Isabella, the sister of the Duke of Florence—but in love with Vittoria, the wife of Camillo. Flamineo assists Brachiano in debauching his sister Vittoria. He kills Camillo, and pretends that he died by accident. Brachiano causes Isabella to be poisoned. Vittoria is tried for adultery, and sentenced to be confined in a house for penitent strumpets. Brachiano gets her from thence and marries her. Flamineo kills his brother Marcello. The Duke of Florence, disguised as a Moor, poisons Brachiano. Two of his friends kill Flamineo and Vittoria."

The story of Vittoria Corombona (Accorambuoni), as Mr. Jourdain de Gatwick has obligingly pointed out to me, is related at large in Casimir Tempesti's " Storia della Vita e Geste di Sisto Quinto," and from one of the authorities cited by this author, Webster probably derived the materials of his tragedy ; though, for that matter, the dramatist lived sufficiently near the date of the events themselves to have learned the story from the 'lips of some one who had gathered it on the spot.

"Paulo Giordano Ursini, Duke di Brachiano (adds Mr. de Gatwick) married, first, Isabella, daughter of Cosmo dei Medici, and sister of Francesco dei Medici, Granduca di Toscana, who, writes Sansovino,[1]

*' mori d'assai giovana età.'*

He married, in 1585, for his second wife, Vittoria Accorambuoni, widow of Francesco Peretti, nephew of the Cardinal of Montalto, afterwards Pope Sextus V. Francesco Peretti, the Camillo of Webster's tragedy, was assassinated in 1582 ; Vittoria was confined in the Castle Sant' Angelo by Pope Gregory XIII. from January, 1583, to April, 1585, and murdered after the death of her husband the Duke. Flaminio, her brother, was also killed. The other characters in Webster's play are all mentioned in the real story : to some he gives their own names, and only slightly changes that of the others."

One memorial of the terrible Duke who partly gave title to this tragedy is still manifest : at Brachiano, in the Papal States, nineteen miles north-west from Rome, the ruins of a fine old castle, once the stronghold of the Brachiani, frown to this day, formidable in their decay.

W. H.

[1] Della Origine et de' Fatti Delle Famiglie illustri D'Italia.

# TO THE READER.

IN publishing this Tragedy, I doe but challenge to myselfe that liberty, which other men have tane before mee; not that I affect praise by it, for, nos hæc nouimus esse nihil, onely, since it was acted in so dull a time of Winter,[1] presented in so open and blacke a theater,[2] that it wanted (that which is the onely grace and setting-out of a tragedy) a full and understanding Auditory; and that since that time I haue noted, most of the people that come to that play-house resemble those ignorant asses (who, visiting stationers' shoppes, their use is not to inquire for good books, but new books), I present it to the generall view with this confidence:

Nec rhoncos metues maligniorum,
Nec scombris tunicas dabis molestas.

If it be objected this is no true drammaticke poem, I shall easily confesse it, non potes in nugas dicere plura meas, ipse ego quam dixi; willingly, and not ignorantly,

---

[1] In the subsequent editions this passage "in so dull a time of winter" is omitted.

[2] *Black a theater.*—Probably, rather, *blank*, i.e. vacant, unsupplied with articles necessary toward theatrical representation.—STEEVENS.

in this kind haue I faulted : For should a man present
to such an auditory, the most sententious tragedy that
euer was written, obseruing all the critticall lawes as
heighth of stile, and grauity of person, inrich it with
the sententious CHORUS, and, as it were lifen [1] Death,
in the passionate and waighty *Nuntius :* yet after all
this diuine rapture, O dura messorum Ilia, the breath
that comes from the uncapable multitude is able to
poison it ; and, ere it be acted, let the author resolue
to fix to every scene this of Horace :

—Hæc hodie porcis comedenda reliuques.

To those who report I was a long time in finishing
this tragedy, I confesse I do not write with a goose-quill
winged with two feathers ; and if they will neede make
it my fault, I must answere them with that of Euripides
to Alcestides, a tragick writer : Alcestides objecting
that Euripides had onely, in three daies composed three
verses, whereas himselfe had written three hundredth :
Thou telst truth (quoth he), but heres the difference,
thine shall onely bee read for three daies, whereas mine
shall continue three ages.

Detraction is the sworne friend to ignorance : for
mine owne part, I haue euer truly cherisht my good
opinion of other mens worthy labours, especially of that
full and haightned stile of maister CHAPMAN, the
labor'd and understanding workes of maister Johnson,
the no lesse worthy composures of the both worthily
excellent maister Beamont and maister Fletcher ; and
lastly (without wrong last to be named), the right happy
and copious industry of m. Shake-speare, m. Decker,

[1] Editions of 1665 and 1672 "enliven."

and m. Heywood, wishing what I write may be read
by their light: protesting that, in the strength of mine
owne judgement, I know them so worthy, that though
I rest silent in my own worke, yet to most of theirs I
dare (without flattery) fix that of Martial,

——*non norunt Hæc monumenta mori.*

In mentem Authoris.—J. WILSON.

*Scire velis quid sit mulier? quo percitet æstro?*
*En tibi, si sapias, cum rule, mille sales.*[1]

[1] These verses "In mentem Authoris," were first printed
in the edition of 1665, with the initials J. W.   In the edition
of 1672, the name, John Wilson, is printed in full.

## On Mr. Webster's most Excellent Tragedy,
### called The White Devil.

" Wee will no more admire Euripides,
    Nor praise the tragick streines of Sophocles;
    For why?  Thou in this Tragedie hast fram'd
    All real worth that can in them be nam'd.
    How lively are thy persons filled, and
    How pretty are thy lines!  Thy verses stand
    Like unto pretious Jewels set in gold,
    And grace thy fluent prose.  I once was told
    By one well skild in Arts, he thought thy play
    Was onely worthy Fame to beare away
    From all before it : Brachianos Ill,
    Murthering his Dutchesse, hath by thy rare skill
    Made him renown'd ; Flamineo such another,
    The Devils darling, Murtherer of his brother :
    His part most strange, (given him to Act by thee)
    Doth gaine him Credit, and not Calumnie :
    Vittoria Corombona, that fam'd Whore,
    Desp'rate Lodovico weltring in his gore,
    Subtile Francisco, all of them shall bee
    Gaz'd at as Comets by Posteritie :
    And thou meane time with never withering Bayes
    Shalt Crowned bee by all that read thy Layes."

      S. Sheppard.  *Epigrams Theological, Philoso-*
        *phical, & Romantick, &c.*  1651.

# THE PERSONS.[1]

MONTICELSO—a Cardinal; afterwards Pope PAUL the Fourth.

FRANCISCO DE MEDICIS, Duke of Florence; in the 5th Act disguis'd for a Moor, under the name of MULI-NASSAR.

BRACHIANO, otherwise PAULO GIORDANO URSINI, Duke of Brachiano, Husband to ISABELLA, and in love with VITTORIA.

GIOVANNI—his Son by ISABELLA.

LODOVICO, an Italian Count, but decay'd.

ANTONELLI, } his Friends, and Dependents of the Duke
GASPARO, } of Florence.

CAMILLO, Husband to VITTORIA.

HORTENSIO, one of BRACHIANO's Officers.

MARCELLO, an Attendant of the Duke of Florence, and Brother to VITTORIA.

FLAMINEO, his Brother; Secretary to BRACHIANO.

JAQUES, a Moor, Servant to GIOVANNI.

ISABELLA, Sister to FRANCISCO DE MEDICIS, and Wife to BRACHIANO.

VITTORIA COROMBONA, a Venetian Lady; first marr'd to CAMILLO, afterwards to BRACHIANO.

CORNELIA, Mother to VITTORIA, FLAMINEO, and MARCELLO.

ZANCHE, a Moor, Servant to VITTORIA.

Ambassadors, Courtiers, Lawyers, Officers, Physitians, Conjurer, Armorer, Attendants.

## THE SCENE—ITALY.

[1] From the edition of 1665.

# THE WHITE DEVIL.

## ACT I.—Scene I.[1]

*Enter Count* Lodovico, Antonelli, *and* Gasparo.

*Lodovico.*

BANISHT!

*Ant.* It griev'd me much to hear the
sentence.

*Lod.* Ha, ha, O Democritus, thy gods
That govern the whole world! courtly reward
And punishment. Fortune's a right whore:
If she give aught, she deals it in small parcels,
That she may take away all at one swoop.
This 'tis to have great enemies! God 'quite them.
Your wolf no longer seems to be a wolf
Than when she's hungry.

*Gas.* You term those enemies,
Are men of princely rank.

*Lod.* Oh, I pray for them:

[1] The division into acts is first made in the edition of 1665.
The further distribution of the acts into scenes, in the
edition of 1672.

The violent thunder is adored by those
Are pasht [1] in pieces by it.

*Ant.* Come, my Lord,
You are justly doom'd ; look but a little back
Into your former life : you have in three years
Ruin'd the noblest earldom.

*Gas.* Your followers
Have swallowed you, like mummia,[2] and being sick
With such unnatural and horrid physic,
Vomit you up i' th' kennel.

*Ant.* All the damnable degrees
Of drinking have you stagger'd through.    One citizen
Is lord of two fair manors, call'd you master,
Only for caviare.

*Gas.* Those noblemen
Which were invited to your prodigal feasts,
(Wherein the phœnix scarce could 'scape your throats)
Laugh at your misery, as fore-deeming you
An idle meteor, which drawn forth, the earth
Would be soon lost i' the air.

---

[1] *Pasht*, explains Gifford, in a note to Massinger's *Virgin Martyr*, "signifies to throw one thing with violence against another."

[2] *Mummia, mummy.* "Mummy is said to have been first brought into use in medicine by the malice of a Jewish physician, who wrote that flesh thus embalmed was good for the cure of divers diseases, and particularly bruises, to prevent the blood's gathering and coagulating. It is, however, believed that no use whatever can be derived from it in medicine, and that all which is sold in the shops, whether brought from Venice, or even directly from the Levant by Alexandria, is factitious, the work of certain Jews, who counterfeit it by drying carcases in ovens, after having prepared them with powder of myrrh, caballin aloes, Jewish pitch, and other coarse or unwholesome drugs."

CHAMBERS' *Dictionary,* voce *Mummy.*

*Ant.* Jest upon you,
And say you were begotten in an earthquake,
You have ruin'd such fair lordships.

*Lod.* Very good.
This well goes with two buckets : I must tend
The pouring out of either.

*Gas.* Worse than these.
You have acted certain murders here in Rome,
Bloody and full of horror.

*Lod.* 'Las, they were flea-bitings :
Why took they not my head then ?

*Gas.* O, my lord !
The law doth sometimes mediate, thinks it good
Not ever to steep violent sins in blood :
This gentle penance may both end your crimes,
And in the example better these bad times.

*Lod.* So, but I wonder then some great men 'scape
This banishment : there's Paulo Giordano Ursini,
The duke of Brachiano, now lives in Rome,
And by close panderism seeks to prostitute
The honour of Vittoria Corombona :
Vittoria, she that might have got my pardon
For one kiss to the duke.

*Ant.* Have a full man within you :
We see that trees bear no such pleasant fruit
There where they grew first, as where they are new set.
Perfumes, the more they are chaf'd, the more they render
Their pleasing scents : and so affliction
Expresseth[1] virtue fully, whether true,
Or else adulterate.

*Lod.* Leave your painted comforts ;

[1] Presses out.

I'll make Italian cut-works[1] in their guts
If ever I return.

   *Gas.* O sir.

   *Lod.* I am patient.
I have seen some ready to be executed,
Give pleasant looks, and money, and grow familiar
With the knave hangman ; so do I ; I thank them,
And would account them nobly merciful,
Would they dispatch me quickly.

   *Ant.* Fare you well ;
We shall find time, I doubt not, to repeal
Your banishment.

   *Lod.* I am ever bound to you.[2]
This is the world's alms ; pray make use of it.
Great men sell sheep, thus to be cut in pieces,
When first they have shorn them bare, and sold their
    fleeces.          *[Exeunt.*

## SCENE II.

*Enter* BRACHIANO, CAMILLO, FLAMINEO, VITTORIA.

*Brach.* Your best of rest.

*Vit. Cor.* Unto my lord the duke,
The best of welcome.   More lights : attend the duke.
        *[Exeunt Camillo and Vittoria.*

*Brach.* Flamineo.

*Flam.* My lord.

*Brach.* Quite lost, Flamineo.

---

[1] A kind of open work, made by cutting out or stamping. —
DYCE.

[2] In the margin of the quarto, opposite these lines, we read
*Enter Senate*, meaning the Sennet, or flourish of trumpets,
&c. preceding the Duke. —COLLIER.

*Flam.* Pursue your noble wishes, I am prompt
As lightning to your service.   O, my lord !
The fair Vittoria, my happy sister,
Shall give you present audience.  Gentlemen, [*Whisper.*
Let the caroch[1] go on, and 'tis his pleasure
You put out all your torches, and depart.

*Brach.* Are we so happy ?

*Flam.* Can it be otherwise ?
Observ'd you not to-night, my honour'd lord,
Which way soe'er you went, she threw her eyes ?
I have dealt already with her chamber-maid,
Zanche the Moor ; and she is wondrous proud
To be the agent for so high a spirit.

*Brach.* We are happy above thought, because 'bove merit.

*Flam.* 'Bove merit ! we may now talk freely : 'bove merit ! what is't you doubt ? her coyness ! that's but the superficies of lust most women have ; yet why should ladies blush to hear that nam'd, which they do not fear to handle ? O they are politic ; they know our desire is increased by the difficulty of enjoying ; whereas satiety is a blunt, weary, and drowsy passion.  If the buttery-hatch at court stood continually open, there would be nothing so passionate crowding, nor hot suit after the beverage.

*Brach.* O but her jealous husband——

*Flam.* Hang him ; a gilder that hath his brains perisht with quick-silver is not more cold in the liver.  [2]The great barriers moulted not more feathers, than he hath

---

[1] Great coach.
[2] i. e. more feathers were not dislodged from the helmets of the combatants in the great tilting match.

shed hairs, by the confession of his doctor. [1]An Irish
gamester that will play himself naked, and then wage
all downwards, at hazard, is not more venturous. So
unable to please a woman, that, like a Dutch doublet,
all his back is shrunk into his breeches.
Shroud you within this closet, good my lord;
Some trick now must be thought on to divide
My brother-in-law from his fair bed-fellow.

*Brach.* O should she fail to come.

*Flam.* I must not have your lordship thus unwisely
amorous. I myself have loved a lady, and pursued her
with a great deal of under-age protestation, whom some
three or four gallants that have enjoyed would with all
their hearts have been glad to have been rid of. 'Tis
just like a summer bird-cage in a garden: the birds that
are without despair to get in, and the birds that are
within despair and are in a consumption, for fear they
shall never get out. Away, away, my lord.

[Exit Brach.

Enter CAMILLO.

See here he comes. This fellow by his apparel
Some men would judge a politician;
But call his wit in question, you shall find it
Merely an ass [2]in's foot cloth.

---

[1] *An Irish gamester will play himself naked.*—Barnaby Rich,
in his *New Description of Ireland*, 1610, says, "there is (i. e.
in Ireland) a certaine brotherhood, called by the name of
*Karrowes*, and these be common gamsters, that do only
exercise playing at cards, and they will play away their
mantels, and their shirts from their backs, and when they
have nothing left them, they will trusse themselves in straw;
this is the life they lead, and from this they will not be re-
claimed."—REED.

[2] i. e. in his housings, his accoutrements.—STEEVENS.

How now, brother? what, travelling to bed to your
kind wife?

*Cam.* I assure you, brother, no ; my voyage lies
More northerly, in a far colder clime.
I do not well remember, I protest,
When I last lay with her.

*Flam.* Strange you should lose your count.

*Cam.* We never lay together, but ere morning
There grew a [1]flaw between us.

*Flam.* 'Thad been your part
To have made up that flaw.

*Cam.* True, but she loaths I should be seen in't.

*Flam.* Why, sir, what's the matter?

*Cam.* The duke your master visits me, I thank him ;
And I perceive how, like an earnest bowler,
He very passionately leans that way
He should have his bowl run.

*Flam.* I hope you do not think——

*Cam.* That nobleman bowl booty?[2] faith, his cheek
Hath a most excellent bias : it would fain jump with
    my mistress.

*Flam.* Will you be an ass,
Despite your Aristotle? or a cuckold,
Contrary to your Ephemerides,
Which shews you under what a smiling planet
You were first swaddled?

*Cam.* Pew wew, sir ; tell not me
Of planets nor of Ephemerides.
A man may be made cuckold in the day-time,

---

[1] *Flaw*, a violent storm of wind.  Hence, metaphorically,
a quarrel.—HALLIWELL.
[2] To *play booty*, is to allow one's adversary to win at first, in
order to induce him to continue playing afterwards.—HALLI-
WELL.

When the stars eyes are out.

*Flam.* Sir, good-bye you;
I do commit you to your pitiful pillow
Stuft with horn-shavings.

*Cam.* Brother!

*Flam:* God refuse me,[1]
Might I advise you now, your only course
Were to lock up your wife.

*Cam.* 'Twere very good.

*Flam.* Bar her the sight of revels.

*Cam.* Excellent.

*Flam.* Let her not go to church, but, like a hound
In leam,[2] at your heels.

*Cam.* 'Twere for her honour.

*Flam.* And so you should be certain in one fortnight,
Despite her chastity or innocence,
To be cuckolded, which yet is in suspense.
This is my counsel, and I ask no fee for't.

*Cam.* Come, you know not where my nightcap wrings
me.

*Flam.* Wear it a' th' old fashion; let your large ears
come through, it will be more easy. Nay, I will be bitter: bar your wife of her entertainment: women are
more willingly and more gloriously chaste, when they
are least restrained of their liberty. It seems you would
be a fine capricious, mathematically jealous coxcomb;
take the height of your own horns with a Jacob's staff,
afore they are up. These politic inclosures for paltry

---

[1] *God refuse me.—Refuse me,* or *God refuse me,* appears to
have been among the fashionable modes of swearing in our
author's time.

[2] i. e. a leash, a string. *Leam* is a correction suggested by
Steevens. The original has Leon, which has here no meaning.

mutton, make more rebellion in the flesh, than all the provocative electuaries doctors have uttered since last jubilee

*Cam.* This doth not physic me.

*Flam.* It seems you are jealous : I'll shew you the error of it by a familiar example : I have seen a pair of spectacles fashioned with such perspective art, that lay down but one twelve pence a' th' board, 'twill appear as if there were twenty ; now should you wear a pair of these spectacles, and see your wife tying her shoe, you would imagine twenty hands were taking up of your wife's clothes, and this would put you into a horrible causeless fury.

*Cam.* The fault here, sir, is not in the eyesight.

*Flam.* True, but they that have the yellow jaundice think all objects they look on to be yellow. Jealousy is worse ; her fits presenting to a man, like so many bubbles in a bason of water, twenty several crabbed faces, many times makes his own shadow his cuckold-maker.

*Enter* VITTORIA COROMBONA.

See, she comes ; what reason have you to be jealous of this creature ? what an ignorant ass or flattering knave might he be counted, that should write sonnets to her eyes, or call her brow the snow of Ida, or ivory of Corinth ; or compare her hair to the black-bird's bill, when 'tis like the black-bird's feather ? this is all. Be wise ; I will make you friends, and you shall go to bed together. Marry, look you, it shall not be your seeking. Do you stand upon that, by any means : walk you aloof ; I would not have you seen in't.—Sister [my lord attends you in the banquetting-house[1]] your husband is wondrous discontented.

[1] The passages here marked within brackets are spoken aside to Vittoria.

*Vit. Cor.* I did nothing to displease him ; I carved to him at supper-time.

*Flam.* [You need not have carved him, in faith; they say he is a capon already. I must now seemingly fall out with you]. Shall a gentleman so well descended as Camillo [a lousy slave, that within this twenty years rode with the black guard¹ in the duke's carriage, 'mongst spits and dripping-pans !]—

*Cam.* Now he begins to tickle her.

*Flam.* An excellent scholar [one that hath a head fill'd with calves brains without any sage in them,] come crouching in the hams to you for a night's lodging ? [that hath an itch in's hams, which like the fire at the glass-house hath not gone out this seven years] is he not a courtly gentleman ? [when he wears white satin, one would take him by his black muzzle to be no other creature than a maggot] you are a goodly foil, I confess, . well set out [but cover'd with a false stone—yon counterfeit diamond.]

*Cam.* He will make her know what is in me.

*Flam.* [Come, my lord attends you; thou shalt go to bed to my lord.]

*Cam.* Now he comes to't.

*Flam.* [With a relish as curious as a vintner going to taste new wine.] I am opening your case hard.

[*To Camillo.*

*Cam.* A virtuous brother, o' my credit !

*Flam.* He will give thee a ring with a philosopher's stone in it.

---

¹ i.e. as Gifford explains, in his edition of Ben Johnson, the scullions and other drudges, who rode in the vehicles which carried the furniture and kitchen utensils of great people on their journeys from one of their houses to another.

*Cam.* Indeed, I am studying alchymy.

*Flam.* Thou shalt lie in a bed stuffed with turtle's feathers; swoon in perfumed linen, like the fellow was smothered in roses. So perfect shall be thy happiness, that as men at sea think land, and trees, and ships, go that way they go; so both heaven and earth shall seem to go your voyage. Shall't meet him; 'tis fix'd, with nails of diamonds to inevitable necessity.

*Vit. Cor.* How shall's rid him hence?    [*Aside.*[1]

*Flam.* [I will put [2]brize in's tail, set him gadding presently.] I have almost wrought her to it; I find her coming: but, might I advise you now, for this night I would not lie with her, I would cross her humour to make her more humble.

*Cam.* Shall I, shall I?

*Flam.* It will shew in you a supremacy of judgment.

*Cam.* True, and a mind differing from the tumultuary opinion; for, *quæ negata, grata.*

*Flam.* Right: you are the [3]adamant shall draw her to you, though you keep distance off,

*Cam.* A philosophical reason.

*Flam.* Walk by her a' th' nobleman's fashion, and tell her you will lie with her at the end of the progress.

*Cam.* Vittoria, I cannot be induc'd, or as a man would say, incited——

*Vit. Cor.* To do what, sir?

*Cam.* To lie with you to-night. Your silkworm useth

---

[1] So marked, in old handwriting, in the copy of the edition of 1612, at the British Museum.

[2] i. e. the fly that stings cattle.

[3] i. e. the magnet.

to fast every third day, and the next following spins the better. To-morrow at night, I am for you.

*Vit. Cor.* You'll spin a fair thread, trust to't.

*Flam.* But do you hear, I shall have you steal to her chamber about midnight.

*Cam.* Do you think so? why look you, brother, because you shall not think I'll gull you, take the key, lock me into the chamber, and say you shall be sure of me.

*Flam.* In troth I will; I'll be your jailor once. But have you ne'er a false door?

*Cam.* A pox on't, as I am a Christian! tell me to-morrow how scurvily she takes my unkind parting.

*Flam.* I will.

*Cam.* Didst thou not mark the jest of the silk-worm? Good-night; in faith, I will use this trick often.

*Flam.* Do, do, do.            [*Exit Camillo.*
So, now you are safe. Ha, ha, ha, thou intanglest thyself in thine own work like a silk-worm.

*Enter* BRACHIANO.

Come, sister, darkness hides your blush. Women are like curst[1] dogs: civility[2] keeps them tied all day-time, but they are let loose at midnight; then they do most good, or most mischief. My lord, my lord!

ZANCHE *brings out a carpet, spreads it, and lays on it two fair cushions.*

*Brach.* Give credit: I could wish time would stand
        still,
And never end this interview, this hour;

---

[1] Ill-conditioned.            [2] Social order.

But all delight doth itself soons't devour.

*Enter* CORNELIA *listening.*[1]

Let me into your bosom, happy lady,
Pour out, instead of eloquence, my vows.
Loose me not, madam, for if you forego me,
I am lost eternally.
  *Vit. Cor.* Sir, in the way of pity,
I wish you heart-whole.
  *Brach.* You are a sweet physician.
  *Vit. Cor.* Sure, sir, a loathed cruelty in ladies
Is as to doctors many funerals:
It takes away their credit.
  *Brach.* Excellent creature!
We call the cruel, fair; what name for you
That are so merciful?
  *Zan.* See now they close.
  *Flam.* Most happy union.
  *Cor.* [2]My fears are fall'n upon me: oh, my heart!
My son the pander! now I find our house
Sinking to ruin. Earthquakes leave behind,
Where they have tyranniz'd, iron, or lead, or stone;
But woe to ruin, violent lust leaves none.
  *Brach.* What value is this jewel?
  *Vit. Cor.* 'Tis the ornament of a weak fortune.
  *Brach.* In sooth, I'll have it; nay, I will but change
My jewel for your jewel.
  *Flam.* Excellent;
His jewel for her jewel: well put in, duke.

---

[1] This direction as to listening is in manuscript in the copy of 1612 just mentioned.
[2] Aside.

*Brach.* Nay, let me see you wear it.

*Vit. Cor.* Here, sir?

*Brach.* Nay, lower, you shall wear my jewel lower.

*Flam.* That's better : she must wear his jewel lower.

*Vit. Cor.* To pass away the time, I'll tell your grace
A dream I had last night.

*Brach.* Most wishedly.

*Vit. Cor.* A foolish idle dream :
Methought I walk'd about the mid of night
Into a church-yard, where a goodly yew-tree
Spread her large root in ground : under that yew,
As I sate sadly leaning on a grave,
Checquer'd with cross sticks, there came stealing in
Your duchess and my husband ; one of them
A pick-ax bore, th' other a rusty spade,
And in rough terms they 'gan to challenge me
About this yew.

   *Brach.* That tree?

*Vit. Cor.* This harmless yew;
They told me my intent was to root up
That well-grown yew, and plant i' the stead of it
A wither'd black-thorn ; and for that they vow'd
To bury me alive.   My husband straight
With pick-ax 'gan to dig, and your fell duchess
With shovel, like a fury, voided out
The earth and scatter'd bones : lord, how methought
I trembled ! and yet for all this terror
I could not pray.

   *Flam.* No ; the devil was in your dream.

   *Vit. Cor.* When to my rescue there arose, methought,
A whirlwind, which let fall a massy arm

From that strong plant ;
And both were struck dead by that sacred yew,
In that base shallow grave that was their due.

   *Flam.* Excellent devil !
She hath taught him in a dream
To make away his duchess and her husband.

   *Brach.* Sweetly shall I interpret this your dream.
You are lodg'd within his arms who shall protect you
From all the fevers of a jealous husband,
From the poor envy of our phlegmatic duchess.
I'll seat you above law, and above scandal ;
Give to your thoughts the invention of delight,
And the fruition ; nor shall government
Divide me from you longer, than a care
To keep you great : you shall to me at once,
Be dukedom, health, wife, children, friends, and all.

   *Cor.*[1] Woe to light hearts, they still fore-run our fall!

   *Flam.* What fury raised thee up? away, away.

                        *Exit Zanche.*

   *Cor.* What make you here, my lord, this dead of night?
Never dropp'd mildew on a flower here till now.

   *Flam.* I pray, will you go to bed then,
Lest you be blasted?

   *Cor.* O that this fair garden
Had with all poison'd herbs of Thessaly
At first been planted ; made a nursery
For witchcraft, rather than a burial plot
For both your honours !

   *Vit. Cor.* Dearest mother, hear me.

   *Cor.* O, thou dost make my brow bend to the earth,

              [1] (advancing.)

Sooner than nature ! See the curse of children !
In life they keep us frequently in tears ;
And in the cold grave leave us in pale fears.

*Brach.* Come, come, I will not hear you.

*Vit. Cor.* Dear, my lord.

*Cor.* Where is thy duchess now, adulterous duke ?
Thou little dream'st this night she's come to Rome.

*Flam.* How ! come to Rome !

*Vit. Cor.* The duchess !

*Brach.* She had been better—

*Cor.* The lives of princes should like dials move,
Whose regular example is so strong,
They make the times by them go right, or wrong.

*Flam.* So, have you done ?

*Cor.* Unfortunate Camillo !

*Vit. Cor.* I do protest, if any chaste denial,
If any thing but blood could have allay'd
His long suit to me—

*Cor.* I will join with thee,
To the most woeful end e'er mother kneel'd :
If thou dishonour thus thy husband's bed,
Be thy life short as are the funeral tears
In great men's—

*Brach.* Fie, fie, the woman's mad.

*Cor.* Be thy act, Judas-like ; betray in kissing :
May'st thou be envied during his short breath,
And pitied like a wretch after his death !

*Vit. Cor.* O me accurs'd !                    [*Exit.*

*Flam.* Are you out of your wits ? my lord,
I'll fetch her back again.

*Brach.* No, I'll to bed :

Send doctor Julio to me presently.
Uncharitable woman ! thy rash tongue
Hath rais'd a fearful and prodigious storm :
Be thou the cause of all ensuing harm.          [*Exit.*

   *Flam.* Now, you that stand so much upon your
      honour,
Is this a fitting time a' night, think you,
To send a duke home without e'er a man ?
I would fain know where lies the mass of wealth
Which you have hoarded for my maintenance,
That I may bear my beard out of the level
Of my lord's stirrup.
   *Cor.* What ! because we are poor
Shall we be vicious ?
   *Flam.* Pray, what means have you
To keep me from the gallies, or the gallows ?
My father prov'd himself a gentleman,
Sold all's land, and, like a fortunate fellow,
Died ere the money was spent.   You brought me up
At Padua, I confess, where I protest,
For want of means—the university judge me—
I have been fain to heel my tutor's stockings,
At least seven years ; conspiring with a beard,
Made me a graduate ; then to this duke's service,
I visited the court, whence I return'd
More courteous, more lecherous by far,
But not a suit the richer.   And shall I,
Having a path so open, and so free
To my preferment, still retain your milk
In my pale forehead ? no, this face of mine
I'll arm, and fortify with lusty wine,
  Gainst shame and blushing.

*Cor.* O, that I ne'er had borne thee!

*Flam.* So would I;
I would the common'st courtezan in Rome
Had been my mother, rather than thyself.
Nature is very pitiful to whores,
To give them but few children, yet those children
Plurality of fathers; they are sure
They shall not want.  Go, go,
Complain unto my great lord cardinal;
It may be he will justify the act.
Lycurgus wonder'd much, men would provide
Good stallions for their mares, and yet would suffer
Their fair wives to be barren.

*Cor.* Misery of miseries!                        [*Exit.*

*Flam.* The duchess come to court!  I like not that.
We are engag'd to mischief, and must on;
As rivers to find out the ocean
Flow with crook bendings beneath forced banks,
Or as we see, to aspire some mountain's top,
The way ascends not straight, but imitates
The subtle foldings of a winter's snake,
So who knows policy and her true aspect,
Shall find her ways winding and indirect.        [*Exit.*

## ACT II.[1]—Scene I.

*Enter* Francisco de Medicis, *cardinal* Monticelso, Marcello, Isabella, *young* Giovanni, *with little* Jaques *the Moor.*

### *Francisco de Medicis.*

AVE you not seen your husband since you arrived?

*Isab.* Not yet, sir.

*Fran. de Med.* Surely he is wondrous kind;
If I had such a dove-house as Camillo's,
I would set fire on't were't but to destroy
The pole-cats that haunt to it—My sweet cousin!

*Giov.* Lord uncle, you did promise me a horse,
And armour.

*Fran. de Med.* That I did, my pretty cousin.
Marcello, see it fitted.

*Mar.* My lord, the duke is here.

*Fran. de Med.* Sister, away; you must not yet be seen.

*Isab.* I do beseech you, entreat him mildly,
Let not your rough tongue
Set us at louder variance; all my wrongs
Are freely pardon'd; and I do not doubt,
As men, to try the precious unicorn's horn,[2]

---

[1] Not marked in the 4to. of 1612. The *Act* is marked in the 4to. of 1665, the *Scene* not until the edition of 1672.

[2] The horn of the unicorn was considered an infallible antidote against poison: the animal, aware of this quality of its horn, was reported always to dip it into the water before he drank, in order to counteract anything noxious contained

Make of the powder a preservative circle,
And in it put a spider, so these arms
Shall charm his poison, force it to obeying,
And keep him chaste from an infected straying.

    *Fran. de Med.* I wish it may.   Be gone : 'void the
    chamber.

                 [*Exeunt all but Monticelso and Francisco.*

            *Enter* BRACHIANO *and* FLAMINEO.

You are welcome ; will you sit ?—I pray, my lord,
Be you my orator, my heart's too full ;
I'll second you anon.

    *Mont.* Ere I begin,
Let me entreat your grace forego all passion,
Which may be raised by my free discourse.

    *Brach.* As silent as i' th' church : you may  proceed.

    *Mont.* It is a wonder to your noble friends,
That you, having as 'twere enter'd the world
With a free sceptre in your able hand,
And having to th' use of nature, well applied,
High gifts of learning, should in your prime age
Neglect your awful throne for the soft down
Of an insatiate bed.   O, my lord,
The drunkard after all his lavish cups

therein ; on which account, other beasts watched his drinking, that they might judge of the purity of their beverage.
In such estimation was this counter-poison, that Andrea
Racci, a Florentine physician, relates it had been sold by
the apothecaries for £24 sterling per ounce, when the current
value of the same quantity of gold was only £2 6s. 3d.
Ambrose Parè, an eminent French surgeon, who flourished
towards the end of the sixteenth century, exposed the cheat
of its quack-salving vendors.   What the *Unicorn's horn* was
supposed to be, what was sold for it, and the real unicorn as
well as the fancied unicorn, are treated of largely by Sir
Thomas Brown, *Vulgar Errors*, c. ~~xxiii~~ b. 3.

                      XXIII

Is dry, and then is sober ! so at length,
When you awake from this lascivious dream,
Repentance then will follow, like the sting
Plac'd in the adder's tail.   Wretched are princes
When fortune blasteth but a petty flower
Of their unwieldly crowns, or ravisheth
But one pearl from their sceptre ; but alas !
When they to wilful shipwreck lose good fame,
All princely titles perish with their name.

   *Brach.* You have said, my lord.

   *Mont.* Enough to give you taste
How far I am from flattering your greatness.

   *Brach.* Now, you that are his second, what say you ?
Do not like young hawks fetch a course about ;
Your game flies fair, and for you.

   *Fran. de Med.* Do not fear it :
I'll answer you in your own hawking phrase.
Some eagles that should gaze upon the sun
Seldom soar high, but take their lustful ease ;
Since they from dunghill birds their prey can seize.
You know Vittoria ?

   *Brach.* Yes.

   *Fran. de Med.* You shift your shirt there,
When you retire from tennis ?

   *Brach.* Happily.[1]

   *Fran. de Med.* Her husband is lord of a poor fortune,
Yet she wears cloth of tissue.

   *Brach.* What of this ?
Will you urge that, my good lord cardinal,
As part of her confession at next shrift,

---

   [1] *Happily*—haply, possibly.

And know from whence it sails?

*Fran. de Med.* She is your strumpet.

*Brach.* Uncivil sir, there's hemlock in thy breath,
And that black slander.   Were she a whore of mine,
All thy loud cannons, and thy borrow'd Switzers,
Thy gallies, nor thy sworn confederates,
Durst not supplant her.

*Fran. de Med.* Let's not talk on thunder.
Thou hast a wife, our sister: would I had given
Both her white hands to death, bound and lock'd fast
In her last winding sheet, when I gave thee
But one.

*Brach.* Thou had'st given a soul to God then.

*Fran. de Med.* True:
Thy ghostly father, with all his absolution,
Shall ne'er do so by thee.

*Brach.* Spit thy poison.

*Fran. de Med.* I shall not need; lust carries her sharp
    whip
At her own girdle.   Look to't, for our anger
Is making thunder-bolts.

*Brach.* Thunder! in faith,
They are but crackers.

*Fran. de Med.* We'll end this with the cannon.

*Brach.* Thou'lt get nought by it, but iron in thy
    wounds,
And gunpowder in thy nostrils.

*Fran. de Med.* Better that,
Than change perfumes for plasters.

*Brach.* Pity on thee!
'Twere good you'd shew your slaves, or men condemn'd,
Your new-plowd forehead-defiance! and I'll meet thee,

Even in a thicket of thy ablest men.

*Mont.* My lords, you shall not word it any further
Without a milder limit.

*Fran. de Med.* Willingly.

*Brach.* Have you proclaim'd a triumph, that you bait
A lion thus?

*Mont.* My lord!

*Brach.* I am tame, I am tame, sir.

*Fran. de Med.* We send unto the duke for conference
'Bout levies 'gainst the pirates; my lord duke
Is not at home: we come ourself in person;
Still my lord duke is busied.    But, we fear,
When Tiber to each prowling passenger
Discovers flocks of wild ducks, then, my lord—
'Bout moulting time I mean—we shall be certain
To find you sure enough, and speak with you.

*Brach.* Ha!

*Fran. de Med.* A mere tale of a tub: my words are
idle.
But to express the sonnet by natural reason,
When stags grow melancholic you'll find the season.

*Enter* GIOVANNI.

*Mont.* No more, my lord; here comes a champion
Shall end the difference between you both;
Your son, the prince Giovanni.    See, my lords, *Bra*
What hopes you store in him; this is a casket
For both your crowns, and should be held like dear.
Now is he apt for knowledge; therefore know
It is a more direct and even way,
To train to virtue those of princely blood,
By examples than by precepts: if by examples,

Whom should he rather strive to imitate
Than his own father? be his pattern then,
Leave him a stock of virtue that may last,
Should fortune rend his sails, and split his mast.

    *Brach.* Your hand, boy: growing to a soldier?

    *Giov.* Give me a pike.

    *Fran. de Med.* What, practising your pike so young,
       fair cousin?

    *Giov.* Suppose me one of Homer's frogs, my lord,
Tossing my bull-rush thus.   Pray, sir, tell me,
Might not a child of good discretion
Be leader to an army?

    *Fran. de Med.* Yes, cousin, a young prince
Of good discretion might.

    *Giov.* Say you so?
Indeed I have heard, 'tis fit a general
Should not endanger his own person oft;
So that he make a noise when he's a'horseback,
Like a Danske[1] drummer,—O, 'tis excellent!—
He need not fight! methinks his horse as well
Might lead an army for him.   If I live,
I'll charge the French foe in the very front
Of all my troops, the foremost man.

    *Fran. de Med.* What! what!

    *Giov.* And will not bid my soldiers up, and follow,
But bid them follow me.

    *Brach.* Forward lap-wing!
He flies with the shell on's head.[2]

    *Fran. de Med.* Pretty cousin!

---

[1] *Danske,*—Danish.
    i. e. ere he's scarce hatched.

*Giov.* The first year, uncle, that I go to war,
All prisoners that I take, I will set free,
Without their ransom.

*Fran. de Med.* Ha! without their ransom!
How then will you reward your soldiers,
That took those prisoners for you?

*Giov.* Thus, my lord:
I'll marry them to all the wealthy widows
That fall[1] that year.

*Fran. de Med.* Why then, the next year following,
You'll have no men to go with you to war.

*Giov.* Why then I'll press the women to the war,
And then the men will follow.

*Mont.* Witty prince!

*Fran. de Med.* See a good habit makes a child a man,
Whereas a bad one makes a man a beast.
Come, you and I are friends.

*Brach.* Most wishedly:
Like bones which, broke in sunder, and well set,
Knit the more strongly.

*Fran. de Med.* Call Camillo hither.——
You have receiv'd the rumour, how count Lodowick
Is turn'd a pirate?

*Brach.* Yes.

*Fran. de Med.* We are now preparing
Some ships to fetch him in.   Behold your duchess.
We now will leave you, and expect from you
Nothing but kind intreaty.

*Brach.* You have charm'd me.

   [*Exeunt Francisco, Monticelso, and Giovanni.*

---

[1] i. e. *fall in.*

*Enter* ISABELLA.

You are in health, we see.

   *Isab.* And above health,
To see my lord well.

   *Brach.* So: I wonder much
What amorous whirlwind hurried you to Rome.

   *Isab.* Devotion, my lord.

   *Brach.* Devotion!
Is your soul charg'd with any grievous sin?

   *Isab.* 'Tis burden'd with too many; and I think
The oftener that we cast our reckonings up,
Our sleeps will be the sounder.

   *Brach.* Take your chamber.

   *Isab.* Nay, my dear lord, I will not have you angry!
Doth not my absence from you, now two months,
Merit one kiss?

   *Brach.* I do not use to kiss:
If that will dispossess your jealousy,
I'll swear it to you.

   *Isab.* O my loved lord,
I do not come to chide: my jealousy!
I am to learn what that Italian means.
You are as welcome to these longing arms,
As I to you a virgin.[1]

   *Brach.* O, your breath!
Out upon sweet-meats and continued physic,
The plague is in them!

   *Isab.* You have oft, for these two lips,
Neglected cassia, or the natural sweets

---

[1] i. e. when first you married me.

Of the spring-violet : they are not yet much wither'd.
My lord I should be merry : these your frowns
Show in a helmet lovely ; but on me,
In such a peaceful interview, methinks
They are too too roughly knit.

    *Brach.* O, dissemblance ! [1]
Do you bandy factions 'gainst me ? have you learnt
The trick of impudent baseness to complain
Unto your kindred ?

    *Isab.* Never, my dear lord.

    *Brach.* Must I be hunted out ? or was't your trick
To meet some amorous gallant here in Rome,
That must supply our discontinuance ?

    *Isab.* I pray, sir, burst my heart ; and in my death
Turn to your ancient pity, though not love.

    *Brach.* Because your brother is the corpulent duke,
That is, the great duke, 'sdeath, I shall not, shortly,
Racket away five hundred crowns at tennis,
But it shall rest 'pon record !   I scorn him
Like a shav'd Polack :[2] all his reverend wit
Lies in his wardrobe ; he's a discreet fellow,
When he's made up in his robes of state.
Your brother, the great duke, because h'as gallies,
And now and then ransacks a Turkish fly-boat,
(Now all the hellish furies take his soul !)
First made this match : accursed be the priest
That sang the wedding-mass, and even my issue !

---

[1] Dissembling woman !
[2] Polander.  In Moryson's *Itinerary*, 1617, it is said, "The Polonians *shave* all their heads close, excepting the haire of the forehead, which they nourish very long, and cast backe to the hinder part of the head."—REED.

*Isab.* O, too too far you have curs'd !

*Brach.* Your hand I'll kiss ;
This is the latest ceremony of my love.
Henceforth I'll never lie with thee ; by this,
This wedding-ring, I'll ne'er more lie with thee !
And this divorce shall be as truly kept,
As if the judge had doomed it.    Fare you well :
Our sleeps are sever'd.

*Isab.* Forbid it, the sweet union
Of all things blessed ! why, the saints in heaven
Will knit their brows at that.

*Brach.* Let not thy love
Make thee an unbeliever ; this my vow
Shall never, on my soul, be satisfied [1]
With my repentance : let thy brother rage
Beyond a horrid tempest, or sea-fight,
My vow is fixed.

*Isab.* O my winding-sheet !
Now shall I need thee shortly.    Dear, my lord,
Let me hear once more, what I would not hear :
Never ?

*Brach.* Never.

*Isab.* O my unkind lord ! may your sins find mercy,
As I upon a woful widow'd bed
Shall pray for you, if not to turn your eyes
Upon your wretched wife and hopeful son,
Yet that in time you'll fix them upon heaven !

*Brach.* No more ; go, go, complain to the great duke.

*Isab.* No, my dear lord ; you shall have present witness
How I'll work peace between you.    I will make

---

[1] In the sense of *released.*

Myself the author of your cursed vow ;
I have some cause to do it, you have none. ·
Conceal it, I beseech you, for the weal
Of both your dukedoms, that you wrought the means
Of such a separation : let the fault
Remain with my supposed jealousy,
And think with what a piteous and rent heart
I shall perform this sad ensuing part.

*Enter* FRANCISCO, FLAMINEO, MONTICELSO, *and* CAMILLO.

 *Brach.* Well, take your course.—My honourable bro-
  ther !
 *Fran.* Sister !—This is not well, my lord.—Why,
  sister !—
She merits not this welcome.
 *Brach.* Welcome, say !
She hath given me[1] a sharp welcome.
 *Fran.* Are you foolish ?
Come, dry your tears : is this a modest course
To better what is naught, to rail and weep ?
Grow to a reconcilement, or, by heaven,
I'll ne'er more deal between you.
 *Isab.* Sir, you shall not ;
No, though Vittoria, upon that condition,
Would become honest.
 *Fran.* Was your husband loud
Since we departed ?
 *Isab.* By my life, sir, no,
I swear by that I do not care to lose.
Are all these ruins of my former beauty

---

[1] *me*—supplied from an old interlineation in the 4to. of 1612.

Laid out for a whore's triumph?

*Fran.* Do you hear?
Look upon other women, with what patience
They suffer these slight wrongs, and with what justice
They study to requite them : take that course.

*Isab.* O that I were a man, or that I had power
To execute my apprehended wishes!
I would whip some with scorpions.

*Fran.* What! turn'd fury!

*Isab.* To dig the strumpet's eyes out; let her lie
Some twenty month's a dying; to cut off
Her nose and lips, pull out her rotten teeth;
Preserve her flesh like mummia, for trophies
Of my just anger!   Hell, to my affliction,
Is mere snow-water.   By your favour, sir ;—
Brother, draw near, and my lord cardinal ;—
Sir, let me borrow of you but one kiss;
Henceforth I'll never lie with you, by this,
This wedding-ring.

*Fran.* How, ne'er more lie with him!

*Isab.* And this divorce shall be as truly  kept
As if in thronged court a thousand ears
Had heard it, and a thousand lawyers' hands
Seal'd to the separation.

*Brach.* Ne'er lie with me!

*Isab.* Let not my former dotage
Make thee an unbeliever; this my vow
Shall never on my soul be satisfied
With my repentance : *manet alta mente repostum.*

*Fran.* Now, by my birth, you are a foolish, mad,
And  jealous woman.

*Brach.* You see 'tis not my seeking.

*Fran.* Was this your circle of pure unicorn's horn,
You said should charm your lord! now horns upon thee,
For jealousy deserves them! Keep your vow
And take your chamber.

*Isab.* No, sir, I'll presently to Padua;
I will not stay a minute.

*Mont.* O good madam!

*Brach.* 'Twere best to let her have her humour;
Some half day's journey will bring down her stomach,
And then she'll turn in post.

*Fran.* To see her come
To my lord cardinal for a dispensation
Of her rash vow, will beget excellent laughter.

*Isab.* Unkindness, do thy office; poor heart, break:
"Those are the killing griefs, which dare not speak."

[*Exit.*

*Mar.* Camillo's come, my lord.

*Enter* CAMILLO.

*Fran.* Where's the commission?

*Mar.* 'Tis here.

*Fran.* Give me the signet.

*Flam.* My Lord, do you mark their whispering? I
will compound a medicine, out of their two heads,
stronger than garlick, deadlier than stibium:[1] the can-
tharides, which are scarce seen to stick upon the flesh,
when they work to the heart, shall not do it with more
silence or invisible cunning.

---

[1] *stibium*—an ancient name for antimony.—REED.

*Enter* DOCTOR.

*Brach.* About the murder?

*Flam.* They are sending him to Naples, but I'll send him to Candy.[1]   Here's another property too.

*Brach.* O, the doctor!

*Flam.* A poor quack-salving knave, my lord; one that should have been lashed for's lechery, but that he confessed a judgment, had an execution laid upon him, and so put the whip to a *non plus.*

*Doc.* And was cozened, my lord, by an arranter knave than myself, and made pay all the colourable execution.

*Flam.* He will shoot pills into a man's guts shall make them have more ventages than a cornet or a lamprey; he will poison a kiss; and was once minded for his masterpiece, because Ireland breeds no poison, to have prepared a deadly vapour in a Spaniard's fart, that should have poisoned all Dublin.

*Brach.* O saint Anthony's fire!

*Doc.* Your secretary is merry, my lord.

*Flam.* O thou cursed antipathy to nature! Look, his eye's bloodshed, like a needle a chirurgeon stitcheth a wound with.   Let me embrace thee, toad, and love thee, O thou abominable, loathsome gargarism,[2] that will fetch up lungs, lights, heart, and liver, by scruples!

*Brach.* No more.—I must employ thee, honest doctor: You must to Padua, and by the way, Use some of your skill for us.

---

_[1] A play upon the verb *Candy*, itself from *canleo*, to bleach, make white.
[2] Gargle.

*Doc.* Sir, I shall.

*Brach.* But for Camillo?

*Flam.* He dies this night, by such a politic strain,
Men shall suppose him by's own engine slain.
But for your duchess' death—

*Doc.* I'll make her sure.

*Brach.* Small mischiefs are by greater made secure.

*Flam.* Remember this, you slave; when knaves
come to preferment, they rise as gallowses are raised
i'th' Low Countries, one upon another's shoulders.

[*Exeunt.*

[1] *Mont.* Here is an emblem, nephew, pray peruse it:
'Twas thrown in at your window.

*Cam.* At my window!
Here is a stag, my lord, hath shed his horns,
And, for the loss of them, the poor beast weeps :
The word, *Inopem me copia fecit.*

*Mont.* That is,
Plenty of horns hath made him poor of horns.

*Cam.* What should this mean?

*Mont.* I'll tell you; 'tis given out
You are a cuckold.

*Cam.* Is it given out so?
I had rather such report as that, my lord,
Should keep within doors.

*Fran.* Have you any children?

*Cam.* None, my lord.

*Fran.* You are the happier :
I'll tell you a tale.

[1] Monticelso, Camillo, and Francisco, having retired to the
back of the stage on the entrance of the Doctor, here come
forward again.—COLLIER.

*Cam.* Pray, my lord.

*Fran.* An old tale.
Upon a time Phœbus, the god of light,
Or him we call the Sun, would need be married:
The gods gave their consent, and Mercury
Was sent to voice it to the general world.
But what a piteous cry there straight arose
Amongst smiths and felt-makers, brewers and cooks,
Reapers and butter-women, amongst fishmongers,
And thousand other trades, which are annoy'd
By his excessive heat! 'twas lamentable.
They came to Jupiter all in a sweat,
And do forbid the bans.    A great fat cook
Was made their speaker, who intreats of Jove
That Phœbus might be gelded; for if now,
When there was but one sun, so many men
Were like to perish by his violent heat,
What should they do if he were married,
And should beget more, and those children
Make fire-works like their father?    So say I;
Only I will apply it to your wife;
Her issue, should not providence prevent it,
Would make both nature, time, and man repent it.

*Mont.* Look you, cousin,
Go, change the air for shame; see if your absence
Will blast your cornucopia.    Marcello
Is chosen with you joint commissioner,
For the relieving our Italian coast
From pirates.

*Mar.* I am much honour'd in't.

*Cam.* But, sir,

Ere I return, the stag's horns may be sprouted
Greater than those are shed.

*Mont.* Do not fear it;
I'll be your ranger.

*Cam.* You must watch i'th'nights;
Then's the most danger.

*Fran.* Farewell, good Marcello:
All the best fortunes of a soldier's wish
Bring you a ship-board.

*Cam.* Were I not best, now I am turn'd soldier,
Ere that I leave my wife, sell all she hath,
And then take leave of her?

*Mont.* I expect good from you,
Your parting is so merry.

*Cam.* Merry, my lord! a'th' captain's humour right,
I am resolved to be drunk this night.        [*Exeunt.*

*Fran.* So, 'twas well fitted; now shall we discern
How his wish'd absence will give violent way
To duke Brachiano's lust.

*Mont.* Why, that was it;
To what scorn'd purpose else should we make choice
Of him for a sea-captain? and, besides,
Count Lodowick, which was rumour'd for a pirate,
Is now in Padua.

*Fran.* Is't true?

*Mont.* Most certain.
I have letters from him, which are suppliant
To work his quick repeal from banishment:
He means to address himself for pension
Unto our sister duchess.

*Fran.* O, 'twas well!

We shall not want his absence past six days :
I fain would have the duke Brachiano run
Into notorious scandal ; for there's nought
In such curst dotage, to repair his name,
Only the deep sense of some deathless shame.

*Mont.* It may be objected, I am dishonourable
To play thus with my kinsman ; but I answer,
For my revenge I'd stake a brother's life,
That being wrong'd, durst not avenge himself.

*Fran.* Come, to observe this strumpet.

*Mont.* Curse of greatness !
Sure he'll not leave her ?

*Fran.* There's small pity in't :
Like mistletoe on sear elms spent by weather,
Let him cleave to her, and both rot together.    [*Exeunt.*


## ACT III.—Scene I.

*Enter* Brachiano, *with one · in the habit of a conjurer.*

### Brachiano.

NOW, sir, I claim your promise : 'tis dead mid-
night,
        The time prefix'd to show me, by your art,
How the intended murder of Camillo,
And our loath'd duchess, grow to action.

*Con.* You have won me, by your bounty, to a deed
I do not often practise.   Some there are,
Which by sophistic tricks, aspire that name
Which I would gladly lose, of necromancer ;
As some that use to juggle upon cards,

Seeming to conjure, when indeed they cheat ;
Others that raise up their confederate spirits
'Bout wind-mills, and endanger their own necks
For making of a squib ; and some there are
Will keep a curtal[1] to shew juggling tricks,
And give out 'tis a spirit ; besides these,
Such a whole ream of almanack-makers, figure-flingers,
Fellows, indeed, that only live by stealth,
Since they do merely lie about stol'n goods,
They'd make men think the devil were fast and loose,
With speaking fustian Latin.   Pray, sit down ;
Put on this night-cap, sir, 'tis charm'd ; and now
I'll shew you, by my strong commanding art,
The circumstance that breaks your duchess' heart.

*A dumb Show.*

*Enter suspiciously* Julio *and* Christophero : *they draw
a curtain where Brachiano's picture is ; they put on
spectacles of glass, which cover their eyes and noses, and
then burn perfumes afore the picture, and wash the lips
of the picture ; that done, quenching the fire, and putting off their spectacles, they depart laughing.*

*Enter* Isabella *in her night-gown, as to bed-ward, with
lights after her, count* Lodovico, Giovanni, Guid-
Antonio, *and others waiting on her : she kneels down
as to prayers, then draws the curtain of the picture,
does three reverences to it, and kisses it thrice ; she*

---

[1] This refers to *Banks'* celebrated horse, so often mentioned
in old writers.   The term *curtal* was applied to a docked
horse, or any cropped animal.

*faints, and will not suffer them to come near it; dies;*
*sorrow expressed in Giovanni, and in count Lodovico.*
*She's conveyed out solemnly.*

*Brach.* Excellent ! then she's dead.

*Con.* She's poisoned
By the fumed picture.   'Twas her custom nightly,
Before she went to bed, to go and visit
Your picture, and to feed her eyes and lips
On the dead shadow : doctor Julio,
Observing this, infects it with an oil,
And other poison'd stuff, which presently
Did suffocate her spirits.

*Brach.* Methought I saw
Count Lodowick there.

*Con.* He was ; and by my art,
I find he did most passionately doat
Upon your duchess.   Now turn another way,
And view Camillo's far more politic [1] fate.
Strike louder, music, from this charmed ground,
To yield, as fits the act, a tragic sound !

*The second dumb Show.*

*Enter* FLAMINEO, MARCELLO, CAMILLO, *with four more,*
*as captains: they drink healths, and dance; a vaulting*
*horse is brought into the room; Marcello and two more*
*whispered out of the room, while Flamineo and Camillo*
*strip themselves into their shirts, as to vault; they com-*
*pliment who shall begin ; as Camillo is about to vault,*
*Flamineo pitcheth him upon his neck, and, with the*
*help of the rest, writhes his neck about ; seems to see if*

[1] i. e. ingeniously contrived.

*it be broke, and lays him folded double, as 'twere under
the horse; makes shews to call for help; Marcello comes
in, laments; sends for the cardinal and duke, who come
forth with armed men; wonder at the act; command
the body to be carried home; apprehend Flamineo,
Marcello, and the rest, and go, as 'twere, to apprehend
Vittoria.*

*Brach.* 'Twas quaintly done; but yet each circumstance
I taste not fully.

*Con.* O, 'twas most apparent!
You saw them enter, charg'd with their deep healths
To their boon voyage; and, to second that,
Flamineo calls to have a vaulting horse
Maintain their sport; the virtuous Marcello
Is innocently plotted forth the room;
Whilst your eye saw the rest, and can inform you
The engine of all.

*Brach.* It seems Marcello and Flamineo
Are both committed.

*Con.* Yes, you saw them guarded;
And now they are come with purpose to apprehend
Your mistress, fair Vittoria.   We are now
Beneath her roof: 'twere fit we instantly
Make out by some back postern.

*Brach.* Noble friend,
You bind me ever to you: this shall stand
As the firm seal annexed to my hand;
It shall inforce a payment.

*Con.* Sir, I thank you.        [*Exit Brachiano.*
Both flowers and weeds spring, when the sun is warm,
And great men do great good, or else great harm. [*Exit.*

## SCENE II.

*Enter* FRANCISCO DE MEDICIS, *and* MONTICELSO, *their Chancellor and Register.*

*Fran.* You have dealt discreetly, to obtain the presence
Of all the grave lieger ambassadors
To hear Vittoria's trial.

*Mont.* 'Twas not ill ;
For, sir, you know we have nought but circumstances
To charge her with, about her husband's death :
Their approbation, therefore, to the proofs
Of her black lust shall make her infamous
To all our neighbouring kingdoms.   I wonder
If Brachiano will be here ?

*Fran.* O fie ! 'Twere impudence too palpable. [*Exeunt.*

*Enter* FLAMINEO, *and* MARCELLO *guarded, and*
*a* LAWYER.

*Lawyer.* What, are you in by the week ?[2] so, I will try now whether thy wit be close prisoner.   Methinks none should sit upon thy sister, but old whore-masters.

*Flam.* Or cuckolds ; for your cuckold is your most terrible tickler of lechery.   Whore-masters would serve, for none are judges at tilting, but those that have been old tilters.

*Lawyer.* My lord duke and she have been very private.

*Flam.* You are a dull ass ; 'tis threatened they have been very public.

---

[1] Resident ambassadors.
[2] This phrase appears to signify an engagement for a time limited.—STEEVENS.

*Lawyer.* If it can be proved they have but kissed one another—

*Flam.* What then?

*Lawyer.* My lord cardinal will ferret them.

*Flam.* A cardinal, I hope, will not catch conies.[1]

*Lawyer.* For to sow kisses, (mark what I say,) to sow kisses is to reap lechery; and, I am sure, a woman that will endure kissing is half won.

*Flam.* True, her upper part, by that rule; if you will win her nether part too, you know what follows.

*Lawyer.* Hark! the ambassadors are 'lighted.

*Flam.* I do put on this feigned garb or mirth,
To gull suspicion.

*Mar.* O my unfortunate sister!
I would my dagger-point had cleft her heart
When she first saw Brachiano: you, 'tis said,
Were made his engine, and his stalking horse,
To undo my sister.

*Flam.* I am a kind of path
To her, and mine own preferment.

*Mar.* Your ruin.

*Flam.* Hum! thou art a soldier,
Followest the great duke, feed'st his victories,
As witches do their serviceable spirits,
Even with thy prodigal blood: what hast got?
But, like the wealth of captains, a poor handful,
Which in thy palm thou bear'st, as men hold water;
Seeking to gripe it fast, the frail reward
Steals through thy fingers.

---

[1] To *conycatch*, to cheat a simple person; conies (rabbits) being simple animals.—NARES.

*Mar.* Sir!

*Flam.* Thou hast scarce maintenance
To keep thee in fresh shamois.[1]

*Mar.* Brother!

*Flam.* Hear me:
And thus, when we have even pour'd ourselves
Into great fights, for their ambition,
Or idle spleen, how shall we find reward?
But as we seldom find the mistletoe
Sacred to physic, or the builder oak,[2]
Without a mandrake by it; so in our quest of gain,
Alas, the poorest of their forc'd dislikes
At a limb proffers, but at heart it strikes!
This is lamented doctrine.

*Mar.* Come, come.

*Flam.* When age shall turn thee
White as a blooming hawthorn——

*Mar.* I'll interrupt you:
For love of virtue bear an honest heart,
And stride o'er every politic respect,
Which, where they most advance, they most infect.
Were I your father, as I am your brother,
I should not be ambitious to leave you
A better patrimony.

*Flam.* I'll think on't.
The lord ambassadors.

> [*Here there is a passage of the lieger ambassadors*
> *over the stage severally.*

---

[1] i. e. shoes made of the wild goat's skin.—STEEVENS.
[2] The epithet of "*builder* oak" is originally Chaucer's:
   "*The bilder oke*, and eke the hardy ashe
      Tho piller elme," &c.—*Assemblie of Foules*: COLLIER.

*Enter* FRENCH AMBASSADOR.

*Lawyer.* O my sprightly Frenchman! Do you know him? he's an admirable tilter.

*Flam.* I saw him at last tilting: he shewed like a pewter candlestick fashioned [1] like a man in armour, holding a tilting staff in his hand, little bigger than a candle of twelve i'th' pound.

*Lawyer.* O, but he's an excellent horseman!

*Flam.* A lame one in his lofty tricks; he sleeps a horseback, like a poulter. [2]

*Enter* ENGLISH *and* SPANISH.

*Lawyer.* Lo you, my Spaniard!

*Flam.* He carries his face in's ruff, as I have seen a serving-man carry glasses in a cypress [3] hatband, monstrous steady, for fear of breaking; he looks like the claw of a blackbird, first salted, and then broiled in a candle. [*Exeunt.*

*The Arraignment of* VITTORIA. [4]

*Enter* FRANCISCO, MONTICELSO, *the six lieger Ambassadors,* BRACHIANO, VITTORIA, *and a Guard.*

*Mont.* Forbear, my lord, here is no place assign'd
This business, by his holiness, is left          [you.
To our examination.

---

[1] Mr. Steevens observes, that the ancient candlesticks frequently represented human figures holding the sockets for the lights in their extended hands.

[2] *poulter*—poulterer.

[3] A kind of crape.

[4] "This White Devil," as she is called, is made fair as the leprosy, dazzling as the lightning; she is dressed like a bride in her wrongs and her revenge. In the trial scene, in particular, her sudden indignant answers to the questions

*Brach.* May it thrive with you.

[*Lays a rich gown under him.*

*Fran.* A chair there for his lordship.

*Brach.* Forbear your kindness : an unbidden guest
Should travel as Dutch women go to church,
Bear their stools with them.

*Mont.* At your pleasure, sir.
Stand to the table, gentlewoman.    Now, signior,
Fall to your plea.

*Lawyer. Domine judex, converte oculos in hanc pestem,
mulierum corruptissimam.*

*Vit.* What's he?

*Fran.* A lawyer that pleads against you.

*Vit.* Pray, my lord, let him speak his usual tongue,
I'll make no answer else.

*Fran.* Why, you understand Latin.

*Vit.* I do, sir, but amongst this auditory
Which come to hear my cause, the half or more
May be ignorant in't

*Mont.* Go on, sir.

*Vit.* By your favour,
I will not have my accusation clouded
In a strange tongue : all this assembly
Shall hear what you can charge me with.

*Fran.* Signior,
You need not stand on't much; pray, change your language.

that are asked her startle the hearers.    Nothing can be
imagined finer than the whole conduct and conception of
this scene, than her scorn of her accusers and of herself.
The sincerity of her sense of guilt triumphs over the
hypocrisy of their affected and official contempt of it.—
HAZLITT, *Literature of the Age of Elizabeth.*

*Mont.* O, for God's sake—Gentlewoman, your credit
Shall be more famous by it.

*Lawyer.* Well then, have at you.

*Vit.* I am at the mark, sir; I'll give aim[1] to you,
And tell you how near you shoot.

*Lawyer.* Most literated judges, please your lordships
So to connive your judgments to the view
Of this debauch'd and diversivolent woman ;
Who such a black concatenation
Of mischief hath effected, that to extirp
The memory of't, must be the consummation
Of her, and her projections.

*Vit.* What's all this ?

*Lawyer.* Hold your peace !
Exorbitant sins must have exulceration.

*Vit.* Surely, my lords, this lawyer here hath swallow'd
Some 'pothecaries bills, or proclamations ;
And now the hard and undigestible words
Come up, like stones we use give hawks for physic.
Why, this is Welsh to Latin.[2]

*Lawyer.* My lords, the woman
Knows not her tropes, nor figures, nor is perfect
In the academic derivation
Of grammatical elocution.

*Fran.* Sir, your pains
Shall be well spar'd, and your deep eloquence
Be worthily applauded amongst those
Which understand you.

---

[1] "He who *gave aim* was stationed near the butts, to tell
the archers, after every discharge, how wide, or how short,
the arrow fell of the mark."—Nares.

[2] i. e. this is a Welsh jargon, worse than his Latin.

*Lawyer.* My good lord.

*Fran.* Sir,

Put up your papers in your fustian bag,

                     *[Francisco speaks this as in scorn.*

Cry mercy, sir, 'tis buckram, and accept

My notion of your learn'd verbosity.

*Lawyer.* I most graduatically thank your lordship :
I shall have use for them elsewhere.

*Mont.* I shall be plainer with you, and paint out
Your follies in more natural red and white
Than that upon your cheek.

*Vit.* O, you mistake !
You raise a blood as noble in this cheek
As ever was your mother's.

*Mont.* I must spare you, till proof cry whore to that.
Observe this creature here, my honour'd lords,
A woman of a most prodigious spirit,
In her effected.

*Vit.* My honourable lord,
It doth not suit a reverend cardinal
To play the lawyer thus.

*Mont.* O, your trade instructs your language !
You see, my lords, what goodly fruit she seems ;
Yet like those apples[1] travellers report

---

[1] This account is taken from Maundeville's *Travels.* "And
also the Cytees there weren lost, because of Synne. And
there besyden growen trees, that beren fulle *faire Apples,
and faire of colour to beholde ; but whoso brekethe hem, or cut-
tethe hem in two, he schalle fynde within hem Coles and Cyndres ;*
in tokene that, be Wrathe of God, the Cytees and the Lond
weren brente and sonken into Helle. Sum men clepen that
See, the Lake Dalfetidee ; summe the Flom of Develes ;
and sume that Flom that is ever stynkynge. And in to that
See, sonken the 5 Cytees, be wrathe of God ; that is to seyne,
*Sodom, Gomorre,* Aldama, Seboym, and Segor."—REED.

To grow where Sodom and Gomorrah stood,
I will but touch her, and you straight shall see
She'll fall to soot and ashes.

   *Vit.* Your envenom'd 'pothecary should do't.

   *Mont.* I am resolv'd,[1]
Were there a second paradise to lose,
This devil would betray it.

   *Vit.* O poor charity!
Thou art seldom found in scarlet.

   *Mont.* Who knows not how, when several night by
     night
Her gates were chok'd with coaches, and her rooms
Outbrav'd the stars with several kind of lights;
When she did counterfeit a prince's court
In music, banquets, and most riotous surfeits;
This whore forsooth was holy.

   *Vit.* Ha! whore! what's that?

   *Mont.* Shall I expound whore to you? sure I shall
I'll give their perfect character. They are first,
Sweet-meats which rot the eater; in man's nostrils
Poison'd perfumes. They are cozening alchymy;
Shipwrecks in calmest weather. What are whores!
Cold Russian winters, that appear so barren,
As if that nature had forgot the spring.
They are the true material fire of hell:
Worse than those tributes i'th' Low Countries paid,
Exactions upon meat, drink, garments, sleep,
Ay, even on man's perdition, his sin.
They are those brittle evidences of law,
Which forfeit all a wretched man's estate
For leaving out one syllable. What are whores!

          [1] i. e. convinced.—DYCE.

They are those flattering bells have all one tune,
At weddings and at funerals.   Your rich whores
Are only treasuries by extortion fill'd,
And emptied by curs'd riot.   They are worse,
Worse than dead bodies which are begg'd at gallows,
And wrought upon by surgeons, to teach man
Wherein he is imperfect.   What's a whore!
She's like the guilty counterfeited coin,
Which, whosoe'er first stamps it, brings in trouble
All that receive it.

    *Vit.* This character 'scapes me.

    *Mont.* You, gentlewoman!
Take from all beasts and from all minerals
Their deadly poison—

    *Vit.* Well, what then?

    *Mont.* I'll tell thee;
I'll find in thee a 'pothecary's shop,
To sample them all.

    *Fr. Am.* She hath liv'd ill.

    *Eng. Am.* True, but the cardinal's too bitter.

    *Mont.* You know what whore is.   Next the devil
       adultery,
Enters the devil murder.

    *Fran.* Your unhappy husband
Is dead.

    *Vit.* O, he's a happy husband!
Now he owes nature nothing.

    *Fran.* And by a vaulting engine.

    *Mont.* An active plot; he jump'd into his grave,

    *Fran.* What a prodigy was't,
That from some two yards' height, a slender man
Should break his neck!

*Mont.* I'th' rushes![1]

*Fran.* And what's more,
Upon the instant lose all use of speech,
All vital motion, like a man had lain
Wound up three days.    Now mark each circumstance.

*Mont.* And look upon this creature[2] was his wife!
She comes not like a widow; she comes arm'd
With scorn and impudence: is this a mourning-habit?

*Vit.* Had I foreknown his death, as you suggest,
1 would have bespoke my mourning.

*Mont.* O, you are cunning!

*Vit.* You shame your wit and judgment,
To call it so.    What! is my just defence
By him that is my judge call'd impudence?
Let me appeal then from this Christian court.[3]
To the uncivil[4] Tartar.

*Mont.* See, my lords,
She scandals our proceedings.

*Vit.* Humbly thus,
Thus low, to the most worthy and respected
Lieger ambassadors, my modesty
And woman-hood I tender; but withal,
So intangled in a cursed accusation,
That my defence, of force, like Portia's,[5]

---

[1] i. e. on the rushes, which then, in lieu of carpets, covered the floors of rooms.

[2] (who.)

[3] i. e. this *Court Christian*, the name, in England, of the Ecclesiastical Courts, where causes of adultery are cognizable.—REED.

[4] i. e. the savage, uncivilized.

[5] The original has *Perseus*, an evident misprint. The emendation was suggested to Mr. Dyce by Mr. Mitford, the allusion being to Shakespeare's *Merchant of Venice* (1597).—DYCE.

Must personate masculine virtue.   To the point.
Find me but guilty, sever head from body,
We'll part good friends : I scorn to hold my life
At yours, or any man's intreaty, sir.

*Eng. Am.* She hath a brave spirit.

*Mont.* Well, well, such counterfeit jewels
Make true ones oft suspected.

*Vit.* You are deceiv'd :
For know, that all your strict-combined heads,
Which strike against this mine of diamonds,
Shall prove but glassen hammers : they shall break.
These are but feigned shadows of my evils.
Terrify babes, my lord, with painted devils,
I am past such needless palsy: For your names
Of whore and murderess, they proceed from you,
As if a man should spit against the wind :
The filth returns in's face.

*Mont.* Pray you, mistress, satisfy me one question :
Who lodg'd beneath your roof that fatal night
Your husband brake his neck ?

*Brach.* That question
Inforceth me break silence : I was there.

*Mont.* Your business ?

*Brach.* Why, I came to comfort her,
And take some course for settling her estate,
Because I heard her husband was in debt
To you, my lord.

*Mont.* He was.

*Brach.* And 'twas strangely fear'd,
That you would cozen her.

*Mont.* Who made you overseer ?

*Brach.* Why, my charity, my charity, which should
    flow
From every generous and noble spirit,
To orphans and to widows.
    *Mont.* Your lust !
    *Brach.* Cowardly dogs bark loudest : sirrah priest,
I'll talk with you hereafter.   Do you hear ?
The sword you frame of such an excellent temper,
I'll sheathe in your own bowels.
There are a number of thy coat resemble
Your common post-boys.
    *Mont.* Ha !
    *Brach.* Your mercenary post-boys ;
Your letters carry truth, but 'tis your guise
To fill your mouths with gross and impudent lies.
    *Serv.* My lord, your gown.
    *Brach.* Thou liest, 'twas my stool :
Bestow't upon thy master, that will challenge [1]
The rest a'th' household-stuff ; for Brachiano
Was ne'er so beggarly to take a stool
Out of another's lodging : let him make
Vallance for his bed on't, or a demy foot-cloth
For his most reverend moile.[2]   Monticelso,
*Nemo me impune lacessit.*           [*Exit.*
    *Mont.* Your champion's gone.
    *Vit.* The wolf may prey the better.
    *Fran.* My lord, there's great suspicion of the murder,
But no sound proof who did it.   For my part,
I do not think she hath a soul so black
To act a deed so bloody ; if she have,

---

[1] Claim as due.        [2] *moile,*—mule.

As in cold countries husbandmen plant vines,
And with warm blood manure them; even so
One summer she will bear unsavoury fruit,
And ere next spring wither both branch and root.
To act of blood let pass; only descend
To matter of incontinence.

    *Vit.* I discern poison
Under your gilded pills.

    *Mont.* Now the duke's gone, I will produce a letter
Wherein 'twas plotted, he and you should meet
At an apothecary's summer-house,
Down by the river Tiber,—view't my lords,—
Where after wanton bathing and the heat
Of a lascivious banquet—I pray read it,
I shame to speak the rest.

    *Vit.* Grant I was tempted;
Temptation to lust proves not the act:
*Casta est quam nemo royavit.*
You read his hot love to me, but you want
My frosty answer.

    *Mont.* Frost i'th' dog-days! strange!

    *Vit.* Condemn you me for that the duke did love me?
So may you blame some fair and crystal river,
For that some melancholic distracted man
Hath drown'd himself in't.

    *Mont.* Truly drown'd, indeed.

    *Vit.* Sum up my faults, I pray, and you shall find,
That beauty and gay clothes, a merry heart,
And a good stomach to feast, are all,
All the poor crimes that you can charge me with.
In faith, my lord, you might go pistol flies,
The sport would be more noble.

*Mont.* Very good.

*Vit.* But take your course : it seems you've beggar'd
    me first,
And now would fain undo me.   I have houses,
Jewels, and a poor remnant of crusadoes ; [1]
Would those would make you charitable !

*Mont.* If the devil
Did ever take good shape, behold his picture.

*Vit.* You have one virtue left,
You will not flatter me.

*Fran.* Who brought this letter ?

*Vit.* I am not compell'd to tell you.

*Mont.* My lord duke sent to you a thousand ducats
The twelfth of August.

*Vit.* 'Twas to keep your cousin
From prison ; I paid use[2] for't.

*Mont.* I rather think,
'Twas interest for his lust.

*Vit.* Who says so but yourself ?
If you be my accuser,
Pray cease to be my judge : come from the bench ;
Give in your evidence 'gainst me, and let these
Be moderators.[3]   My lord cardinal,
Were your intelligencing ears as loving
As to my thoughts, had you an honest tongue,
I would not care though you proclaim'd them all.

*Mont.* Go to, go to.
After your goodly and vainglorious banquet,

---

[1] *crusadoes,*—an old Portuguese coin, so called from the
cross stamped on it.
[2] Interest.
[3] Presidents, Judges.

I'll give you a choke-pear.

*Vit.* A' your own grafting?

*Mont.* You were born in Venice, honourably descended
From the Vittelli : 'twas my cousin's fate,
Ill may I name the hour, to marry you ;
He bought you of your father.

*Vit.* Ha !

*Mont.* He spent there in six months
Twelve thousand ducats, and (to my acquaintance[1])
Receiv'd in dowry with you not one julio :[2]
'Twas a hard pennyworth, the ware being so light.
I yet but draw the curtain ; now to your picture :
You came from thence a most notorious strumpet,
And so you have continued.

*Vit.* My lord !

*Mont.* Nay, hear me,
You shall have time to prate.　My lord Brachiano—
Alas !　I make but repetition,
Of what is ordinary and Rialto talk,
And ballated,[3] and would be play'd a'th' stage,
But that vice many times finds such loud friends,
That preachers are charm'd silent.
You, gentlemen, Flamineo and Marcello,
The court hath nothing now to charge you with,
Only you must remain upon your sureties
For your appearance.

*Fran.* I stand for Marcello.

*Flam.* And my lord duke for me.

*Mont.* For you, Vittoria, your public fault,

---

[1] i. e. knowledge.
[2] A coin of about six-pence value.—REED.
[3] Made the subject of ballads.

Join'd to th' condition of the present time,
Takes from you all the fruits of noble pity,
Such a corrupted trial have you made
Both of your life and beauty, and been styl'd
No less an ominous fate than blazing stars
To princes.   Hear your sentence : you are confin'd
Unto a house of convertites, and your bawd—

*Flam.* Who, I?
*Mont.* The Moor.
*Flam.* O, I am a sound man again.
*Vit.* A house of convertites ! what's that ?
*Mont.* A house of penitent whores.
*Vit.* Do the noblemen in Rome
Erect it for their wives, that I am sent
To lodge there ?
*Fran.* You must have patience.
*Vit.* I must first have vengeance
I fain would know if you have your salvation
By patent, that you proceed thus.
*Mont.* Away with her,
Take her hence.
*Vit.* A rape ! a rape !
*Mont.* How ?
*Vit.* Yes, you have ravish'd justice ;
Forc'd her to do your pleasure.
*Mont.* Fie, she's mad !
*Vit.* Die with those pills in your most cursed maw,
Should bring you health ! or while you sit o'th' bench,
Let your own spittle choke you !
*Mont.* She's turn'd fury.
*Vit.* That the last day of judgment may so find you,

And leave you the same devil you were before!
Instruct me, some good horse-leech, to speak treason;
For since you cannot take my life for deeds,
Take it for words.  O woman's poor revenge,
Which dwells but in the tongue!  I will not weep;
No, I do scorn to call up one poor tear
To fawn on your injustice: bear me hence
Unto this house of—what's your mitigating title?

*Mont.* Of convertites.

*Vit.* It shall not be a house of convertites;
My mind shall make it honester to me
Than the Pope's palace, and more peaceable
Than thy soul, though thou art a cardinal.
Know this, and let it somewhat raise your spite,
Through darkness diamonds spread their richest light.[1]

[*Exit.*

*Enter* BRACHIANO.

*Brach.* Now you and I are friends, sir, we'll shake
In a friend's grave together; a fit place,      [hands
Being th' emblem of soft peace, t'atone[2] our hatred.

[1] "This White Devil of Italy sets off a bad cause so
speciously, and pleads with such an innocence-resembling
boldness, that we seem to see that matchless beauty of her
face which inspires such gay confidence into her; and are
ready to expect, when she has done her pleadings, that her
very judges, her accusers, the grave ambassadors who
sit as spectators, and all the court, will rise and make proffer
to defend her in spite of the utmost conviction of her guilt;
as the shepherds in Don Quixote make proffer to follow the
beautiful shepherdess Marcela, 'without reaping any profit
out of her manifest resolution made there in their hearing.'
So sweet and lovely does she make the shame,
Which, like a canker in the fragrant rose,
Does spot the beauty of her budding name."
C. LAMB.  *Spec. of Eng. Dram. Poets*, p. 229.

[2] *t'atone,*—reconcile, i. e. bring into tune.

*Fran.* Sir, what's the matter?

*Brach.* I will not chase more blood from that lov'd cheek ;

You have lost too much already ; fare you well.   [*Exit.*

*Fran.* How strange these words sound ! what's the interpretation?

*Flam.* [*Aside.*] Good ; this is a preface to the discovery of the duchess's death : he carries it well.   Because now I cannot counterfeit a whining passion for the death of my lady, I will feign a mad humour for the disgrace of my sister ; and that will keep off idle questions.   Treason's tongue hath a villanous palsy in't ; I will talk to any man, hear no man, and for a time appear a politic madman.                      [*Exit.*

*Enter* GIOVANNI, *and Count* LODOVICO.

*Fran.* How now, my noble cousin? what, in black !

*Giov.* Yes, uncle, I was taught to imitate you
In virtue, and you must imitate me
In colours of your garments.   My sweet mother
Is——

*Fran.* How? where?

*Giov.* Is there ; no, yonder : indeed, sir, I'll not tell
For I shall make you weep.                        [you,

*Fran.* Is dead?

*Giov.* Do not blame me now,
I did not tell you so.

*Lod.* She's dead, my lord.

*Fran.* Dead !

*Mont.* Bless'd lady, thou art now above thy woes !
Wilt please your lordships to withdraw a little?[1]

----

[1] To the ambassadors, who withdraw accordingly.

*Giov.* What do the dead do, uncle? do they eat,
Hear music, go a hunting, and be merry,
As we that live?

*Fran.* No, coz; they sleep.

*Giov.* Lord, lord, that I were dead!
I have not slept these six nights. When do they wake?

*Fran.* When God shall please.

*Giov.* Good God, let her sleep ever!
For I have known her wake an hundred nights,
When all the pillow where she laid her head
Was brine-wet with her tears. I am to complain to you,
      sir;
I'll tell you how they have us'd her now she's dead:
They wrapp'd her in a cruel fold of lead,
And would not let me kiss her.

*Fran.* Thou did'st love her.

*Giov.* I have often heard her say she gave me suck,
And it should seem by that she dearly lov'd me,
Since princes seldom do it.

*Fran.* O, all of my poor sister that remains!
Take him away for God's sake?          [*Exit Giovanni.*

*Mont.* How now, my lord?

*Fran.* Believe me, I am nothing but her grave;
And I shall keep her blessed memory
Longer than thousand epitaphs.

### *Enter* FLAMINEO *as distracted.*

*Flam.* We endure the strokes like anvils or hard
      steel,
Till pain itself make us no pain to feel.
Who shall do me right now? is this the end of service
I'd rather go weed garlic; travel through France, and
be mine own ostler; wear sheep-skin linings, or shoes

that stink of blacking; be entered into the list of the forty thousand pedlars in Poland.

*Enter Savoy* Ambassador.

Would I had rotted in some surgeon's house at Venice, built upon the pox as well as on piles, ere I had served Brachiano!

*Savoy Amb.* You must have comfort.

*Flam.* Your comfortable words are like honey : they relish well in your mouth that's whole, but in mine that's wounded, they go down as if the sting of the bee were in them. O, they have wrought their purpose cunningly, as if they would not seem to do it of malice! In this a politician imitates the devil, as the devil imitates a cannon; wheresoever he comes to do mischief, he comes with his backside towards you.

*Enter French and English* Ambassadors.

*French Amb.* The proofs are evident.

*Flam.* Proof! 'twas corruption. O gold, what a god art thou! and O man, what a devil art thou to be tempted by that cursed mineral! Yon diversivolent lawyer, mark him! knaves turn informers, as maggots turn to flies, you may catch gudgeons with either. A cardinal! I would he would hear me : there's nothing so holy but money will corrupt and putrify it, like victual under the line.[1] You are happy in England, my lord; here they sell justice with those weights they press men to death with. O horrible salary!

*Eng. Amb.* Fie, fie, Flamineo.

---

[1] i. e. the equinoctial line.

*Flam.* Bells ne'er ring well, till they are at their full pitch ; and I hope yon cardinal shall never have the grace to pray well, till he come to the scaffold.   If they were racked now to know the confederacy : but your noblemen are privileged from the rack ; and well may, for. a little thing would pull some of them a'pieces afore they came to their arraignment.   Religion, O how it is commedled [1] with policy !   The first blood shed in the world happened about religion.   Would I were a Jew !

*Mar.* O, there are too many !

*Flam.* You are deceived ; there are not Jews enough, priests enough, nor gentlemen enough.

*Mar.* How ?

*Flam.* I'll prove it ; for if there were Jews enough, so many Christians would not turn usurers ; if priests enough, one should not have six benefices ; and if gentlemen enough, so many early mushrooms, whose best growth sprang from a dunghill, should not aspire to gentility.   Farewell : let others live by begging : be thou one of them practise the art of Wolner in England,[2] to swallow all's given thee : and yet let one

---

[1] *commedled,—co-mingled.*   To meddle, anciently, signified to *mix* or *mingle.*—STEEVENS.

[2] As to this *Wolner,* we find in the Registers of the Stationers Company, edited by Collier for the Shakespeare Society, the following particulars :—

"Rd of Henry Denham, for his lycense for the pryntinge of a boke intituled pleasante tayles of the lyfe of Richard Wolner." [Woolner, or Wolner, was a great humourist, and a greater eater, whose name became proverbial.   "Three meales of a lazirillo make the fourth of a Woolner," says G. Hervey in his *Pierces Supererogation,* 1593 ; and S. Rowlands in his *Knave of Clubs,* 1611, has,—

"Plying his victuals thus an hour at least,
       Like unto Woolner the same ravening beast "

A droll, dry story is told of him in Taylor the water-poet's *Wit and Mirth,* 1629, which also found its way into Sir J. Har-

purgation make thee as hungry again as fellows that
work in a saw-pit. I'll go hear the screech-owl.  [*Exit.*

*Lod.* This was Brachiano's pander; and 'tis strange
That in such open, and apparent guilt
Of his adulterous sister, he dare utter
So scandalous a passion.  I must wind him.

*Re-enter* FLAMINEO.

*Flam.* How dares this banish'd count return to Rome,
His pardon not yet purchas'd ! I have heard
The deceased duchess gave him pension,
And that he came along from Padua
I'th' train of the young prince.  There's somewhat in't:
Physicians, that cure poisons, still do work
With counter-poisons.

*Mar.* Mark this strange encounter.

*Flam.* The god of melancholy turn thy gall to poison,
And let the stigmatic[1] wrinkles in thy face,
Like to the boisterous waves in a rough tide,

rington's *Brief View of the State of the Church,* 1653, and is
there thus narrated :—" When he (Day, Bishop of Winches-
ter) was first Dean of Windsor, there was a singing man in
the quire, one Woolner, a pleasant fellow, but famous for his
eating rather than his singing, and for the swallow of his
throat than for the sweetness of his note.  Master Dean sent
a man to reprove him for not singing with his fellows : the
messenger thought all were worshipful, at least, that did
then wear white surplices, and told him, Mr. Dean would
pray his worship to sing ! 'Thank Mr. Dean,' quoth Woolner,
'and tell him I am as merry as they that sing !' Which answer though it would have offended some men, yet, hearing
him to be such as I have described, he was soon pacified."
No copy of Denham's publication regarding Woolner is ex-
tant ; its popularity, no doubt, prevented its preservation,
excepting when a joke, as in the instance just quoted, has
been transmitted to us second or third hand.

[1] *stigmatic,* i. e. marked as with a brand of infamy.—STEEVENS

One still overtake another.

 *Lod.* I do thank thee,
And I do wish ingeniously [1] for thy sake,
The dog-days all year long.

 *Flam.* How croaks the raven ?
Is our good duchess dead ?

 *Lod.* Dead.

 *Flam.* O fate !
Misfortune comes like the coroner's business
Huddle upon huddle.

 *Lod.* Shalt thou and I join house-keeping ?

 *Flam.* Yes, content :
Let's be unsociably sociable.

 *Lod.* Sit some three days together, and discourse ?

 *Flam.* Only with making faces ;
Lie in our clothes.

 *Lod.* With faggots for our pillows.

 *Flam.* And be lousy.

 *Lod.* In taffata linings, that's genteel melancholy ;
Sleep all day.

 *Flam.* Yes ; and, like your melancholic hare,
Feed after midnight.
We are observed : see how yon couple grieve.

 *Lod.* What a strange creature is a laughing fool !
As if man were created to no use
But only to shew his teeth.

 *Flam.* I'll tell thee what,
It would do well instead of looking-glasses,
To set one's face each morning by a saucer
Of a witch's congeal'd blood.

---

   [1] *ingeniously,* for *ingenuously.*

*Lod.* Precious rogue!
We'll never part.

*Flam.* Never, till the beggary of courtiers,
The discontent of churchmen, want of soldiers,
And all the creatures that hang manacled,
Worse than strappadoed, on the lowest felly
Of fortune's wheel, be taught, in our two lives,
To scorn that world which life of means deprives.

*Enter* ANTONELLI.[1]

*Anto.* My lord, I bring good news. The Pope, on's
death-bed,
At th' earnest suit of the great duke of Florence,
Hath sign'd your pardon, and restor'd unto you——

*Lod.* I thank you for your news. Look up again,
Flamineo, see my pardon.

*Flam.* Why do you laugh?
There was no such condition in our covenant.

*Lod.* Why?

*Flam.* You shall not seem a happier man than I:
You know our vow, sir; if you will be merry,
Do it i'th' like posture, as if some great man
Sate while his enemy were executed:
Though it be very lechery unto thee,
Do't with a crabbed politician's face.

*Lod.* Your sister is a damnable whore.

*Flam.* Ha!

*Lod.* Look you, I spake that laughing.

*Flam.* Dost ever think to speak again?

*Lod.* Do you hear?

[1] And with him Gasparo, though the entrance is not
marked in the quartos.

Wilt sell me forty ounces of her blood
To water a mandrake?

*Flam.* Poor lord, you did vow
To live a lousy creature.

*Lod.* Yes.

*Flam.* Like one
That had for ever forfeited the day-light,
By being in debt.

*Lod.* Ha, ha!

*Flam.* I do not greatly wonder you do break,
Your lordship learn'd 't long since.   But I'll tell you.

*Lod.* What?

*Flam.* And 't shall stick by you.

*Lod.* I long for it.

*Flam.* This laughter scurvily becomes your face:
If you will not be melancholy, be angry.   [*Strikes him.*
See, now I laugh too.

*Mar.* You are to blame: I'll force you hence.

*Lod.* Unhand me.   [*Exeunt Marcello and Flamineo.*
That e'er I should be forc'd to right myself,
Upon a pander!

*Anto.* My lord.

*Lod.* H' had been as good met with his fist a thun-
    derbolt.

*Gas.* How this shews!

*Lod.* Uds'death! how did my sword miss him?
These rogues that are most weary of their lives
Still 'scape the greatest dangers.
A pox upon him; all his reputation,
Nay, all the goodness of his family,
Is not worth half this earthquake:

I learn'd it of no fencer to shake thus :
Come, I'll forget him, and go drink some wine. [*Exeunt.*

### SCENE III.

*Enter* FRANCISCO *and* MONTICELSO.

*Mont.* Come, come, my lord, untie your folded
    thoughts,
And let them dangle loose, as a bride's hair.[1]
Your sister's poison'd.
    *Fran.* Far be it from my thoughts
To seek revenge.
    *Mont.* What, are you turn'd all marble ?
    *Fran.* Shall I defy him, and impose a war,
Most burthensome on my poor subjects' necks,
Which at my will I have not power to end ?
You know for all the murders, rapes, and thefts,
Committed in the horrid lust of war,
He that unjustly caus'd it first proceed,
Shall find it in his grave, and in his seed.
    *Mont.* That's not the course I'd wish you ; pray
    observe me.
We see that undermining more prevails
Than doth the cannon.   Bear your wrongs conceal'd,
And, patient as the tortoise, let this camel
Stalk o'er your back unbruis'd : sleep with the lion,
And let this brood of secure foolish mice
Play with your nostrils, till the time be ripe
For th' bloody audit, and the fatal gripe :
Aim like a cunning fowler, close one eye,

    [1] Brides formerly walked to church with their hair hang-
ing loose behind.—STEEVENS.

That you the better may your game espy.

    *Fran.* Free me, my innocence, from treacherous acts!
I know there's thunder yonder ; and I'll stand,
Like a safe valley, which low bends the knee
To some aspiring mountain : since I know
Treason, like spiders weaving nets for flies,
By her foul work is found, and in it dies.
To pass away these thoughts, my honour'd lord,
It is reported you possess a book,
Wherein you have quoted, by intelligence,
The names of all notorious offenders
Lurking about the city.

    *Mont.* Sir, I do ;
And some there are which call it my black-book.
Well may the title hold ; for though it teach not
The art of conjuring, yet in it lurk
The names of many devils.

    *Fran.* Pray let's see it.

    *Mont.* I'll fetch it to your lordship.        [*Exit.*

    *Fran.* Monticelso,
I will not trust thee, but in all my plots
I'll rest as jealous as a town besieg'd.
Thou canst not reach what I intend to act :
Your flax soon kindles, soon is out again,
But gold slow heats, and long will hot remain.

    *Enter* MONTICELSO, *presents* FRANCISCO *with a book.*

    *Mont.* 'Tis here, my lord.

    *Fran.* First, your intelligencers, pray let's see.

    *Mont.* Their number rises strangely ;
And some of them

You'd take for honest men.
Next are panders.
These are your pirates ; and these following leaves
For base rogues, that undo young gentlemen,
By taking up commodities ;[1] for politic bankrupts ;
For fellows that are bawds to their own wives,
Only to put off horses, and slight jewels,
Clocks, defac'd plate, and such commodities,
At birth of their first children.

   *Fran.* Are there such ?

   *Mont.* These are for impudent bawds,
That go in men's apparel ; for usurers
That share with scriveners for their good reportage
For lawyers that will antedate their writs :
And some divines you might find folded there,
But that I slip them o'er for conscience' sake.
Here is a general catalogue of knaves :
A man might study all the prisons o'er,
Yet never attain this knowledge.

   *Fran.* Murderers ?
Fold down the leaf, I pray ;
Good, my lord, let me borrow this strange doctrine.

   *Mont.* Pray, use't, my lord.

   *Fran.* I do assure your lordship,
You are a worthy member of the state,
And have done infinite good in your discovery
Of these offenders.

   *Mont.* Somewhat, sir.

---

[1] Usurers formerly defrauded necessitous borrowers by furnishing them with goods and wares, to be converted into cash at a great loss to the borrower. This was done to avoid the penal Statutes against Usury.—REED.

*Fran.* O God!
Better than tribute of wolves paid in England;
'Twill hang their skins o'th hedge.

*Mont.* I must make bold
To leave your lordship.

*Fran.* Dearly, sir, I thank you:
If any ask for me at court, report
You have left me in the company of knaves.

[*Exit Monticelso.*

I gather now by this, some cunning fellow
That's my lord's officer, and that lately skipp'd
From a clerk's desk up to a justice' chair,
Hath made this knavish summons, and intends,
As th' Irish rebels wont were to sell heads,
So to make prize of these. And thus it happens:
Your poor rogues pay for't which have not the means
To present bribe in fist; the rest o'th' band
Are raz'd out of the knaves' record; or else
My lord he winks at them with easy will;
His man grows rich, the knaves are the knaves still.
But to the use I'll make of it; it shall serve
To point me out a list of murderers,
Agents for any villany. Did I want
Ten leash of courtezans, it would furnish me;
Nay, laundress three armies. That in so little paper
Should lie th' undoing of so many men!
'Tis not so big as twenty declarations.
See the corrupted use some make of books:
Divinity, wrested by some factious blood,
Draws swords, swells battles, and o'erthrows all good.
To fashion my revenge more seriously,

Let me remember my dead sister's face :
Call for her picture? no, I'll close mine eyes,
And in a melancholic thought I'll frame

*Enter* Isabella's *ghost.*

Her figure 'fore me.   Now I ha't—how strong
Imagination works ! how she can frame
Things which are not ! methinks she stands afore me,
And by the quick idea of my mind,
Were my skill pregnant, I could draw her picture.
Thought as a subtle juggler, makes us deem
Things supernatural, which have cause
Common as sickness.   'Tis my melancholy.
How cam'st thou by thy death?—how idle am.I
To question mine own idleness !—did ever
Man dream awake till now ?—remove this object ;
Out of my brain with't : what have I to do
With tombs, or death-beds, funerals, or tears,
That have to meditate upon revenge ?    [*Exit Ghost.*[1]
So, now 'tis ended, like an old wife's story.
Statesmen think often they see stranger sights
Than madmen.   Come, to this weighty business.
My tragedy must have some idle mirth in't,
Else it will never pass.   I am in love,
In love with Corombona ; and my suit
Thus halts to her in verse.—                [*He writes.*
I have done it rarely : O the fate of princes !
I am so us'd to frequent flattery,
That, being alone, I now flatter myself :
But it will serve ; 'tis seal'd.   Bear this

[1] Supplied by Mr. Dyce.

*Enter* SERVANT.

To the house of convertites, and watch your leisure
To give it to the hands of Corombona,
Or to the matron, when some followers
Of Brachiano may be by.   Away.        [*Exit Servant.*
He that deals all by strength, his wit is shallow;
When a man's head goes through, each limb will follow.
The engine for my business, bold count Lodowick;
'Tis gold must such an instrument procure,
With empty fist no man doth falcons lure.
Brachiano, I am now fit for thy encounter:
Like the wild Irish, I'll ne'er think thee dead
Till I can play at football with thy head.
*Flectere si nequeo superos, Acheronta movebo.*      [*Exit.*


## ACT IV.—SCENE I.[1]

*Enter the* MATRON, *and* FLAMINEO.

*Matron.*

SHOULD it be known the duke hath such
        recourse
        To your imprison'd sister, I were like
T' incur much damage by it.
    *Flam.* Not a scruple.
The Pope lies on his death-bed, and their heads
Are troubled now with other business
Than guarding of a lady.

[1] Supplied from the 4to. of 1672.

*Enter* SERVANT.

*Servant.* Yonder's Flamineo in conference
With the matrona.—Let me speak with you :
I would entreat you to deliver for me
This letter to the fair Vittoria.
　*Matron.* I shall, sir.

*Enter* BRACHIANO.

*Servant.* With all care and secresy ;
Hereafter you shall know me, and receive
Thanks for this courtesy.　　　　　　　　　*[Exit.*
　*Flam.* How now ? what's that ?
　*Matron.* A letter.
　*Flam.* To my sister ?　I'll see't deliver'd.
　*Brach.* What's that you read, Flamineo ?
　*Flam.* Look.
　*Brach.* Ha !　"To the most unfortunate, his best
　　respected Vittoria."
Who was the messenger ?
　*Flam.* I know not.
　*Brach.* No ! who sent it ?
　*Flam.* Ud'sfoot ! you speak, as if a man
Should know what fowl is coffin'd in a bak'd meat
Afore you cut it up.
　*Brach.* I'll open't, were't her heart.　What's here
　　subscrib'd !
Florence ! this juggling is gross and palpable.
I have found out the conveyance.　Read it, read it.
　*Flam.* "Your tears I'll turn to triumphs, be but mine ;
Your prop is fallen : I pity, that a vine,

Which princes heretofore have long'd to gather,
Wanting supporters, now should fade and wither."
(Wine, i'faith, my lord, with lees would serve his turn.)
" Your sad imprisonment I'll soon uncharm,
And with a princely uncontrolled arm
Lead you to Florence, where my love and care
Shall hang your wishes in my silver hair."
(A halter on his strange equivocation !)
" Nor for my years return me the sad willow,
Who prefer blossoms before fruit that's mellow ? "
(Rotten, on my knowledge, with lying too long i'th'
        bed-straw.)
" And all the lines of age this line convinces ; [1]
The gods never wax old, no more do princes."
A pox on't, tear it; let's have no more atheists, for
        God's sake.

*Brach.* Ud'sdeath ! . I'll cut her into atomies.
And let th' irregular north-wind sweep her up,
And blow her int' his nostrils : where's this whore ?

*Flam.* What ? what do you call her ?

*Brach.* O, I could be mad !
Prevent the curs'd disease [2] she'll bring me to,
And tear my hair off.   Where's this changeable stuff ?

*Flam.* O'er head and ears in water, I assure you ;
She is not for your wearing.

*Brach.* No, you pander ?

*Flam.* What, me, my lord ? am I your dog ?

*Brach.* A blood-hound : do you brave, do you stand
        me ?

_____
[1] Overcomes : a *Latinism*.
[2] i. e. anticipate (*prevenir*) the consequences of the foul
disease she'll give me ;—one of which is, that the hair falls off.

*Flam.* Stand you ! let those that have diseases run ;
I need no plasters.

*Brach.* Would you be kick'd ?

*Flam.* Would you have your neck broke ?
I tell you, duke, I am not in Russia ; [1]
My shins must be kept whole.

*Brach.* Do you know me ?

*Flam.* O my lord, methodically !
As in this world there are degrees of evils,
So in this world there are degrees of devils.
You're a great duke, I your poor secretary.
I do look now for a Spanish fig, or an Italian sallet,[2]
  daily.

*Brach.* Pander, ply your convoy, and leave your
  prating.

[1] It appears from Giles Fletcher's *Russe Commonwealth*, 1591, p. 51, that, on determining an action of debt in that country, "the partie convicted is delivered to the Serjeant, who hath a writte for his warrant out of the Office, to carry him to the *Praveush*, or Righter of Justice, if presently hee pay not the monie, or content not the partie. This *Praveush*, or Righter, is a place neere to the office : where such as have sentence passed against them, and refuse to pay that which is adjudged, are beaten with great cudgels *on the shinnes* and calves of their legges. Every forenoone from eight to eleven they are set on the *Praveush*, and beate in this sort till the monie be payd. The afternoone and night time they are kept in chaines by the Serjeant : except they put in sufficient suerties for their appearance at the *Praveush* at the hower appointed. You shall see fortie or fiftie stand together on the *Praveush* all on a rowe, and their *shinnes* thvs becudgelled and bebasted every morning with a piteous crie. If after a yeare's standing on the Praveush, the partie will not, or lacke wherewithall to satisfie his creditour, it is lawfull for him to sell his wife and children, eyther outright, or for a certaine terme of yeares. And if the price of them doo not amount to the full payment, the creditour may take them to bee his bondslaves, for yeares or for ever, according as the value of the debt requireth."—REED.

[2] Referring to the custom of giving poisoned figs or vegetables to those who were the objects either of the Spanish or Italian revenge.—REED.

*Flam.* All your kindness to me, is like that miserable courtesy of Polyphemus to Ulysses; you reserve me to be devoured last: you would dig turfs out of my grave to feed your larks; that would be music to you. Come, I'll lead you to her.

*Brach.* Do you face me?

*Flam.* O, sir, I would not go before a politic enemy with my back towards him, though there were behind me a whirlpool.

## SCENE II.

*Enter to* VITTORIA, BRACHIANO *and* FLAMINEO.[1]

*Brach.* Can you read, mistress? look upon that letter:
There are no characters, nor hieroglyphics.
You need no comment; I am grown your receiver.
God's precious! you shall be a brave great lady,
A stately and advanced whore.

*Vit.* Say, sir?

*Brach.* Come, come, let's see your cabinet, discover
Your treasury of love-letters. Death and furies!
I'll see them all.

*Vit.* Sir, upon my soul,
I have not any. Whence was this directed?

*Brach.* Confusion on your politic[2] ignorance!
You are reclaim'd, are you? I'll give you the bells,[3]
And let you fly to the devil.

*Flam.* Ware hawk, my lord.

*Vit.* Florence! this is some treacherous plot, my lord;
To me he ne'er was lovely,[4] I protest,

[1] Conjecturally. The old editions mark Enter Vittoria_to Brachiano and Flamineo.
[2] i. e. politicly feigned.          [3] As to a hawk.
[4] The 4to. of 1612 has "thought on"

So much as in my sleep.

   *Brach.* Right! they are plots.
Your beauty!   O ten thousand curses on't!
How long have I beheld the devil in crystal![1]
Thou hast led me, like an heathen sacrifice,
With music, and with fatal yokes of flowers,
To my eternal ruin.   Woman to man
Is either a god, or a wolf.

   *Vit.* My lord.

   *Brach.* Away!
We'll be as differing as two adamants,
The one shall shun the other.   What! dost weep?
Procure but ten of thy dissembling trade,
Ye'd furnish all the Irish funerals
With howling past wild Irish.

   *Flam.* Fie, my lord!

   *Brach.* That hand, that cursed hand, which I have
     wearied
With doating kisses!—O my sweetest duchess,
How lovely art thou now!—My loose thoughts
Scatter like quicksilver: I was bewitch'd;
For all the world speaks ill of thee.

   *Vit.* No matter;
I'll live so now, I'll make that world recant,
And change her speeches.   You did name your duchess.

   *Brach.* Whose death God pardon!

   *Vit.* Whose death God revenge

---

[1] *How long have I beheld the devil in crystal.* The Beril,
which is a kind of crystal, hath a weak tincture of red in it.
Among other tricks of astrologers, the discovery of past or
future events was supposed to be the consequence of looking into it.   See *Aubrey's Miscellanies*, (p. 154, Edition of
1857.)—REED.

On thee, most godless duke!

*Flam.* Now for ten whirlwinds.

*Vit.* What have I gain'd by thee, but infamy?
Thou hast stain'd the spotless honour of my house,
And frighted thence noble society:
Like those, which sick o'th' palsy, and retain
Ill-scenting foxes 'bout them, are still shunn'd
By those of choicer nostrils. What do you call this house?
Is this your palace? did not the judge style it
A house of penitent whores? who sent me to it?
Who hath the honour to advance Vittoria
To this incontinent college? is't not you?
Is't not your high preferment? go, go, brag
How many ladies you have undone like me.
Fare you well, sir; let me hear no more of you!
I had a limb corrupted to an ulcer,
But I have cut it off; and now I'll go
Weeping to heaven on crutches. For your gifts,
I will return them all, and I do wish
That I could make you full executor
To all my sins. O that I could toss myself
Into a grave as quickly! for all thou art worth
I'll not shed one tear more—I'll burst first.

> [*She throws herself upon a bed.*

*Brach.* I have drunk Lethe: Vittoria!
My dearest happiness! Vittoria!
What do you ail, my love? why do you weep?

*Vit.* Yes, I now weep poniards, do you see?

*Brach.* Are not those matchless eyes mine?

*Vit.* I had rather
They were not matchless.

*Brach.* Is not this lip mine ?

*Vit.* Yes ; thus to bite it off, rather than give it thee.

*Flam.* Turn to my lord, good sister.

*Vit.* Hence, you pander !

*Flam.* Pander ! am I the author of your sin ?

*Vit.* Yes ; he's a base thief that a thief lets in.

*Flam.* We're blown up, my lord.

*Brach.* Wilt thou hear me ?
Once to be jealous of thee, is t'express
That I will love thee everlastingly,
And never more be jealous.

 *Vit.* O thou fool,
Whose greatness hath by much o'ergrown thy wit !
What dar'st thou do, that I not dare to suffer,
Excepting to be still thy whore ? for that,
In the sea's bottom sooner thou shalt make
A bonfire.

 *Flam.* O, no oaths, for God's sake !

 *Brach.* Will you hear me ?

 *Vit.* Never.

 *Flam.* What a damn'd imposthume is a woman's will !
Can nothing break it ?   Fie, fie, my lord,
Women are caught as you take tortoises,
She must be turn'd on her back [*Aside*].—Sister, by
  this hand
I am on your side—Come, come, you have wrong'd her :
What a strange credulous man were you, my lord,
To think the duke of Florence would love her !
Will any mercer take another's ware
When once 'tis tows'd and sullied ?   And yet, sister,
How scurvily this forwardness becomes you !

Young leverets stand not long, and women's anger
Should, like their flight, procure a little sport ;
A full cry for a quarter of an hour,
And then be put to th' dead quat.[1]

*Brach.* Shall these eyes,
Which have so long time dwelt upon your face,
Be now put out ?

*Flam.* No cruel landlady i'th' world,
Which lends forth groats to broom-men, and takes use
For them, would do't.
Hand her, my lord, and kiss her : be not like
A ferret, to let go your hold with blowing.

*Brach.* Let us renew right hands.

*Vit.* Hence !

*Brach.* Never shall rage, or the forgetful wine,
Make me commit like fault.

*Flam.* Now you are i'th' way on't, follow't hard.

*Brach.* Be thou at peace with me, let all the world
Threaten the cannon.

*Flam.* Mark his penitence ;
Best natures do commit the grossest faults,
When they're given o'er to jealousy, as best wine,
Dying, makes strongest vinegar.    I'll tell you :
The sea's more rough and raging than calm rivers,
But not so sweet, nor wholesome.    A quiet woman
Is a still water under a great bridge ;
A man may shoot[2] her safely.

---

[1] *Quat*—a corruption of *squat.*
[2] To *shoot the bridge* was a term used by watermen, to signify going through London-bridge at the turning of the tide.
The vessel then went with great velocity, and from thence it
probably was called *shooting.*—REED.

*Vit.* O ye dissembling men !

*Flam.* We suck'd that, sister,
From women's breasts, in our first infancy.

*Vit.* To add misery to misery !

*Brach.* Sweetest !

*Vit.* Am I not low enough ?
Ay, ay, your good heart gathers like a snow-ball,
Now your affection's cold.

*Flam.* Ud'sfoot, it shall melt
To a heart again, or all the wine in Rome
Shall run o'th' lees for't.

*Vit.* Your dog or hawk should be rewarded better
Than I have been.   I'll speak not one word more.

*Flam.* Stop her mouth
With a sweet kiss, my lord.   So,
Now the tide's turn'd, the vessel's come about.
He's a sweet armful.   O, we curl-hair'd men
Are still most kind to women !   This is well.

*Brach.* That you should chide thus !

*Flam.* O, sir, your little chimnies
Do ever cast most smoke !   I sweat for you.
Couple together with as deep a silence,
As did the Grecians in their wooden horse.
My lord, supply your promises with deeds ;
You know that painted meat no hunger feeds.

*Brach.* Stay, ingrateful Rome—[1]

*Flam.* Rome ! it deserves to be call'd Barbary,
For our villanous usage.

*Brach.* Soft ; the same project which the duke of
        Florence,

---

[1] I suspect we should read "Stay *in* ingrateful Rome !"—
DYCE.

(Whether in love or gullery I know not,)
Laid down for her escape, will I pursue.

*Flam.* And no time fitter than this night, my lord.
The Pope being dead, and all the cardinals enter'd
The conclave, for th' electing a new pope ;
The city in a great confusion ;
We may attire her in a page's suit,
Lay her post-horse, take shipping, and amain
For Padua.

*Brach.* I'll instantly steal forth the prince Giovanni,
And make for Padua.   You two with your old mother,
And young Marcello that attends on Florence,
If you can work him to it, follow me :
I will advance you all ; for you, Vittoria,
Think of a duchess' title.

*Flam.* Lo you, sister !
Stay, my lord ; I'll tell you a tale.   The crocodile,
which lives in the river Nilus, hath a worm breeds i'th
teeth of't, which puts it to extreme anguish : a little
bird, no bigger than a wren, is barber-surgeon to this
crocodile ; flies into the jaws of't, picks out the worm,
and brings present remedy.   The fish, glad of ease, but
ingrateful to her that did it, that the bird may not talk
largely of her abroad for non-payment, closeth her chaps,
intending to swallow her, and so put her to perpetual
silence.   But nature, loathing such ingratitude, hath
armed this bird with a quill or prick on the head, top
o'th' which wounds the crocodile i'th' mouth, forceth
her open her bloody prison, and away flies the pretty
tooth-picker from her cruel patient.

*Brach.* Your application is, I have not rewarded
The service you have done me

*Flam.* No, my lord.

You, sister, are the crocodile: you are blemish'd in your fame, my lord cures it; and though the comparison hold not in every particle, yet observe, remember, what good the bird with the prick i'th' head hath done you, and scorn ingratitude.

It may appear to some ridiculous
Thus to talk knave and madman, and sometimes
Come in with a dried sentence, stuft with sage :
But this allows my varying of shapes ;
Knaves do grow great by being great men's apes.

*[Exeunt.*

## SCENE III.

*Enter* FRANCISCO, LODOVICO, GASPARO, *and six Ambassadors.*

*Fran.* So, my lord, I commend your diligence.
Guard well the conclave ; and, as the order is,
Let none have conference with the cardinals.

*Lod.* I shall, my lord.    Room for the ambassadors.

*Gasp.* They're wondrous brave[1] to-day : why do they
wear
These several habits ?

*Lod.* O, sir, they're knights
Of several orders :
That lord i'th' black cloak, with the silver cross,
Is knight of Rhodes ; the next, knight of St. Michael ;
That, of the Golden Fleece ; the Frenchman, there,

Fine.

Knight of the Holy Ghost; my lord of Savoy,
Knight of th' Annunciation; the Englishman
Is knight of th' honour'd Garter, dedicated
Unto their Saint, St. George.    I could describe to you
Their several institutions, with the laws
Annexed to their orders; but that time
Permits not such discovery.

 *Fran.* Where's count Lodowick?

 *Lod.* Here, my lord.

 *Fran.* 'Tis o'th' point of dinner time;
Marshal the cardinals' service.

 *Lod.* Sir, I shall.

   *Enter* SERVANTS, *with several dishes covered.*

Stand, let me search your dish.    Who's this for?

 *Servant.* For my lord cardinal Monticelso.

 *Lod.* Whose this?

 *Servant.* For my lord cardinal of Bourbon.

 *Fr. Amb.* Why doth he search the dishes? to observe
What meat is drest?

 *Eng. Amb.* No, sir, but to prevent
Lest any letters should be convey'd in,
To bribe or to solicit the advancement
Of any cardinal.    When first they enter,
'Tis lawful for the ambassadors of princes
To enter with them, and to make their suit
For any man their prince affecteth best;
But after, till a general election,
No man may speak with them.

 *Lod.* You that attend on the lord cardinals,
Open the window, and receive their viands.

*Cardinal [within].* You must return the service : the
     lord cardinals
Are busied 'bout electing of the Pope ;
They have given o'er scrutiny, and are fallen
To admiration.[1]

*Lod.* Away, away.

*Fran.* I'll lay a thousand ducats you hear news
Of a Pope presently.   Hark ; sure he's elected :
Behold, my lord of Arragon appears
On the church battlements.

                         [*A Cardinal on the terrace.*

*Arragon. Denuntio vobis gaudium magnum : Reve-
rendissimus cardinalis Lorenzo de Monticelso electus est in
sedem apostolicam, et elegit sibi nomen Paulum Quartum.*[2]

*Omnes. Vivat sanctus pater Paulus Quartus !*

*Servant.* Vittoria, my lord—

*Fran.* Well, what of her ?

*Servant.* Is fled the city.

*Fran.* Ha !.

*Servant.* With duke Brachiano.

*Fran.* Fled ! where's the prince Giovanni ?

*Servant.* Gone with his father.

*Fran.* Let the matrona of the convertites
Be apprehended.   Fled ?   O damnable !
How fortunate are my wishes ! why, 'twas this
I only labour'd : I did send the letter
T'instruct him what to do.   Thy fame, fond duke,
I first have poison'd ; directed thee the way

---

[1] So in the quartos.   The sense must be inferred from the
context.
[2] Mr. Dyce points out that the name of Paul IV. was not
Monticelso, but Caraffa.

To marry a whore ; what can be worse ? this follows:
The hand must act to drown the passionate tongue,
I scorn to wear a sword and prate of wrong.

*Enter* MONTICELSO *in state.*

*Mont. Concedimus vobis apostolicam benedictionem,
et remissionem peccatorum.*
My lord reports Vittoria Corombona
Is stol'n from forth the house of convertites
By Brachiano, and they're fled the city.
Now, though this be the first day of our seat,
We cannot better please the divine power,
Than to sequester from the holy church
These cursed persons.   Make it therefore known,
We do denounce excommunication
Against them both : all that are theirs in Rome
We likewise banish.   Set on.                    [*Exit.*
    *Fran.* Come, dear Lodovico ;
You have ta'en the sacrament to prosecute
Th' intended murder.
    *Lod.* With all constancy.
But, sir, I wonder you'll engage yourself
In person, being a great prince.
    *Fran.* Divert me not.
Most of his court are of my faction,
And some are of my council.   Noble friend,
Our danger shall be like in this design :
Give leave part of the glory may be mine.
                              [*Exit Francisco.*

*Enter* MONTICELSO.

*Mont.* Why did the duke of Florence with such care
Labour your pardon ? say.

*Lod.* Italian beggars will resolve you that,
Who, begging of an alms, bid those they beg of,
Do good for their own sakes ; or't may be,
He spreads his bounty with a sowing hand,
Like kings, who many times give out of measure,
Not for desert so much, as for their pleasure.

*Mont.* I know you're cunning.   Come, what devil
        was that
That you were raising ?

*Lod.* Devil ! my lord.

*Mont.* I ask you,
How doth the duke employ you, that his bonnet
Fell with such compliment unto his knee,
When he departed from you ?

*Lod.* Why, my lord,
He told me of a resty Barbary horse
Which he would fain have brought to the career,
The sault, and the ring galliard : now, my lord,
I have a rare French rider.

*Mont.* Take you heed,
Lest the jade break your neck.   Do you put me off
With your wild horse-tricks ?   Sirrah, you do lie.
O, thou'rt a foul black cloud, and thou dost threat
A violent storm !

*Lod.* Storms are i'th' air, my lord ;
I am too low to storm.

*Mont.* Wretched creature !

I know that thou art fashion'd for all ill,
Like dogs, that once get blood, they'll ever kill.
About some murder, was't not?

   *Lod.* I'll not tell you:
And yet I care not greatly if I do;
Marry, with this preparation.   Holy father,
I come not to you as an intelligencer,[1]
But as a penitent sinner: what I utter
Is in confession merely; which, you know,
Must never be reveal'd.

   *Mont.* You have o'erta'en me.

   *Lod.* Sir, I did love Brachiano's duchess dearly,
Or rather I pursued her with hot lust,
Though she ne'er knew on't.   She was poison'd;
Upon my soul she was: for which I have sworn
T' avenge her murder.

   *Mont.* To the duke of Florence?

   *Lod.* To him I have.

   *Mont.* Miserable creature!
If thou persist in this, 'tis damnable.
Dost thou imagine, thou canst slide on blood,
And not be tainted with a shameful fall?
Or, like the black and melancholic yew-tree,
Dost think to root thyself in dead men's graves,
And yet to prosper?   Instruction to thee
Comes like sweet showers to o'er-harden'd ground;
They wet, but pierce not deep.   And so I leave thee,
With all the furies hanging 'bout thy neck,
Till by thy penitence thou remove this evil,
In conjuring from thy breast that cruel devil.   [*Exit*

        [1] Informer.

*Lod.* I'll give it o'er; he says 'tis damnable :
Besides I did expect his suffrage,
By reason of Camillo's death.

*Enter* SERVANT *and* FRANCISCO.

*Fran.* Do you know that count ?
*Servant.* Yes, my lord.
*Fran.* Bear him these thousand ducats to his lodging
Tell him the Pope hath sent them.  Happily [1]
That will confirm more than all the rest.        [*Exit.*
*Servant.* Sir.
*Lod.* To me, sir ?
*Servant.* His Holiness hath sent you a thousand
        crowns,
And wills you, if you travel, to make him
Your patron for intelligence.
*Lod.* His creature ever to be commanded.—
Why now 'tis come about.  He rail'd upon me ;
And yet these crowns were told out, and laid ready,
Before he knew my voyage.  O the art,
The modest form of greatness ! that do sit,
Like brides at wedding-dinners, with their looks turn'd
From the least wanton jest, their puling stomach
Sick of the modesty, when their thoughts are loose,
Even acting of those hot and lustful sports
Are to ensue about midnight : such his cunning !
He sounds my depth thus with a golden plummet.
I am doubly arm'd now.  Now to th' act of blood.
There's but three furies found in spacious hell,
But in a great man's breast three thousand dwell. [*Exit.*

----

[1] Perchance.

## SCENE IV. AT PADUA.

*A passage over the stage of* BRACHIANO, FLAMINEO, MAR-
CELLO, HORTENSIO, COROMBONA, CORNELIA, ZANCHE,
*and others : Flamineo and Hortensio remain.*

*Flam.* In all the weary minutes of my life,
Day ne'er broke up till now.   This marriage
Confirms me happy.
   *Hort.* 'Tis a good assurance.
Saw you not yet the Moor that's come to court?
   *Flam.* Yes, and conferr'd with him i'th' duke's closet.
I have not seen a goodlier personage,
Nor ever talk'd with man better experienc'd
In state affairs, or rudiments of war.
He hath, by report, serv'd the Venetian
In Candy these twice seven years, and been chief
In many a bold design.
   *Hort.* What are those two
That bear him company
   *Flam.* Two noblemen of Hungary, that, living in the
emperor's service as commanders, eight years since, contrary to the expectation of all the court, entered into religion, into the strict order of Capuchins ; but, being not
well settled in their undertaking, they left their order,
and returned to court ; for which, being after troubled
in conscience, they vowed their service against the enemies of Christ, went to Malta, were there knighted, and
in their return back, at this great solemnity, they are
resolved for ever to forsake the world, and settle themselves here in a house of Capuchins in Padua.

*Hort.* 'Tis strange.

*Flam.* One thing makes it so: they have vow'd for ever to wear, next their bare bodies, those coats of mail they served in.

*Hort.* Hard penance!
Is the Moor a Christian?

*Flam.* He is.

*Hort.* Why proffers he his service to our duke?

*Flam.* Because he understands there's like to grow
Some wars between us and the duke of Florence,
In which he hopes employment.
I never saw one in a stern bold look
Wear more command, nor in a lofty phrase
Express more knowing, or more deep contempt
Of our slight airy courtiers.   He talks
As if he had travell'd all the princes' courts
Of Christendom : in all things strives t'express,
That all, that should dispute with him, may know,
Glories, like glow-worms, afar off shine bright,
But look'd to near, have neither heat nor light.
The duke.

*Enter* BRACHIANO, FRANCISCO *disguised like* MULINASSAR,
  LODOVICO *and* GASPARO, *bearing their swords, their*
  *helmets down,* ANTONELLI, FARNESE.

*Brach.* You are nobly welcome. We have heard at full
Your honourable service 'gainst the Turk.
To you, brave Mulinassar, we assign
A competent pension : and are inly sorry,
The vows of those two worthy gentlemen
Make them incapable of our proffer'd bounty.

Your wish is, you may leave your warlike swords
For monuments in our chapel : I accept it,
As a great honour done me, and must crave
Your leave to furnish out our duchess' revels.
Only one thing, as the last vanity
You e'er shall view, deny me not to stay
To see a barriers[1] prepar'd to-night :
You shall have private standings.   It hath pleas'd
The great ambassadors of several princes,
In their return from Rome to their own countries,
To grace our marriage, and to honour me
With such a kind of sport.

    *Fran.* I shall persuade them to stay, my lord.
    *Brach.*[2] Set on there to the presence.
             [*Exeunt Brachiano, Flamineo, and Hortensio.*
    *Lod.* Noble my lord, most fortunately welcome ;
             [*The conspirators here embrace.*
You have our vows, seal'd with the sacrament,
To second your attempts.

    *Gas.* And all things ready ;
He could not have invented his own ruin
(Had he despair'd) with more propriety.

    *Lod.* You would not take my way.
    *Fran.* 'Tis better order'd.
    *Lod.* T' have poison'd his prayer-book, or a pair of
    beads,
The pummel of his saddle, his looking-glass,
Or th' handle of his racket,—O that, that !
That while he had been bandying at tennis,
He might have sworn himself to hell, and strook

   [1] Tilting-match.
   [2] A correction by Mr. Dyce.   The quartos all give the line
to Francisco.

His soul into the hazard !   O, my lord,
I would have our plot be ingenious,
And have it hereafter recorded for example,
Rather than borrow example.

*Fran.* There's no way
More speeding than this thought on.

*Lod.* On then.

*Fran.* And yet methinks that this revenge is poor,
Because it steals upon him like a thief :
To have ta'en him by the casque in a pitch'd field,
Led him to Florence—

*Lod.* It had been rare : and there
Have crown'd him with a wreath of stinking garlic ;
T' have shown the sharpness of his government,
And rankness of his lust.   Flamineo comes.

[*Exeunt Lodovico, Antonelli, and Gasparo.*

*Enter* FLAMINEO, MARCELLO, *and* ZANCHE.

*Mar.* Why doth this devil haunt you, say ?

*Flam.* I know not :
For by this light, I do not conjure for her.
'Tis not so great a cunning as men think,
To raise the devil ; for here's one up already ;
The greatest cunning were to lay him down.

*Mar.* She is your shame.

*Flam.* I prithee pardon her.
In faith, you see, women are like to burs,
Where their affection throws them, there they'll stick.

*Zanche.* That is my countryman, a goodly person ;
When he's at leisure, I'll discourse with him
In our own language.

*Flam.* I beseech you do.      [*Exit Zanche.*

How is't, brave soldier?    O that I had seen
Some of your iron days !    I pray relate
Some of your service to us.

*Fran.* 'Tis a ridiculous thing for a man to be his own
chronicle: I did never wash my mouth with mine own
praise, for fear of getting a stinking breath.

*Mar.* You're too stoical.    The duke will expect other
discourse from you.

*Fran.* I shall never flatter him : I have studied man
too much to do that.    What difference is between the
duke and I? no more than between two bricks, all made
of one clay : only't may be one is placed on the top of a
turret, the other in the bottom of a well, by mere chance.
If I were placed as high as the duke, I should stick as
fast, make as fair a shew, and bear out weather equally.

*Flam.* If this soldier had a patent to beg in churches,
then he would tell them stories.

*Mar.* I have been a soldier too.

*Fran.* How have you thrived?

*Mar.* Faith, poorly.

*Fran.* That's the misery of peace : only outsides are
then respected.    As ships seem very great upon the
river, which shew very little upon the seas, so some men
i'th' court seem Colossuses in a chamber, who, if they
came into the field, would appear pitiful pigmies.

*Flam.* Give me a fair room yet hung with arras, and
some great cardinal to lug me by th' ears, as his endeared
minion.

*Fran.* And thou mayest do the devil knows what
villany.

*Flam.* And safely.

*Fran.* Right : you shall see in the country, in harvest-time, pigeons, though they destroy never so much corn, the farmer dare not present the fowling-piece to them : why? because they belong to the lord of the manor; whilst your poor sparrows, that belong to the lord of heaven, they go to the pot for't.

*Flam.* I will now give you some politic instructions. The duke says he will give you pension; that's but bare promise; get it under his hand. For I have known men that have come from serving against the Turk, for three or four months they have had pension to buy them new wooden legs, and fresh plasters; but after, 'twas not to be had. And this miserable courtesy shews as if a tormentor should give hot cordial drinks to one three quarters dead o'th' rack, only to fetch the miserable soul again to endure more dogdays.

[*Exit Francisco de Medicis.*[1]

*Enter* HORTENSIO, *a* YOUNG LORD, ZANCHE,
*and two more.*

How now, gallants? what, are they ready for the barriers?

*Young Lord.* Yes: the lords are putting on their armour.

*Hort.* What's he?

*Flam.* A new up-start; one that swears like a falconer, and will lie in the duke's ear day by day, like a maker of almanacks: and yet I knew him, since he came to th' court, smell worse of sweat than an under tennis-courtkeeper.

*Hort.* Look you, yonder's your sweet mistress.

*Flam.* Thou art my sworn brother: I'll tell thee, I do love that Moor, that witch, very constrainedly. She

---

[1] The 4tos. do not mark the exit of Francisco; but it is necessary to get rid of him, as he *enters* towards the end of this scene.—DYCE.

knows some of my villany.    I do love her just as a man
holds a wolf by the ears; but for fear of her turning
upon me, and pulling out my throat, I would let her
go to the devil.

*Hort.* I hear she claims marriage of thee.

*Flam.* 'Faith, I made to her some such dark promise;
and, in seeking to fly from't, I run on, like a frighted
dog with a bottle at's tail, that fain would bite it off, and
yet dares not look behind him.    Now, my precious gipsy.

*Zanche.* Ay, your love to me rather cools than heats.

*Flam.* Marry, I am the sounder lover; we have many
wenches about the town heat too fast.

*Hort.* What do you think of these perfumed gallants,
then?

*Flam.* Their satin cannot save them : I am confident
They have a certain spice of the disease;
For they that sleep with dogs shall rise with fleas.

*Zanche.* Believe it, a little painting and gay clothes
make you love me.

*Flam.* How, love a lady for painting or gay apparel?
I'll unkennel one example more for thee.    Æsop had a
foolish dog that let go the flesh to catch the shadow; I
would have courtiers be better divers.

*Zanche.* You remember your oaths?

*Flam.* Lovers' oaths are like mariners' prayers,
uttered in extremity; but when the tempest is o'er, and
that the vessel leaves tumbling, they fall from protesting to drinking.    And yet, amongst gentlemen, protesting and drinking go together, and agree as well as
shoemakers and Westphalia bacon: they are both
drawers on; for drink draws on protestation, and protestation draws on more drink.    Is not this discourse
better now than the morality of your sunburnt
gentleman?

*Enter* CORNELIA.

*Cor.* Is this your perch, you haggard? fly to th' stews.

*Flam.* You should be clapt by th' heels now: strike
  i'th' court!                           [*Exit Cornelia.*[1]

*Zanche.* She's good for nothing, but to make her maids
Catch cold a-nights: they dare not use a bed-staff,
For fear of her light fingers.

*Mar.* You're a strumpet,
An impudent one.

*Flam.* Why do you kick her, say?
Do you think that she's like a walnut tree?
Must she be cudgell'd ere she bear good fruit?

*Mar.* She brags that you shall marry her.

*Flam.* What then?

*Mar.* I had rather she were pitch'd upon a stake,
In some new-seeded garden, to affright
Her fellow crows thence.

*Flam.* You're a boy, a fool
Be guardian to your hound; I am of age.

*Mar.* If I take her near you, I'll cut her throat.

*Flam.* With a fan of feathers?

*Mar.* And, for you, I'll whip
This folly from you.

*Flam.* Are you choleric?
I'll purge't with rhubarb.

*Hort.* O, your brother!

*Flam.* Hang him,

---

[1] The exit of Cornelia is not noted in the 4tos.; but it is
evident from what she says afterwards that she is not on the
stage during the deadly quarrel of her sons.—DYCE.

He wrongs me most, that ought t'offend me least :
I do suspect my mother play'd foul play,
When she conceiv'd thee.

    *Mar.* Now, by all my hopes,
Like the two slaughter'd sons of Oedipus,
The very flames of our affection
Shall turn two ways.  Those words I'll make thee answer
With.thy heart-blood.

    *Flam.* Do, like the geese in the progress ;
You know where you shall find me.

    *Mar.* Very good.           [*Exit Flamineo.*
And thou be'st a noble friend, bear him my sword,
And bid him fit the length on't.

    *Young Lord.* Sir, I shall.    [*Exeunt all but Zanche.*

    *Zanche.* He comes.  Hence petty thought of my dis
        grace !

*Enter* FRANCISCO.

I ne'er lov'd my complexion till now,
'Cause I may boldly say, without a blush,
I love you.

    *Fran.* Your love is untimely sown ; there's a spring
at Michaelmas, but 'tis but a faint one :  I am sunk in
years, and I have vowed never to marry.

    *Zanche.* Alas ! poor maids get more lovers than hus-
bands : yet you may mistake my wealth.  For, as when
ambassadors are sent to congratulate princes, there's
commonly sent along with them a rich present, so that,
though the prince like not the ambassador's person, nor
words, yet he likes well of the presentment ; so I may
come to you in the same manner, and be better loved
for my dowry than my virtue.

*Fran.* I'll think on the motion.

*Zanche.* Do ; I'll now detain you no longer.  At your better leisure, I'll tell you things shall startle your blood :

Nor blame me that this passion I reveal ;

Lovers die inward that their flames conceal.

*Fran.* Of all intelligence this may prove the best :

Sure I shall draw strange fowl from this foul nest.

[*Exeunt*

### SCENE V.

*Enter* MARCELLO *and* CORNELIA.

*Cor.* I hear a whispering all about the court,

You are to fight : who is your opposite ?

What is the quarrel ?

*Mar.* 'Tis an idle rumour.

*Cor.* Will you dissemble ? sure you do not well

To fright me thus : you never look thus pale,

But when you are most angry.  I do charge you,

Upon my blessing—nay, I'll call the duke,

And he shall school you.

*Mar.* Publish not a fear,

Which would convert to laughter : 'tis not so.

Was not this crucifix my father's ?

*Cor.* Yes.

*Mar.* I have heard you say, giving my brother suck

He took the crucifix between his hands,

*Enter* FLAMINEO.

And broke a limb off.

*Cor.* Yes, but 'tis mended.

*Flam.* I have brought your weapon back.

[*Flamineo runs Marcello through.*

*Cor.* Ha! O my horror!

*Mar.* You have brought it home, indeed.

*Cor.* Help! O he's murder'd!

*Flam.* Do you turn your gall up? I'll to sanctuary,
And send a surgeon to you.                          [*Exit.*

*Enter* LODOVICO, HORTENSIO *and* GASPARO.

*Hort.* How! o'th' ground!

*Mar.* O mother, now remember what I told
Of breaking of the crucifix! Farewell.
There are some sins, which heaven doth duly punish
In a whole family. This it is to rise
By all dishonest means! Let all men know,
That tree shall long time keep a steady foot,
Whose branches spread no wilder than the root. [*Dies.*

*Cor.* O my perpetual sorrow!

*Hort.* Virtuous Marcello!
He's dead. Pray leave him, lady: come, you shall.

*Cor.* Alas! he is not dead; he's in a trance. Why
here's nobody shall get anything by his death. Let me
call him again, for God's sake!

*Lod.* I would you were deceived.

*Cor.* O, you abuse me, you abuse me, you abuse me!
how many have gone away thus, for lack of 'tendance!
rear up's head, rear up's head! his bleeding inward will
kill him.

*Hort.* You see he is departed.

*Cor.* Let me come to him; give me him as he is; if
he be turn'd to earth, let me but give him one hearty kiss,
and you shall put us both into one coffin. Fetch a

looking-glass: see if his breath will not stain it; or pull
out some feathers from my pillow, and lay them to his
lips.   Will you lose him for a little pains-taking?

*Hort.* Your kindest office is to pray for him.

*Cor.* Alas! I would not pray for him yet.   He may
live to lay me i'th' ground, and pray for me, if you'll
let me come to him.

*Enter* BRACHIANO, *all armed, save the beaver, with*
FLAMINEO *and others.*

*Brach.* Was this your handy-work?

*Flam.* It was my misfortune.

*Cor.* He lies, he lies! he did not kill him: these have
killed him, that would not let him be better looked to.

*Brach.* Have comfort, my griev'd mother.

*Cor.* O you screech-owl!

*Hort.* Forbear, good madam.

*Cor.* Let me go, let me go.

> [*She runs to Flamineo with her knife drawn,*
> *and coming to him lets it fall.*

The God of heaven forgive thee!   Dost not wonder
I pray for thee?   I'll tell thee what's the reason
I have scarce breath to number twenty minutes;
I'd not spend that in cursing.   Fare thee well:
Half of thyself lies there; and may'st thou live
To fill an hour-glass with his moulder'd ashes,
To tell how thou should'st spend the time to come
In blest repentance!

*Brach.* Mother, pray tell me
How came he by his death? what was the quarrel?

*Cor.* Indeed, my younger boy presum'd too much
Upon his manhood, gave him bitter words,

Drew his sword first; and so, I know not how,
For I was out of my wits, he fell with's head
Just in my bosom.

*Page.* This is not true, madam.

*Cor.* I pray thee, peace.
One arrow's graz'd already; it were vain
T'lose this, for that will ne'er be found again.

*Brach.* Go, bear the body to Cornelia's lodging:
And we command that none acquaint our duchess
With this sad accident. For you, Flamineo,
Hark you, I will not grant your pardon.

*Flam.* No?

*Brach.* Only a lease of your life; and that shall last
But for one day: thou shalt be forc'd each evening
To renew it, or be hang'd.

*Flam.* At your pleasure.

[*Lodovico sprinkles Brachiano's beaver with a poison.*

### *Enter* FRANCISCO.[1]

Your will is law now, I'll not meddle with it.

*Brach.* You once did brave me in your sister's lodging:
I'll now keep you in awe for't. Where's our beaver?

*Fran.* He calls for his destruction. Noble youth,
I pity thy sad fate! Now to the barriers.
This shall his passage to the black lake further;
The last good deed he did, he pardon'd murder. [*Exeunt.*

[*Charges and shouts. They fight at barriers;[2]
first single pairs, then three to three.*

[1] The entrance is not noted in the old editions, but it is obvious.

[2] *Barriers.* "Barriers, from the French *Barres*, a martial sport or exercise of men armed, and fighting together with short swords within certain Barres or lists."—COWEL's *Interpreter.*

## ACT V.[1]—SCENE I.

*Enter* BRACHIANO *and* FLAMINEO, *with others.*

### Brachiano.

AN armourer ! ud's death, an armourer !
*Flam.* Armourer ! where's the armourer ?
*Brach.* Tear off my beaver.
*Flam.* Are you hurt, my lord ?
*Brach.* O, my brain's on fire !

### *Enter* ARMOURER.

The helmet is poison'd.
    *Armourer.* My lord, upon my soul—
    *Brach.* Away with him to torture.
There are some great ones that have hand in this,
And near about me.

### *Enter* VITTORIA COROMBONA.[2]

    *Vit.* O, my lov'd lord ! poison'd !
    *Flam.* Remove the bar.   Here's unfortunate revels !
Call the physicians.

### *Enter two* PHYSICIANS.

A plague upon you !
We have too much of your cunning here already :
I fear the ambassadors are likewise poison'd.
    *Brach.* O, I am gone already ! the infection

---

[1] Supplied from the 4to. of 1665.
[2] Her entrance is only marked in the old editions by the initial preceding what she says.

Flies to the brain and heart.   O thou strong heart !
There's such a covenant 'tween the world and it,
They're loath to break.

 *Giov.* O my most loved father !

 *Brach.* Remove the boy away..
Where's this good woman ?   Had I infinite worlds,
They were too little for thee : must I leave thee ?
What say you, screech-owls, is the venom mortal ?

 *Phys.* Most deadly.

 *Brach.* Most corrupted politic hangman,
You kill without book ; but your art to save
Fails you as oft as great men's needy friends.
I that have given life to offending slaves,
And wretched murderers, have I not power
To lengthen mine own a twelve-month ?
Do not kiss me, for I shall poison thee.
This unction is sent from the great duke of Florence.

 *Fran.* Sir, be of comfort.

 *Brach.* O thou soft natural death, that art joint-twin
To sweetest slumber ! no rough-bearded comet
Stares on thy mild departure ; the dull owl
Beats not against thy casement ; the hoarse wolf
Scents not thy carrion : pity winds thy corse,
Whilst horror waits on princes'.

 *Vit.* I am lost for ever.

 *Brach.* How miserable a thing it is to die

 *Enter* LODOVICO *and* GASPARO, *as Capuchins.*[1]

'Mongst women howling ! what are those ?

---

[1] Their entrance is not marked in the quartos, but it is obvious from the context.

*Flam.* Franciscans :
They have brought the extreme unction.

*Brach.* On pain of death, let no man name death to me :
It is a word infinitely terrible.
Withdraw into our cabinet.

*[Exeunt all but Francisco and Flamineo.*

*Flam.* To see what solitariness is about dying princes!
as heretofore they have unpeopled towns, divorced
friends, and made great houses unhospitable, so now,
O justice! where are their flatterers now? flatterers are
but the shadows of princes' bodies; the least thick
cloud makes them invisible.

*Fran.* There's great moan made for him.

*Flam.* 'Faith, for some few hours salt-water will run
most plentifully in every office o'th' court; but, believe it,
most of them do but weep over their stepmothers' graves.

*Fran.* How mean you?

*Flam.* Why, they dissemble; as some men do that
live within compass o'th' verge.[1]

*Fran.* Come, you have thrived well under him.

*Flam.* 'Faith, like a wolf in a woman's breast ;[2] I have
been fed with poultry : but for money, understand me, I
had as good a will to cozen him as e'er an officer of
them all; but I had not cunning enough to do it.

*Fran.* What didst thou think of him? 'faith, speak
freely.

*Flam.* He was a kind of statesman, that would sooner
have reckoned how many cannon-bullets he had dis-
charged against a town, to count his expense that way,

[1] i. e. of the Jurisdiction of the Court.
[2] The cravings of women during pregnancy were anciently
accounted for by supposing some voracious animal to be
within them.—STEEVENS.

than how many of his valiant and deserving subjects he
　　lost before it.

*Fran.* O, speak well of the duke !

*Flam.* I have done.

### *Enter* LODOVICO.

Wilt hear some of my court-wisdom? To reprehend
princes is dangerous ; and to over-commend some of
them is palpable lying.

*Fran.* How is it with the duke ?

*Lod.* Most deadly ill.
He's fall'n into a strange distraction :
He talks of battles and monopolies,
Levying of taxes ; and from that descends
To the most brain-sick language.　His mind fastens
On twenty several objects, which confound
Deep sense with folly.　Such a fearful end
May teach some men that bear too lofty crest,
Though they live happiest yet they die not best.
He hath conferr'd the whole state of the dukedom
Upon your sister, till the prince arrive
At mature age.

*Flam.* There's some good luck in that yet.

*Fran.* See, here he comes.

### *Enter* BRACHIANO, *presented in a bed,* VITTORIA, *and others.*

There's death in's face already.

*Vit.* O my good lord !

*Brach.* Away, you have abus'd me :
　　　[*These speeches are several kinds of distractions,*
　　　　*and in the action should appear so.*

You have convey'd coin forth our territories,
Bought and sold offices, oppress'd the poor,
And I ne'er dreamt on't. Make up your accounts,
I'll now be mine own steward.

*Flam.* Sir, have patience.

*Brach.* Indeed, I am to blame :
For did you ever hear the dusky raven
Chide blackness ? or was't ever known the devil
Rail'd against cloven creatures ?

*Vit.* O my lord !

*Brach.* Let me have some quails to supper.

*Flam.* Sir, you shall.

*Brach.* No, some fried dog-fish ; your quails feed on
    poison.
That old dog-fox, that politician, Florence !
I'll forswear hunting, and turn dog-killer.
Rare ! I'll be friends with him ; for, mark you, sir, one
    dog
Still sets another abarking. Peace, peace !
Yonder's a fine slave come in now.

*Flam.* Where ?

*Brach.* Why, there,
In a blue bonnet, and a pair of breeches
With a great cod-piece : ha, ha, ha !
Look you, his cod-piece is stuck full of pins,
With pearls o'th' head of them. Do not you know him ?

*Flam.* No, my lord.

*Brach.* Why 'tis the devil.
I know him by a great rose he wears on's shoe,
To hide his cloven foot. I'll dispute with him ;
He's a rare linguist.

*Vit.* My lord, here's nothing.

*Brach.* Nothing! rare! nothing! when I want money,
Our treasury is empty, there is nothing :
I'll not be us'd thus.

*Vit.* O, lie still, my lord!

*Brach.* See, see Flamineo, that kill'd his brother,
Is dancing on the ropes there, and he carries
A money-bag in each hand, to keep him even,
For fear of breaking's neck: and there's a lawyer,
In a gown whipt with velvet, stares and gapes
When the money will fall.  How the rogue cuts capers!
It should have been in a halter.  'Tis there; what's she?

*Flam.* Vittoria, my lord.

*Brach.* Ha, ha, ha! her hair is sprinkl'd with arras
    powder.[1]
That makes her look as if she had sinn'd in the pastry.
What's he?

*Flam.* A divine, my lord.

> [*Brachiano seems here near his end; Lodovico and
> Gasparo, in the habit of Capuchins, present him
> in his bed with a crucifix and hallowed candle.*

*Brach.* He will be drunk ; avoid him : th' argument
Is fearful, when churchmen stagger in't.
Look you, six grey rats that have lost their tails
Crawl up the pillow ; send for a rat-catcher :
I'll do a miracle, I'll free the court
From all foul vermin.   Where's Flamineo?

*Flam.* I do not like that he names me so often,
Especially on's death-bed ; 'tis a sign

---

[1] *Arras Powder.*  There may have been a hair-powder so-called from Arras in France, but I do not remember to have found it mentioned by any writer.  Qy. ought we to read "*orris?*"—DYCE.

I shall not live long.   See, he's near his end.

*Lod.* Pray, give us leave.   *Attende, domine Brachiane.*

*Flam.* See, see how firmly he doth fix his eye
Upon the crucifix.

*Vit.* O hold it constant!
It settles his wild spirits; and so his eyes
Melt into tears.

*Lod. Domine Brachiane, solebas in bello tutus esse tuo
clypeo; nunc hunc clypeum hosti tuo opponas infernali.*

[*By the crucifix.*

*Gas. Olim hastâ valuisti in bello; nunc hanc sacram
hastam vibrabis contra hostem animarum.*

[*By the hallowed taper.*

*Lod. Attende, domine Brachiane, si nunc quoque probas
ea, quæ acta sunt inter nos, flecte caput in dextrum.*

*Gas. Esto securus, domine Brachiane; cogita, quantum
habeas meritorum; denique memineris meam animam pro
tuâ oppignoratam si quid esset periculi.*

*Lod. Si nunc quoque probas ea, quæ acta sunt inter
nos, flecte caput in lævum.*
He is departing: pray stand all apart,
And let us only whisper in his ears
Some private meditations, which our order
Permits you not to hear.

[*Here, the rest being departed, Lodovico and
Gasparo discover themselves.*

*Gas.* Brachiano.

*Lod.* Devil Brachiano, thou art damn'd.

*Gas.* Perpetually.

*Lod.* A slave condemn'd, and given up to the gallows,
Is thy great lord and master.

*Gas.* True ; for thou
Art given up to the devil.

*Lod.* O, you slave !
You that were held the famous politician,
Whose art was poison.

*Gas.* And whose conscience, murder.

*Lod.* That would have broke your wife's neck down
     the stairs,
Ere she was poison'd.

*Gas.* That had your villanous sallets.

*Lod.* And fine embroider'd bottles, and perfumes,
Equally mortal with a winter plague.

*Gas.* Now there's mercury—

*Lod.* And copperas—

*Gas.* And quicksilver—

*Lod.* With other devilish 'pothecary stuff,
A melting in your politic brains : dost hear ?

*Gas.* This is count Lodovico.

*Lod.* This, Gasparo ;
And thou shalt die like a poor rogue.

*Gas.* And stink
Like a dead fly-blown dog.

*Lod.* And be forgotten
Before thy funeral sermon.

*Brach.* Vittoria ! Vittoria !

*Lod.* O, the cursed devil
Comes to himself again ! we are undone.

*Gas.* Strangle him in private.

*Enter* VITTORIA *and the Attendants.*

What ! will you call him again

To live in treble torments? for charity,
For christian charity, avoid the chamber.

                   *[Vittoria and the rest retire.*

  *Lod.* You would prate, sir? This is a true-love-knot
Sent from the duke of Florence.

                   *[Brachiano is strangled.*

  *Gas.* What, is it done?

  *Lod.* The snuff is out. No woman-keeper i'th'world,
Though she had practis'd seven year at the pest-house,[1]
Could have done't quaintlier.   My lords, he's dead.

   Vittoria *and the others come forward.*

  *Omnes.* Rest to his soul!

  *Vit.* O me! this place is hell.             *[Exit.*

  *Fran.* How heavily she takes it!

  *Flam.* O, yes, yes;
Had women navigable rivers in their eyes,
They would dispend them all.   Surely, I wonder
Why we should wish more rivers to the city,
When they sell water so good cheap.   I'll tell thee,
These are but moonish shades of griefs or fears;
There's nothing sooner dry than women's tears.
Why, here's an end of all my harvest; he has given
      me nothing.
Court promises! let wise men count them curs'd
For while you live, he that scores best, pays worst.

  *Fran.* Sure this was Florence' doing.

  *Flam.* Very likely:
Those are found weighty strokes which come from th'
      hand,

---

[1] In allusion to the stranglings done, to save themselves
trouble, by nurses on plague patients.

But those are killing strokes which come from th' head.
O, the rare tricks of a Machiavelian !
He doth not come, like a gross plodding slave,
And buffet you to death ; no, my quaint knave,
He tickles you to death, makes you die laughing,
As if you had swallow'd down a pound of saffron.
You see the feat, 'tis practis'd in a trice ;
To teach court honesty, it jumps on ice.

*Fran.* Now have the people liberty to talk,
And descant on his vices.

*Flam.* Misery of princes,
That must of force be censur'd by their slaves !
Not only blam'd for doing things are ill,
But for not doing all that all men will :
One were better be a thresher.
Ud'sdeath ! I would fain speak with this duke yet.

*Fran.* Now he's dead ?

*Flam.* I cannot conjure ; but if prayers or oaths
Will get to th' speech of him, though forty devils
Wait on him in his livery of flames,
I'll speak to him, and shake him by the hand,
Though I be blasted.                              [*Exit.*

*Fran.* Excellent Lodovico !
What ! did you terrify him at the last gasp ?

*Lod.* Yes, and so idly, that the duke had like
T'have terrified us.

*Fran.*  How ?


*Enter the* MOOR.


*Lod.* You shall hear that hereafter.
See, yon's the infernal, that would make up sport.

Now to the revelation of that secret
She promis'd when she fell in love with you.

*Fran.* You're passionately met in this sad world.

*Zanche.* I would have you look up, sir; these court-
tears
Claim not your tribute to them : let those weep,
That guiltily partake in the sad cause.
I knew last night, by a sad dream I had,
Some mischief would ensue ; yet, to say truth,
My dream most concern'd you.

*Lod.* Shall's fall a dreaming ?

*Fran.* Yes, and for fashion sake I'll dream with her.

*Zanche.* Methought, sir, you came stealing to my bed.

*Fran.* Wilt thou believe me, sweeting? by this light,
I was a-dreamt on thee too ; for methought
I saw thee naked.

*Zanche.* Fie, sir ! as I told you,
Methought you lay down by me.

*Fran.* So dreamt I ;
And lest thou shouldst take cold, I cover'd thee
With this Irish mantle.

*Zanche.* Verily I did dream
You were somewhat bold with me : but to come to't.

*Lod.* How ! how ! I hope you will not go to't here.

*Fran.* Nay, you must hear my dream out.

*Zanche.* Well, sir, forth.

*Fran.* When I threw the mantle o'er thee, thou didst
laugh
Exceedingly, methought.

*Zanche.* Laugh !

*Fran.* And cried'st out, the hair did tickle thee.

*Zanche.* There was a dream indeed !

*Lod.* Mark her, I prithee, she simpers like the suds
A collier hath been wash'd in.

*Zanche.* Come, sir ; good fortune tends you.   I did
   tell you
I would reveal a secret : Isabella,
The duke of Florence' sister, was impoison'd
By a fum'd picture ; and Camillo's neck
Was broke by damn'd Flamineo, the mischance
Laid on a vaulting-horse.

*Fran.* Most strange !

*Zanche.* Most true.

*Lod.* The bed of snakes is broke.

*Zanche.* I sadly do confess, I had a hand
In the black deed.

*Fran.* Thou kept'st their counsel.

*Zanche.* Right ;
For which, urg'd with contrition, I intend
This night to rob Vittoria.

*Lod.* Excellent penitence !
Usurers dream on't while they sleep out sermons.

*Zanche.* To further our escape, I have entreated
Leave to retire me, till the funeral,
Unto a friend i'th' country : that excuse
Will further our escape.   In coin and jewels
I shall at least make good unto your use
An hundred thousand crowns.

*Fran.* O, noble wench !

*Lod.* Those crowns we'll share.

*Zanche.* It is a dowry,
Methinks, should make that sun-burnt proverb false,

And wash the Æthiop white.

*Fran.* It shall; away.

*Zanche.* Be ready for our flight.

*Fran.* An hour 'fore day.                [*Exit Zanche.*

O, strange discovery! why, till now we knew not
The circumstance of either of their deaths.

*Re-enter* ZANCHE.

*Zanche.* You'll wait about midnight in the chapel?

*Fran.* There.                            [*Exit Zanche.*

*Lod.* Why, now our action's justified.

*Fran.* Tush, for justice!

What harms it justice? we now, like the partridge,
Purge the disease with laurel;[1] for the fame
Shall crown the enterprize, and quit[2] the shame. [*Exeunt.*

*Enter* FLAMINEO *and* GASPARO, *at one door; another
way,* GIOVANNI, *attended.*

*Gas.* The young duke: did you e'er see a sweeter prince?

*Flam.* I have known a poor woman's bastard better
favoured: this is behind him; now, to his face, all com-
parisons were hateful. Wise was the courtly peacock, that,
being a great minion, and being compared for beauty by
some dottrels that stood by to the kingly eagle, said the
eagle was a far fairer bird than herself, not in respect
of her feathers, but in respect of her long tallants:[3] his
will grow out in time.—My gracious lord.

---

[1] So Pliny: "Palumbes, gracculi, merulæ, *perdices lauri
folio annuum fastidium purgant.*"—*Nat. Hist.* lib. viii. c. 27.
—REED.

[2] Acquit.

[3] An old form of *talons.*

*Gio.* I pray leave me, sir.

*Flam.* Your grace must be merry; 'tis I have cause to mourn; for wot you, what said the little boy that rode behind his father on horseback?

*Gio.* Why, what said he?

*Flam.* When you are dead, father, said he, I hope then I shall ride in the saddle.   O, 'tis a brave thing for a man to sit by himself! he may stretch himself in the stirrups, look about, and see the whole compass of the hemisphere.  You're now, my lord, i'th' saddle.

*Gio.* Study your prayers, sir, and be penitent:
'Twere fit you'd think on what hath former been;
I have heard grief nam'd the eldest child of sin. [*Exit.*

*Flam.* Study my prayers! he threatens me divinely! I am falling to pieces already.  I care not, though, like Anacharsis, I were pounded to death in a mortar: and yet that death were fitter for usurers, gold and themselves to be beaten together, to make a most cordial cullis[1] for the devil.  He hath his uncle's villanous look already,

### Enter COURTIER.

In decimo sexto.[2]—Now, sir, what are you?

*Cour.* It is the pleasure, sir, of the young duke,
That you forbear the presence, and all rooms
That owe him reverence.

*Flam.* So the wolf and the raven are very pretty fools when they are young.  Is it your office, sir, to keep me out?

*Cour.* So the duke wills.

---

[1] *Cullis.*—The French *coulis*, a strong rich soup or jelly.
[2] i. e. though but in his sixteenth year.

*Flam.* Verily, master courtier, extremity is not to be used in all offices : say, that a gentlewoman were taken out of her bed about midnight, and committed to Castle Angelo, to the tower yonder, with nothing about her but her smock, would it not shew a cruel part in the gentleman-porter to lay claim to her upper garment, pull it o'er her head and ears, and put her in naked ?

*Cour.* Very good : you are merry.　　　　[*Exit.*

*Flam.* Doth he make a court-ejectment of me? a flaming fire-brand casts more smoke without a chimney than within't.　I'll smoor[1] some of them.

### Enter FRANCISCO DE MEDICIS.

How now? thou art sad.

*Fran.* I met even now with the most piteous sight.

*Flam.* Thou meet'st another here, a pitiful
Degraded courtier.

*Fran.* Your reverend mother
Is grown a very old woman in two hours.
I found them winding of Marcello's corse ;
And there is such a solemn melody,
'Tween doleful songs, tears, and sad elegies ;
Such as old grandames, watching by the dead,
Were wont t'outwear the nights with, that, believe me,
I had no eyes to guide me forth the room,
They were so o'ercharg'd with water.

*Flam.* I will see them.

*Fran.* 'Twere much uncharity in you; for your sight
Will add unto their tears.

*Flam.* I will see them :

---

[1] *Smoor*—the Anglo-Saxon *smoran*, to smother.

They are behind the traverse ;[1] I'll discover
Their superstitious howling.

CORNELIA, *the* MOOR, *and three other ladies discovered
winding* MARCELLO'S *corse.   A Song.*

   *Cor.* This rosemary is wither'd ; pray, get fresh.
I would have these herbs grow up in his grave,
When I am dead and rotten.   Reach the bays,
I'll tie a garland here about his head ;
'Twill keep my boy from lightning.   This sheet
I have kept this twenty year, and every day
Hallow'd it with my prayers ; I did not think
He should have wore it.
   *Zanche.* Look you, who are yonder?
   *Cor.* O, reach me the flowers !
   *Zanche.* Her ladyship's foolish.
   *Woman.* Alas, her grief
Hath turn'd her child again !
   *Cor.* You're very welcome :
There's rosemary for you, and rue for you, [*To Flamineo.*
Heart's-ease for you ; I pray make much of it,
I have left more for myself.
   *Fran.* Lady, who's this?
   *Cor.* You are, I take it, the grave-maker.
   *Flam.* So.
   *Zanche.* 'Tis Flamineo.
   *Cor.* Will you make me such a fool? here's a white
      hand :

[1] *The traverse.* " Beside the principal curtains that hung in
the front of the stage, they used others as substitutes for
scenes, which were denominated *traverses.*"—MALONE'S *Hist.
Acc. of the English Stage,* p. 88, ed. Boswell : quoted by Dyce.

Can blood so soon be wash'd out? let me see;
When screech-owls croak upon the chimney-tops,
And the strange cricket i'th' oven sings and hops,
When yellow spots do on your hands appear,
Be certain then you of a corse shall hear.
Out upon't, how 'tis speckled! h'as handled a toad sure.
Cowslip water is good for the memory:
Pray, buy me three ounces of't.

    *Flam.* I would I were from hence.

    *Cor.* Do you hear, sir?
I'll give you a saying which my grandmother
Was wont, when she heard the bell toll, to sing o'er
Unto her lute.

    *Flam.* Do, and you will, do.

    *Cor. Call for the robin-red-breast, and the wren,*
      [*Cornelia doth this in several forms of distraction.*
*Since o'er shady groves they hover,*
*And with leaves and flowers do cover*
*The friendless bodies of unburied men.*
*Call unto his funeral dole*
*The ant, the field-mouse, and the mole,*
*To rear him hillocks that shall keep him warm,*
*And (when gay tombs are robb'd) sustain no harm;*
*But keep the wolf far thence, that's foe to men,*
*For with his nails he'll dig them up again.*
They would not bury him 'cause he died in a quarrel;
But I have an answer for them:
*Let holy churh receive him duly,*
*Since he paid the church-tithes truly.*
His wealth is summ'd, and this is all his store,
This poor men get, and great men get no more.

Now the wares are gone, we may shut up shop.
Bless you all, good people.

[*Exeunt Cornelia and Ladies.*

*Flam.* I have a strange thing in me, to th' which
I cannot give a name, without it be
Compassion.   I pray leave me.        [*Exit Francisco.*
This night I'll know the utmost of my fate ;
I'll be resolv'd what my rich sister means
T'assign me for my service.   I have liv'd
Riotously ill, like some that live in court,
And sometimes when my face was full of smiles,
Have felt the maze of conscience in my breast.
Oft gay and honour'd robes those tortures try :
" We think cag'd birds sing, when indeed they cry."[1]
Ha ! I can stand thee : nearer, nearer yet.

*Enter* BRACHIANO's *Ghost, in his leather cassock and
breeches, boots; a cowl; a pot of lily-flowers, with a
skull in't.*

What a mockery hath death made thee! thou look'st sad.
In what place art thou ? in yon starry gallery ?
Or in the cursed dungeon ?—no ? not speak ?
Pray, sir, resolve me, what religion's best
For a man to die in ? or is it in your knowledge
To answer me how long I have to live ?
That's the most necessary question.
Not answer ? are you still, like some great men
That only walk like shadows up and down,
And to no purpose ; say—

[*The Ghost throws earth upon him, and shews him
the skull.*

___

[1] This line is probably a quotation, and is so marked in
the original copy.—COLLIER.

What's that ?   O fatal ! he throws earth upon me.
A dead man's skull beneath the roots of flowers !
I pray speak, sir : our Italian church-men
Make us believe dead men hold conference
With their familiars, and many times
Will come to bed to them, and eat with them.

*[Exit Ghost.*

He's gone ; and see, the skull and earth are vanish'd.
This is beyond melancholy.   I do dare my fate
To do its worst.   Now to my sister's lodging,
And sum up all these horrors : the disgrace
The prince threw on me ; next the piteous sight
Of my dead brother ; and my mother's dotage ;
And last this terrible vision : all these
Shall with Vittoria's bounty turn to good,
Or I will drown this weapon in her blood.     *[Exit.*

*Enter* FRANCISCO, LODOVICO, *and* HORTENSIO.

*Lod.* My lord, upon my soul you shall no further ;
You have most ridiculously engag'd yourself
Too far already.   For my part, I have paid
All my debts : so, if I should chance to fall,
My creditors fall not with me ; and I vow,
To quit all in this bold assembly,
To the meanest follower.   My lord, leave the city,
Or I'll forswear the murder.               *[Exit.*

*Fran.* Farewell, Lodovico :
If thou dost perish in this glorious act,
I'll rear unto thy memory that fame,
Shall in the ashes keep alive thy name.     *[Exit.*

*Hor.* There's some black deed on foot.   I'll presently
Down to the citadel, and raise some force.

These strong court-factions, that do brook no checks,
In the career oft break the riders' necks.          [*Exit.*

## SCENE II.

*Enter* VITTORIA *with a book in her hand,* ZANCHE; FLA-
MINEO *following them.*

*Flam.* What? are you at your prayers? give o'er.
*Vit.* How, ruffian!
*Flam.* I come to you 'bout wordly business.
Sit down, sit down: nay, stay, blouze, you may hear it:
The doors are fast enough.
*Vit.* Ha! are you drunk?
*Flam.* Yes, yes, with wormwood water; you shall
     taste
Some of it presently.
*Vit.* What intends the fury?
*Flam.* You are my lord's executrix; and I claim
Reward for my long service.
*Vit.* For your service!
*Flam.* Come, therefore, here is pen and ink, set down
What you will give me.
*Vit.* There.                              [*She writes.*
*Flam.* Ha! have you done already?
'Tis a most short conveyance.
*Vit.* I will read it:
I give that portion to thee, and no other,
Which Cain groaned under, having slain his brother.
*Flam.* A most courtly patent to beg by.
*Vit.* You are a villain!
*Flam.* Is't come to this? they say affrights cure
     agues:

Thou hast a devil in thee; I will try
If I can scare him from thee.   Nay, sit still :
My lord hath left me yet two case of jewels,
Shall make me scorn your bounty ; you shall see them.

                                                       [*Exit.*

   *Vit.* Sure he's distracted.
   *Zanche.* O, he's desperate !
For your own safety give him gentle language.
                   [*He re-enters with two case of pistols.*
   *Flam.* Look, these are better far at a dead lift,
Than all your jewel-house.
   *Vit.* And yet, methinks,
These stones have no fair lustre, they are ill set.
   *Flam.* I'll turn the right side towards you : you shall
     see
How they will sparkle.
   *Vit.* Turn this horror from me !
What do you want ? what would you have me do ?
Is not all mine yours ? have I any children ?
   *Flam.* Pray thee, good woman, do not trouble me
With this vain worldly business ; say your prayers :
I made a vow to my deceased lord,
Neither yourself nor I should outlive him
The numbering of four hours.
   *Vit.* Did he enjoin it ? ·
   *Flam.* He did, and 'twas a deadly jealousy,
Lest any should enjoy thee after him,
That urged him vow me to it.   For my death,
I did propound it voluntarily, knowing,
If he could not be safe in his own court,
Being a great duke, what hope then for us ?
   *Vit.* This is your melancholy, and despair.

*Flam.* Away:
Fool thou art, to think that politicians
Do use to kill the effects of injuries
And let the cause live.  Shall we groan in irons,
Or be a shameful and a weighty burthen
To a public scaffold?   This is my resolve:
I would not live at any man's entreaty,
Nor die at any's bidding.
  *Vit.* Will you hear me?
  *Flam.* My life hath done service to other men,
My death shall serve mine own turn: make you ready.
  *Vit.* Do you mean to die indeed?
  *Flam.* With as much pleasure,
As e'er my father gat me.
  *Vit.* Are the doors lock'd?
  *Zanche.* Yes, madam.
  *Vit.* Are you grown an atheist? will you turn your
      body
Which is the goodly palace of the soul,
To the soul's slaughter-house?   O, the cursed devil,
Which doth present us with all other sins
Thrice candied o'er, despair with gall and stibium;
Yet we carouse it off;—cry out for help!—
                                    [*Aside to Zanche.*
Makes us forsake that which was made for man,
The world, to sink to that was made for devils,
Eternal darkness!
  *Zanche.* Help, help!
  *Flam.* I'll stop your throat
With winter plums.
  *Vit.* I prithee yet remember,
Millions are now in graves, which at last day

Like mandrakes shall rise shrieking.

*Flam.* Leave your prating,
For these are but grammatical laments,
Feminine arguments : and they move me,
As some in pulpits move their auditory,
More with their exclamation, than sense
Of reason, or sound doctrine.

*Zanche.* Gentle madam,
Seem to consent, only persuade him teach
The way to death ; let him die first.

*Vit.* 'Tis good, I apprehend it.—
To kill one's self is meat that we must take
Like pills, not chew'd, but quickly swallow it ;
The smart o'th' wound, or weakness of the hand,
May else bring treble torments.

*Flam.* I have held it
A wretched and most miserable life,
Which is not able to die.

*Vit.* O, but frailty !
Yet I am now resolv'd ; farewell, affliction !
Behold, Brachiano, I that while you liv'd
Did make a flaming altar of my heart
To sacrifice unto you, now am ready
To sacrifice heart and all.   Farewell, Zanche !

*Zanche.* How, madam ! do you think that I'll outlive
    you ;
Especially when my best self, Flamineo,
Goes the same voyage ?

*Flam.* O, most loved Moor !

*Zanche.* Only, by all my love, let me entreat you,
Since it is most necessary one of us

Do violence on ourselves, let you or I
Be her sad taster, teach her how to die.

    *Flam.* Thou dost instruct me nobly ; take these
        pistols,
Because my hand is stain'd with blood already :
Two of these you shall level at my breast,
The other 'gainst your own, and so we'll die
Most equally contented : but first swear
Not to outlive me.

    *Vit.* and *Zanche.* Most religiously.

    *Flam.* Then here's an end of me ; farewell, daylight.
And, O contemptible physic ! that dost take
So long a study, only to preserve
So short a life, I take my leave of thee.

                         [*Shewing the pistols.*
These are two cupping-glasses, that shall draw
All my infected blood out.   Are you ready ?

    *Both.* Ready.

    *Flam.* Whither shall I go now ? O Lucian, thy ridicu-
lous purgatory ! to find Alexander the Great cobbling
shoes, Pompey tagging points, and Julius Cæsar making
hair-buttons ! Hannibal selling blacking, and Augustus
crying garlic ! Charlemagne selling lists by the dozen,
and king Pepin crying apples in a cart drawn with one
horse !
Whether I resolve to fire, earth, water, air,
Or all the elements by scruples, I know not,
Nor greatly care—Shoot, shoot,
Of all deaths, the violent death is best ;
For from ourselves it steals ourselves so fast,
The pain, once apprehended, is quite past.

      [*They shoot, and run to him, and tread upon him.*

    *Vit.* What, are you dropt ?

*Flam.* I am mix'd with earth already : as you are noble,
Perform your vows, and bravely follow me.

*Vit.* Whither? to hell?

*Zanche.* To most assur'd damnation?

*Vit.* O, thou most cursed devil!

*Zanche.* Thou art caught—

*Vit.* In thine own engine.   I tread the fire out
That would have been my ruin.

*Flam.* Will you be perjured? what a religious oath
was Styx, that the gods never durst swear by, and violate!   O that we had such an oath to minister, and to
be so well kept in our courts of justice!

*Vit.* Think whither thou art going.

*Zanche.* And remember
What villanies thou hast acted.

*Vit.* This thy death
Shall make me, like a blazing ominous star:
Look up and tremble.

*Flam.* O, I am caught with a springe!

*Vit.* You see the fox comes many times short home ;
'Tis here prov'd true.

*Flam.* Kill'd with a couple of braches![1]

*Vit.* No fitter offering for the infernal furies,
Than one in whom they reign'd while he was living.

*Flam.* O, the way's dark and horrid!   I cannot see :
Shall I have no company?

*Vit.* O yes, thy sins
Do run before thee to fetch fire from hell,
To light thee thither.

*Flam.* O, I smell soot, most stinking soot! the
chimney's a fire :

---

[1] Bitch-hounds.

My liver's parboil'd, like Scotch holly-bread ;
There's a plumber laying pipes in my guts, it scalds.
Wilt thou outlive me !

   *Zanche.* Yes, and drive a stake
Through thy body ; for we'll give it out,
Thou didst this violence upon thyself.

   *Flam.* O, cunning devils ! now I have tried your love,
And doubled all your reaches : I am not wounded.

                       [*Flamineo riseth.*

The pistols held no bullets ; 'twas a plot
To prove your kindness to me ; and I live
To punish your ingratitude.   I knew,
One time or other, you would find a way
To give me a strong potion.   O men,
That lie upon your death-beds, and are haunted
With howling wives ! ne'er trust them ; they'll re-marry
Ere the worm pierce your winding-sheet, ere the spider
Make a thin curtain for your epitaphs.
How cunning you were to discharge ! do you practise
at the artillery-yard ? Trust a woman ! never, never !
Brachiano be my precedent.   We lay our souls to pawn
to the devil for a little pleasure, and a woman makes
the bill of sale.   That ever man should marry !   For
one Hypermnestra that saved her lord and husband,
forty-nine of her sisters cut their husbands' throats all
in one night.   There was a shoal of virtuous horseleeches !   Here are two other instruments.

           *Enter* LODOVICO, GASPARO.[1]

   *Vit.* Help ! help !

   [1] The original entrance marked is, "Enter Lodovico,
Gasparo, Pedro, and Carlo."   There are no such personages

*Flam.* What noise is that? ha! false keys i'th' court!

*Lod.* We have brought you a mask.

*Flam.* A matachin[1] it seems by your drawn swords.
Church-men[2] turned revellers!

*Gas.* Isabella! Isabella!

*Lod.* Do you know us now?[3]

*Flam.* Lodovico! and Gasparo!

*Lod.* Yes; and that Moor the duke gave pension to
Was the great duke of Florence.

*Vit.* O, we are lost!

*Flam.* You shall not take justice forth from my hands,
O, let me kill her!—I'll cut my safety
Through your coats of steel.   Fate's a spaniel,
We cannot beat it from us.   What remains now?
Let all that do ill, take this precedent:
*Man may his fate foresee, but not prevent:*
And of all axioms this shall win the prize,
*'Tis better to be fortunate than wise.*

*Gas.* Bind him to the pillar.

as Pedro and Carlo in the play; and we may assume the
latter names to have been merely those assumed by Lodovico
and Gasparo in their disguise; and to be set forth here to
indicate that they still retain that disguise.

[1] There was a dance called Matachin, thus described by Mr.
Douce: "Such a dance was that well known in France and
Italy by the name of the dance of fools or *Matachins*, who were
habited in short jackets, with gilt paper helmets, long stream-
ers tied to their shoulders, and bells to their legs.   *They carried in their hands a sword* and buckler, with which they
made a clashing noise, and performed various quick and
sprightly evolutions."—*Illust. of Shakespeare.*   Flamineo,
playing upon words, says: "It is not a masque (entertainment) you have brought us, but, as is clear by your drawn
swords, a *Matachin.*"

[2] Lodovico and Gasparo are still in their Capuchin attire.

[3] Lodovico and Gasparo here throw back their cowls and
robes, showing themselves in armour.

*Vit.* O, your gentle pity !
I have seen a black-bird that would sooner fly
To a man's bosom, than to stay[1] the gripe
Of the fierce sparrow-hawk.

*Gas.* Your hope deceives you.

*Vit.* If Florence be i'th'court, would he would kill me !

*Gas.* Fool! princes give rewards with their own hands,
But death or punishment by the hands of others.

*Lod.* Sirrah, you once did strike me ; I'll strike you
Unto the centre.

*Flam.* Thou'lt do it like a hangman, a base hangman,
Not like a noble fellow, for thou see'st
I cannot strike again.

*Lod.* Dost laugh ?

*Flam.* Would'st have me die, as I was born, in
   whining ?

*Gas.* Recommend yourself to heaven.

*Flam.* No, I will carry mine own commendations
   thither.

*Lod.* O, could I kill you forty times a day,
And use't four year together, 'twere too little !
Nought grieves but that you are too few to feed
The famine of our vengeance.   What dost think on ?

*Flam.* Nothing; of nothing: leave thy idle questions.
I am i'th' way to study a long silence :
To prate were idle.   I remember nothing.
There's nothing of so infinite vexation
As man's own thoughts.

*Lod.* O, thou glorious strumpet !
Could I divide thy breath from this pure air
When't leaves thy body, I would suck it up,
And breathe't upon some dunghill.

---

[1] *Stay,*—await.

*Vit.* You my death's-man !
Methinks thou dost not look horrid enough,
Thou hast too good a face to be a hangman :
If thou be, do thy office in right form ;
Fall down upon thy knees, and ask forgiveness.

*Lod.* O, thou hast been a most prodigious comet !
But I'll cut off your train.   Kill the Moor first.

*Vit.* You shall not kill her first ; behold my breast :
I will be waited on in death ; my servant
Shall never go before me.

*Gas.* Are you so brave ?

*Vit.* Yes, I shall welcome death,
As princes do some great ambassadors ;
I'll meet thy weapon half way.

*Lod.* Thou dost tremble :
Methinks, fear should dissolve thee into air.

*Vit.* O, thou art deceiv'd, I am too true a woman !
Conceit[1] can never kill me.   I'll tell thee what,
I will not in my death shed one base tear ;
Or if look pale, for want of blood, not fear.

*Gas.* Thou art my task, black fury.

*Zanche.* I have blood
As red as either of theirs : wilt drink some ?
'Tis good for the falling-sickness.   I am proud ;
Death cannot alter my complexion,
For I shall ne'er look pale.

*Lod.* Strike, strike,
With a joint motion,

*Vit.* 'Twas a manly blow ;
The next thou giv'st, murder some sucking infant ;

---

[1] Fancy, imagination.

And then thou wilt be famous.

*Flam.* O, what blade is't?
A Toledo, or an English fox?[1]
I ever thought a cutler should distinguish
The cause of my death, rather than a doctor.
Search my wound deeper; tent[2] it with the steel
That made it.

*Vit.* O, my greatest sin lay in my blood!
Now my blood pays for't.

*Flam.* Th'art a noble sister!
I love thee now: if woman do breed man,
She ought to teach him manhood: fare thee well.
Know, many glorious women that are fam'd
For masculine virtue, have been vicious,
Only a happier silence did betide them:
She hath no faults, who hath the art to hide them.

*Vit.* My soul, like to a ship in a black storm,
Is driven, I know not whither.

*Flam.* Then cast anchor.
Prosperity doth bewitch men, seeming clear;
But seas do laugh, shew white, when rocks are near.
We cease to grieve, cease to be fortune's slaves,
Nay, cease to die by dying. Art thou gone?
And thou so near the bottom: false report,

---

[1] *A Toledo, or an English Fox? Toledo,* the capital city of New Castile, was formerly much famed for making of sword-blades. *Fox;* a cant term for a sword.—REED. I am informed by Mr. C. Jourdain de Gatwick that the term *Fox* indicates an old broadsword, so called from Andrea Ferrara having stamped some of his blades with a mark which he intended to represent that animal. There is one in the United Service Museum, and one I myself have (adds Mr. Gatwick).

[2] *To tent*—to search, as a wound; from *tent,* a roll of lint employed in examining or purifying a deep wound.—NARES.

Which says that women vie with the nine Muses,
For nine tough durable lives ! I do not look
Who went before, nor who shall follow me ;
No, at myself I will begin and end.
While we look up to heaven, we confound
Knowledge with knowledge. O, I am in a mist !

*Vit.* O, happy they that never saw the court,
Nor ever knew great men but by report ! 　　　[*Dies.*

*Flam.* I recover like a spent taper, for a flash,
And instantly go out.

Let all that belong to great men remember th' old wives'
tradition, to be like the lions i'th' Tower on Candle-
masday ; to mourn if the sun shine, for fear of the
pitiful remainder of winter to come.

'Tis well yet there's some goodness in my death ;
My life was a black charnel. I have caught
An everlasting cold ; I have lost my voice
Most irrecoverably. Farewell, glorious villains.
This busy trade of life appears most vain,
Since rest breeds rest, where all seek pain by pain.
Let no harsh flattering bells resound my knell ;
Strike, thunder, and strike loud, to my farewell ! [*Dies.*

*Enter* AMBASSADORS *and* GIOVANNI.

*Eng. Amb.* This way, this way ! break ope the doors !
　　this way !

*Lod.* Ha ! are we betray'd ?
Why then let's constantly die all together ;
And having finish'd this most noble deed,
Defy the worst of fate, not fear to bleed.

*Eng. Amb.* Keep back the prince : shoot, shoot.

*Lod.* O, I am wounded !
I fear I shall be ta'en.

*Gio.* You bloody villains,
By what authority have you committed
This massacre ?

*Lod.* By thine.

*Gio.* Mine !

*Lod.* Yes ; thy uncle, which is a part of thee, enjoin'd
    us to't :
Thou know'st me, I am sure ; I am Count Lodowick ;
And thy most noble uncle in disguise
Was last night in thy court.

*Gio.* Ha !

*Lod.* Yes, that Moor thy father chose his pensioner.

*Gio.* He turn'd murderer !
Away with them to prison, and to torture :
All that have hands in this shall taste our justice,
As I hope heaven.

*Lod.* I do glory yet,
That I can call this act mine own.   For my part,
The rack, the gallows, and the torturing wheel,
Shall be but sound sleeps to me : here's my rest ;
I limn'd this night-piece, and it was my best.

*Gio.* Remove the bodies.   See, my honour'd lord,
What use you ought make of their punishment.
Let guilty men remember, their black deeds
Do lean on crutches made of slender reeds.

Instead of an Epilogue, only this of Martial supplies me :

*Hæc fuerint nobis præmia, si placui.*

For the action of the Play, 'twas generally well, and I dare affirm, with the joint-testimony of some of their own quality (for the true imitation of life, without striving to make nature a monster) the best that ever became them : whereof as I make a general acknowledgment, so in particular I must remember the well approved industry of my friend Master Perkins,[1] and confess the worth of his action did crown both the beginning and end.

[1] *Master Perkins*—Richard Perkins, an actor of considerable eminence.

# THE
# TRAGEDY
## OF THE DVTCHESSE
## Of Malfy.

*As it was Presented priuatly, at the Black
Friers ; and publiquely at the Globe, By the
Kings Maiesties Seruants.*

The perfect and exact Coppy, with diuerse
*things Printed, that the length of the Play would*
not beare in the Presentment

VVritten by *John Webster.*

Hora.——*Si quid*——
——*Candidus Imperti ; fi non, his utere mecum.*

LONDON :

Printed by NICHOLAS OKES, for IOHN
WATERSON, and are to be sold at the
signe of the Crowne, in *Paules*
Church-yard 1623.

# THE DUCHESS OF MALFI.

THE story of the *Duchess of Malfi* was first told, so far as I know, by Matteo Bandello, in his *Novelle*, Part I. Nov. 26. From him it was adopted by Belleforest, Nov. 19; and either from the original or from the French version it was translated into English, as a portion of that capital collection of "pleasant histories and excellent novels" entitled *The Palace of Pleasure*, which William Painter, then or lately Master of Seven Oaks School, in Kent, occupied several years subsequent to 1562 in translating "out of divers good and commendable authors," and the first tome of which was published by Richard Tottell and William Jones, anno 1566. The second volume of the Collection was "imprinted at London, in Paternoster Rowe, by Henrie Bynneman for Nicholas England, Anno 1567;" and the learned supervisor of the edition of 1813, Mr. Haslewood, has pointed out to how large an extent the various stories contained in these interesting tomes were appropriated, as soon as published, by the dramatic writers to the purposes of the English stage. *The Palace of Pleasure*, indeed, is prominently denounced by Stephen Gosson, in his *Playes Confuted in Five Actions* (1581 or 1582), among the works which "have beene thoroughly ransackt to furnish the playe-houses in London." The story of the *Duchess of Malfi* is also told by Goulart, in his *Thresor d' Histoires Admirables et Memorables de Nostre Temps*, pp. 317-322, of the edition of Geneva, 1620; and in Beard's *Theatre of God's Judgments*, B. ii. Lope de Vega wrote *El Mayordomo de la Duquesa de Amalfi,* 1618.

The plot is shortly this :—The *Duchess,* who is a widow, marries *Antonio,* the steward of her household ; her brothers are so enraged at this, that they employ *Bosola* to murder her and her children, and the brothers themselves come to the same violent end. The scene lies at Malfi, Rome, and other places in Italy.

The second edition of the *Duchess of Malfi* was " printed by J. Raworth, for J. Benson, and are to be sold at his shop in St. Dunstan's Churchyard, in Fleet Street, 1640." It was revived, as an acting-play, at the Lincoln's Inn Fields Theatre in 1664, when Betterton performed *Bosola,* Harris *Duke Ferdinand,* Smith *Antonio,* Young *the Cardinal,* Mrs. Betterton *the Duchess,* and Mrs. Gibbs *Julia.* The play, reports Downes, was excellently acted in all its parts, particularly *Bosola* and *Ferdinand ;* it filled the house eight days successively, and proved one of the best stock tragedies. The tragedy was again printed in 1678 (when Mrs. Shadwell's name stands to the part of *Julia*); and in 1708 appeared, under the editorial care of Hugh Newman, " The Unfortunate Dutchess of Malfi, or the Unnatural Brothers ; a Tragedy, now acted at the Queen's Theatre in the Haymarket, By her Majesties Company of Comedians. Written by Mr. Webster. London, printed for H. N. and are to be sold by John Morphew near Stationers Hall. 1708." This copy was that in use for dramatic representation at the time, and

it exhibits, within inverted commas, " those lines which
were omitted in the acting, by reason of the length of
the play." As a dramatic curiosity, I transcribe from
this copy the Bill of the Play in 1708. It will be seen
that, since 1623, the female *Dramatis Personæ* had
come to be represented by females, instead of, as then
and theretofore, by young men and boys. The innova-
tion, in fact, was first essayed on the 7th of Novem-
ber, 1629, by " some Frenchwomen, or monsters rather
(as horrified Prynne denounces them, in his *Histrio-
mastix*), who attempted to act a French play at the
playhouse in Blackfriars, an impudent, shameful, un-
womanish, graceless, &c. &c. attempt." The attempt,
however, did not succeed until some time afterwards.
But to the Company at the Haymarket in 1708.

### MEN.

| | |
|---|---|
| FERDINAND, Count of Calabria . . | *Mr. Verbruggen.* |
| CARDINAL, his Brother . . . . . | *Mr. Keen.* |
| ANTONIO, Steward of the Household to the Dutchess. . . . . . . | *Mr. Booth.* |
| DELIO, his Friend . . . . . . . | *Mr. Corey.* |
| BOSOLA, Gentleman of the Horse to the Dutchess. . . . . . . | *Mr. Mills.* |
| CASTRUCHIO, an old Lord . . ; . | |
| MARQUESS OF PESCARA . . . . . | *Mr. Fairbank.* |
| COUNT MALATESTE . . . . . . | *Mr. Freeman.* |
| LORD RODERIGO . . . . . . . | *Mr. Kent.* |
| LORD GRISOLAN. . . . . . . . | |
| DOCTOR to the Duke in his Madness . | *Mr. Bowen.* |
| MAD. { ASTROLOGER . . . . . . | *Mr. Trout.* |
| TAYLOR . . . . . . . | *Mr. Pack.* |
| PARSON . . . . . . . | *Mr. Johnson.* |
| DOCTOR . . . . . . . | *Mr. Bullock,* |

WOMEN.

DUTCHESS OF MALFY . . . . . . . *Mrs. Porter.*
CARIOLA, her Woman . . . . . . *Mrs. Powell.*
JULIA, Castruchio's Wife and the Car-
dinal's Mistress . . . . . . . *Mrs. Bradshaw.*

SCENE, *Italy.*

This edition is of great use, from the circumstance
that it gives the various exits and entrances of the
characters in a much more complete and accurate form
than that of the previous quartos, where, at the opening of a scene, all the names are set forth of all the
personages who make their appearance in its course,
although but one or two of them may be present at the
commencement, and even, in some cases, personages
are named who do not make their appearance at all.
It may be as well to observe here that, although in
various instances I have marked the assumed locality
of a scene or subdivision of an act, it is not to be supposed that in our author's time the attention of theatrical audiences was at all distracted from the events
and language of the play by those scenic effects which
are so leading a feature in the dramatic productions of
the present age. "I decidedly concur with Malone,"
writes Mr. Collier (*Annals of the Stage*, iii. 366), "in
the general conclusion that painted moveable scenery
was unknown on our early stage; and it is a fortunate
circumstance (adds Mr. Collier) for the poetry of our
old plays that it was so; the imagination of the auditor
only was appealed to; and we owe to the absence of
painted canvas many of the finer descriptive passages in
Shakespeare, his contemporaries and immediate followers." Scenery we learn, on the same excellent

authority, was not introduced upon the stage until towards 1660.

The *Duchess of Malfi* was worked up by Theobald into a Tragedy called *The Fatal Secret*, which was acted at Covent Garden on the 3rd of April, 1733, with Quin as *Bosola,* and was acted four times. "Theobald's first three acts," writes Mr. Genest, "do not differ very materially from Webster's. In the fourth act he gives the plot a different turn: in Webster's play the *Duchess* is strangled on the stage ; in Theobald's she is carried off the stage for that purpose. In Theobald's last scene the *Duke* and *Cardinal* kill one another by mistake ; the young *Duke* enters ; *Bosola* promises to produce the body of the *Duchess ;* he brings her in alive; *Antonio,* who is disguised as a pilgrim, discovers himself, and the play ends happily. This is effected by making *Bosola* turn out an honest man instead of a villain. The young *Duke*, who is supposed to be about twelve years old, is a new character. Theobald's alteration," adds Mr. Genest, "on the whole is not a bad one, but it is too violent ; he should have retained more of the original play. He tells us, in his preface : 'I have retained the names of the characters ; I have adopted as much of Webster's tale as I conceived for my purpose, and as much of his writing as I could turn to account. I have nowhere spared myself out of indolence, but have often engrafted his thoughts and language, because I was conscious I could not so well supply them from my own fund.' "

W. Hazlitt.

TO THE

# RIGHT HONOURABLE GEORGE HARDING,

## BARON BERKELEY, OF BERKELEY CASTLE,

### AND KNIGHT OF THE ORDER OF THE BATH TO THE ILLUSTRIOUS PRINCE CHARLES.

My noble Lord,

THAT I may present my excuse why, being a stranger to your lordship, I offer this poem to your patronage, I plead this warrant: men who never saw the sea, yet desire to behold that regiment of waters, choose some eminent river to guide them thither, and make that, as it were, their conduct or postilion: by the like ingenious means has your fame arrived at my knowledge, receiving it from some of worth, who both in contemplation and practice owe to your honour their clearest service. I do not altogether look up at your title; the ancien'st nobility being but a relic of time past, and the truest honour indeed being for a man to confer honour on himself, which your learning strives to propagate, and shall make you arrive at the dignity of a great example. I am confident this work is not unworthy your honour's perusal, for by such poems as this poets have kissed the hands of great princes, and drawn their gentle eyes to look down upon their sheets of paper, when the poets themselves were bound up in their winding-sheets. The like courtesy from your lordship shall make you live in your grave, and laurel spring out of it, when the ignorant scorners of the Muses, that like worms in libraries seem to live only to destroy learning, shall wither neglected and forgotten. This work and myself I humbly present to your approved censure,[1] it being the utmost of my wishes to have your honourable self my·weighty and perspicuous comment; which grace so done me shall ever be acknowledged

By your lordship's
in all duty and
observance,
JOHN WEBSTER.

[1] Judgment, from the Latin *censeo*.

IN THE JUST WORTH OF THAT WELL DESERVER,
MR. JOHN WEBSTER, AND UPON THIS
MASTER-PIECE OF TRAGEDY.

IN this thou imitat'st one rich and wise,
That sees his good deeds done before he
dies:
As he by works, thou by this work of fame
Hast well provided for thy living name.
To trust to others' honourings is worth's crime,
Thy monument is rais'd in thy life-time;
And 'tis most just, for every worthy man
Is his own marble, and his merit can
Cut him to any figure, and express
More art than death's cathedral palaces,
Where royal ashes keep their court.   Thy note
Be ever plainness, 'tis the richest coat:
Thy epitaph only the title be,
Write *Duchess*, that will fetch a tear for thee;
For who e'er saw this *Duchess* live and die,
That could get off under a bleeding eye.
In Tragœdiam.
Ut lux ex tenebris ictu percussa tonantis,
Illa, ruina malis, claris fit vita poetis.
Thomas Middletonus,
Poeta et Chron.[1]
Londinensis.

[1] Middleton was City Chronologer.

## TO HIS FRIEND MR. JOHN WEBSTER,

### UPON HIS DUCHESS OF MALFI.

I never saw thy *Duchess* till the day
That she was lively bodied in thy play :
Howe'er she answer'd her low-rated love
Her brothers' anger did so fatal prove,
Yet my opinion is, she might speak more,
But never in her life so well before.

Wil. Rowley.

## TO THE READER OF THE AUTHOR,

### AND HIS DUCHESS OF MALFI.

Crown him a poet, whom nor Rome nor Greece
Transcend in all their's for a masterpiece ;
In which, whiles words and matter change, and men
Act one another, he, from whose clear pen
They all took life, to memory hath lent
A lasting fame, to raise his monument.

John Ford.

# THE ACTORS' NAMES.

| | |
|---|---|
| BOSOLA. | *J. Lowin.* |
| FERDINAND. | 1. *R. Burbidge*, 2. *J. Taylor.* |
| CARDINAL. | 1. *H. Cundaile*, 2. *R. Robinson.* |
| ANTONIO. | 1. *W. Ostler*, 2. *R. Benfeild.* |
| DELIO. | *J. Underwood.* |
| FOROBOSCO. | *N. Towley.* |
| MALATESTE. | |
| THE MARQUIS OF PESCARA. } | *J. Rice.* |
| RODERIGO. | |
| SILVIO. | *T. Pollard.* |
| GRISOLAN. | |
| The Several Madmen. | *N. Towley, J. Underwood, &c.* |
| THE DUCHESS. | *R. Sharpe.* |
| The Cardinal's Mistress | *J. Thompson.* |
| DOCTOR. | |
| CARIOLA. } | *R. Pallant.* |
| Court Officers. | |
| Three Young Children. | |
| Two Pilgrims. | |

# THE DUCHESS OF MALFI.

## ACT I.—Scene I.

*Enter* Antonio, *and* Delio.

### *Delio.*

OU are welcome to your country, dear·
    Antonio ;
You have been long in France, and you.
    return
A very formal Frenchman in your habit.
How do you like the French court ?
  *Ant.* I admire it :
In seeking to reduce both state and people
To a fixt order, their judicious king
Begins at home ; quits[1] first his royal palace
Of flattering sycophants, of dissolute
And infamous persons, which he sweetly terms
His master's masterpiece, the work of heaven ;
Considering duly, that a prince's court
Is like a common fountain, whence should flow
Pure silver drops in general, but if't chance

[1] Clears.

Some curs'd example poison't near the head,
Death and diseases through the whole land spread.
And what is't makes this blessed government,
But a most provident council, who dare freely
Inform him the corruption of the times?
Though some o'th' court hold it presumption
To instruct princes what they ought to do,
It is a noble duty to inform them
What they ought to foresee.   Here comes Bosola,
The only court-gall; yet I observe his railing
Is not for simple love of piety:
Indeed he rails at those things which he wants;
Would be as lecherous, covetous, or proud,
Bloody, or envious, as any man,
If he had means to be so.   Here's the Cardinal.

*Enter* BOSOLA *and* CARDINAL.

*Bos.* I do haunt you still.
*Card.* So.
*Bos.* I have done you better service[1]
Than to be slighted thus.
Miserable age, where only the reward
Of doing well, is the doing of it!
*Card.* You enforce your merit too much.
*Bos.* I fell into the gallies in your service,
Where, for two years together, I wore
Two towels instead of a shirt, with a knot on the
      shoulder,

[1] I print the following speeches of Bosola, as well as other portions of the Tragedy, in the blank verse marked by the quartos, and which, however and by whomsoever compiled, exhibit, as Mr. Dyce remarks, manifest traces of the metre in which it is most probable the whole was at first composed.

After the fashion of a Roman mantle.
Slighted thus!   I will thrive some way: '
Black-birds fatten best in hard weather;
Why not I in these dog-days?
 *Card.* Would you could become honest!
 *Bos.* With all your divinity do but direct me
The way to it.   I have known many travel far for it,
And yet return as arrant knaves as they went forth,
Because they carried themselves always along with
  them.       [*Exit Cardinal.*
Are you gone?
Some fellows, they say, are possessed with the devil,
But this great fellow were able to possess the greatest
Devil, and make him worse.
 *Ant.* He hath denied thee some suit?
 *Bos.* He and his brother are like plum-trees that
  grow crooked
Over standing-pools; they are rich, and o'erladen with
Fruit, but none but crows, pies, and caterpillars feed
On them.   Could I be one of their flattering panders, I
Would hang on their ears like a horseleech, till I were
  full, and
Then drop off.   I pray leave me.
Who would rely upon these miserable dependencies,
  in expectation to
Be advanced to-morrow?   What creature ever fed
  worse, than hoping
Tantalus? nor ever died any man more fearfully, than
  he that hoped
For a pardon.   There are rewards for hawks and dogs,
When they have done us service: but for a soldier that
  hazards his

Limbs in a battle, nothing but a kind of geometry is
     his last
Supportation.
  *Delio.* Geometry !
  *Bos.* Ay, to hang in a fair pair of slings, take his
     latter swing in the
World upon an honourable pair of crutches, from
     hospital
To hospital.   Fare ye well, sir: and yet do not you
     scorn us, for
Places in the court are but like beds in the hospital,
     where this
Man's head lies at that man's foot, and so lower and
     lower.                                    [*Exit.*
  *Delio.* I knew this fellow seven years in the gallies
For a notorious murder ; and 'twas thought
The Cardinal suborn'd it : he was releas'd
By the French general, Gaston de Foix,
When he recover'd Naples.
  *Ant.* 'Tis great pity,
He should be thus neglected : I have heard
He's very valiant.   This foul melancholy
Will poison all his goodness ; for, I'll tell you,
If too immoderate sleep be truly said
To be an inward rust unto the soul,
It then doth follow want of action
Breeds all black malecontents, and their close rearing,
Like moths in cloth, do hurt for want of wearing.

## SCENE II.

*Enter* ANTONIO, DELIO, FERDINAND, CASTRUCCIO, SILVIO.

  *Delio.* The presence 'gins to fill : you promis'd me

To make me the partaker of the natures
Of some of your great courtiers.

 *Ant.* The lord cardinal's,
And other strangers, that are now in court?
I shall : here comes the great Calabrian Duke.

 *Ferd.* Who took the ring oftenest?[1]

 *Silvio.* Antonio Bologna, my lord.

 *Ferd.* Our sister Duchess' great master of her household :
Give him the jewel.   When shall we leave this sportive
  action,
And fall to action indeed?

 *Cast.* Methinks, my lord,
You should not desire to go to war in person.

 *Ferd.* Now, for some gravity : why, my lord?

 *Cast.* It is fitting a soldier arise to be a prince, but
  not necessary
A prince descend to be a captain.

 *Ferd.* No?

 *Cast.* No, my lord ;
He were far better do it by a deputy.

 *Ferd.* Why should he not as well sleep, or eat by a
  deputy?
This might take idle, offensive, and base office from him,
Whereas the other deprives him of honour.

 *Cast.* Believe my experience : that realm is never
  long in quiet,
Where the ruler is a soldier.

 *Ferd.* Thou toldest me
Thy wife could not endure fighting.

 *Cast.* True, my lord.

    [1] i. e. in the tilting at the ring.

*Ferd.* And of a jest she broke of a captain
She met full of wounds : I have forgot it.

   *Cast.* She told him, my lord, he was a pitiful fellow,
    to lie
Like the children of Ismael, all in tents.[1]

   *Ferd.* Why, there's a wit were able to undo
All the chirurgeons o'th' city, for although
Gallants should quarrel, and had drawn their weapons,
And were ready to go to it, yet her persuasions would
Make them put up.

   *Cast.* That she would, my lord.
How do you like my Spanish gennet ?

   *Rod.* He is all fire.

   *Ferd.* I am of Pliny's opinion, I think he was begot
    by the wind ;
He runs as if he were ballassed with quicksilver.

   *Silvio.* True, my lord, he reels from the tilt often.

   *Rod. Gris.* Ha, ha, ha !

   *Ferd.* Why do you laugh ? methinks you that are
    courtiers
Should be my touchwood, take fire when I give fire ;
That is, not laugh but when I laugh, were the subject
    never so witty.

   *Cast.* True, my lord ; I myself have heard a very
    good jest,
And have scorned to seem to have so silly a wit, as to
    understand it.

   *Ferd.* But I can laugh at your fool, my lord.

   *Cast.* He cannot speak, you know, but he makes
    faces :
My lady cannot abide him.

---

[1] *Tent* is a roll of lint used in searching a wound.

*Ferd.* No?

*Cast.* Nor endure to be in merry company ; for she
    says
Too much laughing, and too much company, fills her
Too full of the wrinkle.

*Ferd.* I would then have a mathematical instrument
Made for her face,
That she might not laugh out of compass. I shall shortly
Visit you at Milan, Lord Silvio.

*Silvio.* Your grace shall arrive most welcome.

*Ferd.* You are a good horseman, Antonio : you have
    excellent
Riders in France : what do you think of good horse-
    manship ?

*Ant.* Nobly, my lord : as out of the Grecian horse
    issued
Many famous princes, so out of brave horsemanship
Arise the first sparks of growing resolution, that raise
The mind to noble action.

*Ferd.* You have bespoke it worthily.

*Silvio.* Your brother, the lord Cardinal, and sister
    Duchess.

*Enter* CARDINAL, DUCHESS, CARIOLA, *and* JULIA.

*Card.* Are the gallies come about ?

*Gris.* They are, my lord.

*Ferd.* Here's the Lord Silvio is come to take his leave.

*Delio.* Now, sir, your promise : what's that Cardinal ?
I mean his temper? they say he's a brave fellow,
Will play his five thousand crowns at tennis, dance,
Court ladies, and one that hath fought single combats.

*Ant.* Some such flashes superficially hang on him, for
    form ;

But observe his inward character: he is a melancholy
Churchman ; the spring in his face is nothing but the
Engendering of toads ; where he is jealous of any man,
He lays worse plots for him than ever was imposed on
Hercules, for he strews in his way flatterers, panders,
Intelligencers, atheists, and a thousand such political
Monsters.   He should have been Pope, but instead of
Coming to it by the primitive decency of the church,
He did bestow bribes so largely, and so impudently, as
        if he would
Have carried it away without heaven's knowledge.
Some good he hath done——

    *Delio.* You have given too much of him: what's his
        brother?

    *Ant.* The duke there ? a most perverse and turbulent
        nature :
What appears in him mirth is merely outside ;
If he laugh heartily, it is to laugh
All honesty out of fashion.

    *Delio.* Twins?

    *Ant.* In quality.
He speaks with others' tongues, and hears men's suits
With others' ears ; will seem to sleep o' th' bench
Only to entrap offenders in their answers ;
Dooms men to death by information,
Rewards by hearsay.

    *Delio.* Then the law to him
Is like a foul black cobweb to a spider,
He makes it his dwelling and a prison
To entangle those shall feed him.

    *Ant.* Most true :

He never pays debts unless they be shrewd turns,
And those he will confess that he doth owe.
Last, for his brother there, the cardinal,
They that do flatter him most say oracles
Hang at his lips; and verily I believe them,
For the devil speaks in them.
But for their sister, the right noble duchess,
You never fix'd your eye on three fair medals
Cast in one figure, of so different temper.
For her discourse, it is so full of rapture,
You only will begin then to be sorry
When she doth end her speech, and wish, in wonder,
She held it less vain-glory, to talk much,
Than your penance to hear her: whilst she speaks,
She throws upon a man so sweet a look,
That it were able to raise one to a galliard[1]
That lay in a dead palsy, and to dote
On that sweet countenance; but in that look
There speaketh so divine a continence,
As cuts off all lascivious and vain hope.
Her days are practis'd in such noble virtue,
That sure her nights, nay more, her very sleeps,
Are more in heaven, than other ladies' shrifts.
Let all sweet ladies break their flattering glasses,
And dress themselves in her.

   *Delio.* Fie, Antonio,
You play the wire-drawer with her commendations.

   *Ant.* I'll case the picture up: only thus much,
All her particular worth, grows to this sum;
She stains the time past, lights the time to come.

---

[1] A quick and lively dance.

*Cari.* You must attend my lady in the gallery,
Some half an hour hence.

 *Ant.* I shall.    [*Exeunt Antonio and Delio.*

 *Ferd.* Sister, I have a suit to you.

 *Duch.* To me, sir?

 *Ferd.* A gentleman here, Daniel de Bosola,
One that was in the gallies——

 *Duch.* Yes, I know him.

 *Ferd.* A worthy fellow h'is: pray let me entreat for
The provisorship of your horse.

 *Duch.* Your knowledge of him
Commends him and prefers him.

 *Ferd.* Call him hither.    [*Exit Attendant.*
We are now upon parting.—Good Lord Silvio,
Do us commend to all our noble friends
At the leaguer.

 *Silvio.* Sir, I shall.

 *Ferd.* You are for Milan

 *Silvio.* I am.

 *Duch.* Bring the carroches :[1] we'll bring you down
  to the haven.
      [*Exeunt all but the Cardinal and*
          *Ferdinand.*

 *Card.* Be sure you entertain that Bosola
For your intelligence : I would not be seen in't ;
And therefore many times I have slighted him,
When he did court our furtherance, as this morning.

 *Ferd.* Antonio, the great master of her household,
Had been far fitter.

 *Card.* You are deceiv'd in him :

---

[1] Large coaches.

His nature is too honest for such business.
He comes : I'll leave you.                                    [*Exit.*

*Enter* BOSOLA.

*Bos.* I was lur'd to you.

*Ferd.* My brother here, the cardinal could never
Abide you.

*Bos.* Never since he was in my debt.

*Ferd.* May be some oblique character in your face
Made him suspect you.

*Bos.* Doth he study physiognomy ?
There's no more credit to be given to th' face,
Than to a sick man's urine, which some call
The physician's whore, because she cozens him.
He did suspect me wrongfully.

*Ferd.* For that
You must give great men leave to take their times.
Distrust doth cause us seldom be deceiv'd :
You see, the oft shaking of the cedar-tree
Fastens it more at root.

*Bos.* Yet, take heed ;
For to suspect a friend unworthily,
Instructs him the next way to suspect you,
And prompts him to deceive you.

*Ferd.* There's gold.

*Bos.* So,
What follows ? never rain'd such showers as these
Without thunderbolts i'th' tail of them : whose throat
        must I cut ?

*Ferd.* Your inclination to shed blood rides post
Before my occasion to use you.  I give you that
To live i'th' court here, and observe the duchess ;

To note all the particulars of her 'haviour,
What suitors do solicit her for marriage,
And whom she best affects.   She's a young widow :
I would not have her marry again.
    *Bos.* No, sir?
    *Ferd.* Do not you ask the reason ; but be satisfied
I say I would not.
    *Bos.* It seems you would create me
One of your familiars.
    *Ferd.* Familiar ! what's that?
    *Bos.* Why, a very quaint invisible devil in flesh ;
An intelligencer.
    *Ferd.* Such a kind of thriving thing
I would wish thee ; and ere long, thou may'st arrive
At a higher place by't.
    *Bos.* Take your devils,
Which hell calls angels:[1] these curs'd gifts would make
You a corrupter, me an impudent traitor ;
And should I take these, they'd take me to hell.
    *Ferd.* Sir, I'll take nothing from you, that I have
        given :
There is a place that I procur'd for you
This morning, the provisorship o' th' horse ;
Have you heard on't?
    *Bos.* No.
    *Ferd.* 'Tis yours: is't not worth thanks ?
    *Bos.* I would have you curse yourself now, that
        your bounty
(Which makes men truly noble) e'er should make
Me a villain.   O, that to avoid ingratitude
For the good deed you have done me, I must do

---

[1] *Angel* was a gold coin, in value about 8*s.*

All the ill man can invent ! Thus the devil
Candies all sins o'er; and what heaven terms vile
That names he complemental.

*Ferd.* Be yourself;
Keep your old garb of melancholy; 'twill express
You envy those that stand above your reach,
Yet strive not to come near 'em : this will gain
Access to private lodgings, where yourself
May, like a politic dormouse——

*Bos.* As I have seen some,
Feed in a lord's dish, half asleep, not seeming
To listen to any talk ; and yet these rogues
Have cut his throat in a dream. What's my place ?
The provisorship o'th' horse ? say, then, my corruption
Grew out of horse-dung: I am your creature.

*Ferd.* Away.

*Bos.* Let good men, for good deeds, covet good fame,
Since place and riches, oft are bribes of shame :
Sometimes the devil doth preach. [*Exit.*

　　*Enter* DUCHESS, CARDINAL, *and* CARIOLA.[1]

*Card.* We are to part from you; and your own dis-
　　cretion
Must now be your director.

*Ferd.* You are a widow :
You know already what man is ; and therefore
Let not youth, high promotion, eloquence——

*Card.* No,
Nor anything without the addition, honour,
Sway your high blood.

*Ferd.* Marry ! they are most luxurious,[2]

---

[1] Supplied by Mr. Dyce.　　　　[2] Lascivious.

Will wed twice.

*Card.* O, fie !

*Ferd.* Their livers are more spotted
Than Laban's sheep.

*Duch.* Diamonds are of most value,
They say, that have past through most jewellers' hands.

*Ferd.* Whores, by that rule, are precious.

*Duch.* Will you hear me ?
I'll never marry.

*Card.* So most widows say ;
But commonly that motion lasts no longer
Than the turning of an hour-glass : the funeral sermon
And it, end both together.

*Ferd.* Now hear me :
You live in a rank pasture here, i'th' court ;
There is a kind of honey-dew that's deadly ;
'Twill poison your fame ; look to't : be not cunning ;
For they whose faces do belie their hearts,
Are witches ere they arrive at twenty years,
Ay, and give the devil suck.

*Duch.* This is terrible good counsel.

*Ferd.* Hypocrisy is woven of a fine small thread,
Subtler than Vulcan's engine :[1] yet, believ't,
Your darkest actions, nay, your privat'st thoughts,
Will come to light.

*Card.* You may flatter yourself,
And take your own choice ; privately be married
Under the eves of night—

*Ferd.* Think't the best voyage
That e'er you made ; like the irregular crab,

---

[1] i. e. the net in which he caught Mars and Venus. —DYCE.

Which, though't goes backward, thinks that it goes right,
Because it goes its own way : but observe,
Such weddings may more properly be said
To be executed, than celebrated.

 *Card.* The marriage night
Is the entrance into some prison.

 *Ferd.* And those joys,
Those lustful pleasures, are like heavy sleeps
Which do forerun man's mischief.

 *Card.* Fare you well.
Wisdom begins at the end : remember it.   [*Exit.*

 *Duch.* I think this speech between you both was
  studied,
It came so roundly off.

 *Ferd.* You are my sister ;
This was my father's poinard, do you see ?
I'd be loath to see't look rusty, 'cause 'twas his.
I would have you to give o'er these chargeable revels,
A visor and a mask are whispering rooms
That were never built for goodness ;—fare ye well,
And beware that part,[1] which like the lamprey,
Hath never a bone in't.

 *Duch.* Fie, sir.

 *Ferd.* Nay,
I mean the tongue ; variety of courtship :
What cannot a neat knave with a smooth tale
Make a woman believe ? Farewell, lusty widow. [*Exit.*

 *Duch.* Shall this move me ?  If all my royal kindred
Lay in my way unto this marriage,
I'd make them my low footsteps : and even now,

---

[1] From the edition of 1708.  The editions of 1623 and 1640
read : "and women like that part."

Even in this hate, as men in some great battles,
By apprehending danger, have achiev'd
Almost impossible actions,—I have heard soldiers say
    so,—
So I through frights and threatenings will assay
This dangerous venture.  Let old wives report
I wink'd, and chose a husband.  Cariola,
To thy known secrecy I have given up
More than my life—my fame.
  *Cari.* Both shall be safe :
For I'll conceal this secret from the world,
As warily as those that trade in poison
Keep poison from their children.
  *Duch.* Thy protestation
Is ingenious[1] and hearty : I believe it.
Is Antonio come ?
  *Cari.* He attends you.
  *Duch.* Good dear soul,
Leave me ; but place thyself behind the arras,
Where thou may'st overhear us.  Wish me good speed,
For I am going into a wilderness
Where I shall find nor path, nor friendly clew,
To be my guide.          [*Exit Cariola.*

*Enter* ANTONIO.

I sent for you : sit down ;
Take pen and ink, and write : are you ready ?
  *Ant.* Yes.
  *Duch.* What did I say ?
  *Ant.* That I should write somewhat.
  *Duch.* O, I remember.

[1] For *ingenious.*  The terms were often transposed by early writers.—HALLIWELL.

After these triumphs and this large expence,
It's fit, like thrifty husbands, we inquire
What's laid up for to-morrow.

   *Ant.* So please your beauteous excellence.

   *Duch.* Beauteous! Indeed I thank you :
I look young for your sake ;
You have ta'en my cares upon you.

   *Ant.* I'll fetch your grace
The particulars of your revenue and expence.

   *Duch.* O, you are
An upright treasurer ; but you mistook :
For when I said I meant to make inquiry
What's laid up for to-morrow, I did mean
What's laid up yonder for me.

   *Ant.* Where ?

   *Duch.* In heaven.
I am making my will, (as 'tis fit princes should,
In perfect memory,) and, I pray, sir, tell me
Were not one better make it smiling, thus,
Than in deep groans, and terrible ghastly looks,
As if the gifts we parted with procur'd
That violent distraction ?

   *Ant.* O, much better.

   *Duch.* If I had a husband now, this care were quit :
But I intend to make you overseer.
What good deed shall we first remember ? say.

   *Ant.* Begin with that first good deed begun i'th' world
After man's creation, the sacrament of marriage :
I'd have you first provide for a good husband ;
Give him all.

   *Duch.* All ?

*Ant.* Yes, your excellent self.

*Duch.* In a winding sheet?

*Ant.* In a couple.

*Duch.* St. Winifred, that were a strange will!

*Ant.* 'Twere strange if there were no will in you
To marry again.

*Duch.* What do you think of marriage?

*Ant.* I take't, as those that deny purgatory,
It locally contains, or heaven, or hell,
There's no third place in't.

*Duch.* How do you affect it?

*Ant.* My banishment, feeding my melancholy,
Would often reason thus.

*Duch.* Pray, let's hear it.

*Ant.* Say a man never marry, nor have children,
What takes that from him? only the bare name
Of being a father, or the weak delight
To see the little wanton ride a cock-horse
Upon a painted stick, or hear him chatter
Like a taught starling.

*Duch.* Fie, fie, what's all this?
One of your eyes is blood-shot; use my ring to't,
They say 'tis very sovereign: 'twas my wedding ring
And I did vow never to part with it
But to my second husband.

*Ant.* You have parted with it now.

*Duch.* Yes, to help your eye-sight.

*Ant.* You have made me stark blind.

*Duch.* How?

*Ant.* There is a saucy and ambitious devil,
Is dancing in this circle.

*Duch.* Remove him.

*Ant.* How?

*Duch.* There needs small conjuration, when your finger

May do it; thus; is it fit?                    [*He kneels.*

*Ant.* What said you?

*Duch.* Sir,

This goodly roof of yours, is too low built;

I cannot stand upright in't nor discourse,

Without I raise it higher: raise yourself;

Or, if you please, my hand to help you: so.

*Ant.* Ambition, madam, is a great man's madness,

That is not kept in chains, and close-pent rooms,

But in fair lightsome lodgings, and is girt

With the wild noise of prattling visitants,

Which makes it lunatic beyond all cure.

Conceive not I am so stupid but I aim

Whereto your favours tend: but he's a fool,

That being a-cold, would thrust his hands i'th' fire

To warm them.

*Duch.* So now the ground's broke,

You may discover what a wealthy mine

I make you lord of.

*Ant.* O, my unworthiness!

*Duch.* You were ill to sell yourself:

This darkening of your worth is not like that

Which tradesmen use i'th' city; their false lights

Are to rid bad wares off: and I must tell you,

If you will know where breathes a complete man,

(I speak it without flattery,) turn your eyes,

And progress through yourself.

*Ant.* Were there nor heaven nor hell,

I should be honest : I have long serv'd virtue,
And ne'er ta'en wages of her.

*Duch.* Now she pays it.
The misery of us that are born great !
We are forc'd to woo, because none dare woo us ;
And as a tyrant doubles with his words,
And fearfully equivocates, so we
Are forc'd to express our violent passions
In riddles, and in dreams, and leave the path
Of simple virtue, which was never made
To seem the thing it is not.   Go, go brag
You have left me heartless ; mine is in your bosom :
I hope 'twill multiply love there.   You do tremble :
Make not your heart so dead a piece of flesh,
To fear, more than to love me.   Sir, be confident :
What is't distracts you ? This is flesh and blood, sir ;
'Tis not the figure cut in alabaster,
Kneels at my husband's tomb.   Awake, awake, man !
I do here put off all vain ceremony,
And only do appear to you a young widow
That claims you for her husband, and like a widow,
I use but half a blush in't.

*Ant.* Truth speak for me :
I will remain the constant sanctuary
Of your good name.

*Duch.* I thank you, gentle love :
And 'cause  you shall not come to me in debt,
Being now my steward, here upon your lips
I sign your *Quietus est.*   This you should have begg'd
　　now ;
I have seen children oft eat sweetmeats thus,
As fearful to devour them too soon.

*Ant.* But for your brothers?

*Duch.* Do not think of them :
All discord without this circumference
Is only to be pitied, and not fear'd :
Yet, should they know it, time will easily
Scatter the tempest.

*Ant.* These words should be mine,
And all the parts you have spoke, if some part of it
Would not have savour'd flattery.

*Duch.* Kneel.

*Enter* CARIOLA.

*Ant.* Ha !

*Duch.* Be not amaz'd, this woman's of my counsel :
I have heard lawyers say, a contract in a chamber
*Per verba presenti* is absolute marriage.
Bless, heaven, this sacred gordian, which let violence
Never untwine !

*Ant.* And may our sweet affections, like the spheres,
Be still in motion.

*Duch.* Quickening, and make
The like soft music.

*Ant.* That we may imitate the loving palms,
Best emblem of a peaceful marriage
That never bore fruit divided.

*Duch.* What can the church force more?

*Ant.* That fortune may not know an accident
Either of joy, or sorrow, to divide
Our fixed wishes.

*Duch.* How can the church build faster?
We now are man and wife, and 'tis the church
That must but echo this.   Maid, stand apart :

I now am blind.

    *Ant.* What's your conceit in this?

    *Duch.* I would have you lead your fortune by the
        hand

Unto your marriage bed :

(You speak in me this, for we now are one :)

We'll only lie, and talk together, and plot

T'appease my humourous kindred ; and if you please,

Like the old tale in Alexander and Lodowick,

Lay a naked sword between us, keep us chaste.

O, let me shrowd my blushes in your bosom,

Since 'tis the treasury of all my secrets !    [*Exeunt.*

    *Cari.* Whether the spirit of greatness, or of woman

Reign most in her, I know not ; but it shews

A fearful madness : I owe her much of pity.    [*Exit.*

## ACT II.—SCENE I.

*Enter* BOSOLA *and* CASTRUCCIO.

### Bosola.

YOU say, you would fain be taken for an
        eminent courtier ?

    *Cast.* 'Tis the very main of my ambition.

    *Bos.* Let me see : you have a reasonable good face
        for't already,

And your night-cap expresses your ears sufficient largely.

I would have you learn to twirl the strings of your band

With a good grace, and in a set speech, at th' end of
        every sentence,

To hum three or four times, or blow your nose till it
    smart again,
To recover your memory.  When you come to be a
    president
In criminal causes, if you smile upon a prisoner, hang
    him, but if
You frown upon him, and threaten him, let him be sure
    to 'scape
The gallows.
    *Cast.* I would be a very merry president.
    *Bos.* Do not sup a' nights ; 'twill beget you
An admirable wit.
    *Cast.* Rather it would make me have a good stomach
    to quarrel ;
For they say, your roaring boys [1] eat meat seldom,
And that makes them so valiant.
But how shall I know whether the people take me
For an eminent fellow ?
    *Bos.* I will teach a trick to know it :
Give out you lie a-dying, and if you
Hear the common people curse you,
Be sure you are taken for one of the prime night-caps. [2]
             *Enter an* OLD LADY. [3]
You come from painting now.
    *Old Lady.* From what ?
    *Bos.* Why, from your scurvy face-physic.
To behold thee not painted, inclines somewhat near

---

[1] The cant term for bullying bucks of our author's time.
[2] *Night-caps,*—another term for the bullies of the time.
[3] This entrance is supplied by Mr. Dyce.  In the original,
all the persons who appear during the scenes are named
together at its commencement.

A miracle : these in thy face here, were deep ruts,
And foul sloughs, the last progress.
There was a lady in France, that having had the small-
pox,
Flay'd the skin off her face, to make it more level ;
And whereas before she looked like a nutmeg-grater,
After she resembled an abortive hedgehog.

*Old Lady.* Do you call this painting ?

*Bos.* No, no, but you call't careening of an old
Morphewed[1] lady, to make her disembogue again :
There's rough-cast phrase to your plastic.

*Old Lady.* It seems you are well acquainted with
my closet.

*Bos.* One would suspect it for a shop of witchcraft,
To find in it the fat of serpents, spawn of snakes, Jews'
spittle,
And their young childrens' ordure ;  and all these for
the face.
I would sooner eat a dead pigeon, taken from the soles
of the feet
Of one sick of the plague, than kiss one of you fasting.
Here are two of you, whose sin of your youth is the very
Patrimony of the physician ; makes him renew
His foot-cloth with the spring, and change his
High-priced courtezan with the fall of the leaf.
I do wonder you do not loathe yourselves.
Observe my meditation now.
What thing is in this outward form of man
To be belov'd ?   We account it ominous,
If nature do produce a colt, or lamb,

---

[1] Leperous.

A fawn, or goat, in any limb resembling
A man, and fly from't as a prodigy.
Man stands amaz'd to see his deformity
In any other creature but himself.
But in our own flesh, though we bear diseases
Which have their true names only ta'en from beasts,
As the most ulcerous wolf and swinish measle,
Though we are eaten up of lice and worms,
And though continually we bear about us
A rotten and dead body, we delight
To hide it in rich tissue ; all our fear,
Nay all our terror, is, lest our physician
Should put us in the ground, to be made sweet.
Your wife's gone to Rome : you two couple, and get you
To the wells at Lucca, to recover your aches.    I
Have other work on foot.

           [*Exeunt Castruccio and the Old Lady.*[1]

I observe our duchess
Is sick a-days, she pukes, her stomach seethes,
The fins of her eyelids look most teeming blue,
She wanes i'th' cheek, and waxes fat i'th' flank,
And, contrary to our Italian fashion,
Wears a loose-bodied gown ; there's something in't.
I have a trick may chance discover it,
A pretty one : I have bought some apricocks,[2]
The first our spring yields—

        *Enter* ANTONIO *and* DELIO.

  *Delio.* And so long since married !
You amaze me.

---

[1] Supplied by Mr. Dyce.
[2] His reason for bringing apricots will appear further on.

*Ant.* Let me seal your lips for ever :
For did I think, that anything but th' air
Could carry these words from you, I should wish
You had no breath at all.—Now, sir, in your contem-
      plation ?
You are studying to become a great wise fellow.

*Bos.* O, sir, the opinion of wisdom,
Is a foul tetter, that runs
All over a man's body : if simplicity
Direct us to have no evil,
It directs us to a happy being : for the subtlest folly
Proceeds from the subtlest wisdom :
Let me be simply honest.

    *Ant.* I do understand your inside.

    *Bos.* Do you so ?

    *Ant.* Because you would not seem to appear to th'
      world
Puft up with your preferment, you continue
This out-of-fashion melancholy : leave it, leave it.

    *Bos.* Give me leave to be honest in any phrase, in any
Complement whatsoever.  Shall I confess myself to you?
I look no higher than I can reach :
They are the gods that must ride on winged horses.
A lawyer's mule, of a slow pace, will both suit
My disposition and business : for, mark me,
When a man's mind rides faster than his horse can
      gallop,
They quickly both tire.

    *Ant.* You would look up to heaven, but I think
The devil, that rules i'th' air stands in your light.

    *Bos.* O, sir, you are lord of the ascendant,
Chief man with the duchess ; a duke was your
Cousin-german removed.  Say you were lineally

Descended from King Pepin, or he himself,
What of this? search the heads of the greatest rivers
In the world, you shall find them
But bubbles of water.    Some would think
The souls of princes were brought forth
By some more weighty cause, than those of meaner
      persons:
They are deceived, there's the same hand to them;
The like passions sway them;
The same reason
That makes a vicar to go to law for a tithe-pig,
And undo his neighbours, makes them spoil
A whole province, and batter down
Goodly cities with the cannon.

*Enter* DUCHESS *and* LADIES.[1]

*Duch.* Your arm, Antonio: do I not grow fat?
I am exceeding short-winded.    Bosola,
I would have you, sir, provide for me a litter;
Such a one as the Duchess of Florence rode in.

    *Bos.* The duchess us'd one when she was great with
      child.

    *Duch.* I think she did.  Come hither, mend my ruff:
Here, when?[2] thou art such a tedious lady; and
Thy breath smells of lemon pills: would thou hadst
    done!
Shall I swoon under thy fingers?    I am
So troubled with the mother.[3]

    *Bos.* I fear too much.

    *Duch.* I have heard you say, that the French courtiers

[1] Supplied by Mr. Dyce.
[2] An exclamation of impatience—*When* will you have done?
[3] Hysterical passions.

Wear their hats on fore the king.

*Ant.* I have seen it.

*Duch.* In the presence?

*Ant.* Yes.

*Duch.* Why should not we bring up that fashion?
'Tis ceremony more than duty, that consists
In the removing of a piece of felt:
Be you the example to the rest o'th' court,
Put on your hat first.

*Ant.* You must pardon me:
I have seen, in colder countries than in France,
Nobles stand bare to th' prince; and the distinction
Methought shew'd reverently.

*Bos.* I have a present for your grace.

*Duch.* For me, sir?

*Bos.* Apricocks, madam.

*Duch.* O, sir, where are they?
I have heard of none to[1] year.

*Bos.* Good, her colour rises.

*Duch.* Indeed I thank you: they are wondrous fair
    ones:
What an unskilful fellow is our gardener!
We shall have none this month.

*Bos.* Will not your grace pare them?

*Duch.* No: they taste of musk, methinks; indeed
    they do.

*Bos.* I know not: yet I wish your grace had par'd 'em.

*Duch.* Why?

*Bos.* I forgot to tell you, the knave gardener,
Only to raise his profit by them the sooner,

---

[1] An expression now rustic, but quite analogous with the
*to-day* which retains its position in genteel society.

Did ripen them in horse-dung.

*Duch.* O, you jest.—
You shall judge : pray, taste one.

*Ant.* Indeed, madam,
I do not love the fruit.

*Duch.* Sir, you are loath
To rob us of our dainties : 'tis a delicate fruit ;
They say they are restorative.

*Bos.* 'Tis a pretty art,
This grafting.

*Duch.* 'Tis so : a bettering of nature.

*Bos.* To make a pippin grow upon a crab,
A damson on a black-thorn.  How greedily she eats them !
A whirlwind strike off these bawd farthingales !
For, but for that, and the loose-bodied gown,
I should have discover'd apparently
The young springal cutting a caper in her belly.

*Duch.* I thank you, Bosola : they were right good ones,
If they do not make me sick.

*Ant.* How now, madam ?

*Duch.* This green fruit and my stomach are not
        friends :
How they swell me !

*Bos.* Nay, you are too much swell'd already.

*Duch.* O, I am in an extreme cold sweat !

*Bos.* I am very sorry.                    [*Exit.*

*Duch.* Lights to my chamber.   O, good Antonio,
I fear I am undone !

*Delio.* Lights there, lights.        [*Exit Duchess.*

*Ant.* O my most trusty Delio, we are lost !
I fear she's fallen in labour ; and there's left
No time for her remove.

*Delio.* Have you prepar'd
Those ladies to attend her? and procur'd
That politic safe conveyance for the midwife,
Your duchess plotted?

*Ant.* I have.

*Delio.* Make use then of this forc'd occasion:
Give out that Bosola hath poison'd her
With these apricocks; that will give some colour
For her keeping close.

*Ant.* Fie, fie, the physicians
Will then flock to her.

*Delio.* For that you may pretend
She'll use some prepar'd antidote of her own,
Lest the physicians should re-poison her.

*Ant.* I am lost in amazement: I know not what to
    think on't.                    [*Exeunt.*


## SCENE II.

### *Enter* BOSOLA.

*Bos.* So, so, there's no question but her tetchiness
And most vulturous eating of the apricocks, are
Apparent signs of breeding.

### *Enter an* OLD LADY.[1]

Now?

*Old Lady.* I am in haste, sir.

*Bos.* There was a young waiting-woman, had a mon-
    strous desire
To see the glass-house—

---

[1] Supplied by Mr. Dyce.

*Old Lady.* Nay, pray let me go.

*Bos.* And it was only to know what strange instru-
    ment it was,
Should swell up a glass to the fashion of a woman's belly.

 *Old Lady.* I will hear no more of the glass-house.
You are still abusing women.

*Bos.* Who I? no, only, by the way, now and then,
Mention your frailties.   The orange-tree
Bears ripe and green fruit and blossoms,
Altogether : and some of you
Give entertainment for pure love, but more,
For more precious reward.   The lusty
Spring smells well ; but drooping autumn tastes well.
    If we
Have the same golden showers, that rained in the time
    of Jupiter
The thunderer, you have the same Danaes still, to hold up
Their laps to receive them.   Didst thou never study
The mathematics ?

 *Old Lady.* What's that, sir ?

*Bos.* Why, to know the trick how to make a many
    lines meet
In one centre.   Go, go, give your foster-daughters good
    counsel :
Tell them, that the devil takes delight to hang at a
    woman's girdle,
Like a false rusty watch, that she cannot discern
How the time passes.         *[Exit Old Lady.*

    *Enter* Antonio, Roderigo, *and* Grisolan.

*Ant.* Shut up the court-gates.

*Rod.* Why, sir? what's the danger ?

*Ant.* Shut up the posterns presently, and call
All the officers o'th' court.

*Gris.* I shall instantly.    [*Exit.*

*Ant.* Who keeps the key o'th' park gate ?

*Rod.* Forobosco.

*Ant.* Let him bring't presently.

#### Enter GRISOLAN *and* SERVANTS.

*First Serv.* O, gentlemen o'th' court, the foulest treason!

*Bos.* If that these apricocks should be poison'd now,
Without my knowledge !

*Serv.* There was taken even now a Switzer in the
duchess' bed-chamber—

*Second Serv.* A Switzer !

*Serv.* With a pistol in his great cod-piece.

*Bos.* Ha, ha, ha !

*Serv.* The cod-piece was the case for't.

*Second Serv.* There was a cunning traitor ; who
would have search'd his cod-piece ?

*Serv.* True, if he had kept out of the ladies' chambers :
and all the moulds of his buttons were leaden bullets.

*Second Serv.* O, wicked cannibal ! a firelock in's cod-
piece !

*Serv.* 'Twas a French plot, upon my life.

*Second Serv.* To see what the devil can do !

*Ant.* Are all the officers here ?

*Servants.* We are.

*Ant.* Gentlemen,
We have lost much plate you know ; and but this
evening
Jewels, to the value of four thousand ducats,
Are missing in the duchess' cabinet.

Are the gates shut?

*Serv.* Yes.

*Ant.* 'Tis the duchess' pleasure
Each officer be lock'd into his chamber
Till the sun-rising; and to send the keys
Of all their chests, and of their outward doors
Into her bed-chamber.   She is very sick.

*Rod.* At her pleasure.

*Ant.* She entreats you tak't not ill: the innocent
Shall be the more approv'd by it.

*Bos.* Gentlemen o'th' wood-yard, where's your
    Switzer now?

*Serv.* By this hand 'twas credibly reported by one
    o'th' blackguard.[1]          [*Exeunt Gentlemen.*

*Delio.* How fares it with the duchess?

*Ant.* She's expos'd
Unto the worst of torture, pain and fear.

*Delio.* Speak to her all happy comfort.

*Ant.* How I do play the fool with mine own danger!
You are this night, dear friend, to post to Rome:
My life lies in your service.

*Delio.* Do not doubt me.

*Ant.* O, 'tis far from me! and yet fear presents me
Somewhat that looks like danger.

*Delio.* Believe it,
'Tis but the shadow of your fear, no more:
How superstitiously we mind our evils!
The throwing down salt, or crossing of a hare,
Bleeding at nose, the stumbling of a horse,
Or singing of a cricket, are of power

---

[1] One of the scullions or lower servants.

To daunt whole man in us.   Sir, fare you well :
I wish you all the joys of a blest father ;       ·
And, for my faith, lay this unto your breast,
Old friends, like old swords, still are trusted best. [*Exit.*

### *Enter* CARIOLA.

*Cari.* Sir, you are the happy father of a son :
Your wife commends him to you.
    *Ant.* Blessed comfort !
For heaven' sake tend her well : I'll presently
Go set a figure for's nativity.                          [*Exeunt.*


## SCENE III.

### *Enter* BOSOLA, *with a dark lantern.*

*Bos.* Sure I did hear a woman shriek : list, ha !
And the sound came, if I receiv'd it right,
From the duchess' lodgings.   There's some stratagem
In the confining all our courtiers
To their several wards : I must have part of it ;
My intelligence will freeze else.   List, again !
It may be 'twas the melancholy bird,
Best friend of silence and of solitariness,
The owl, that scream'd so.   Ha ! Antonio !

### *Enter* ANTONIO.

*Ant.* I heard some noise.   Who's there ?   what art
    thou ? speak.
    *Bos.* Antonio ? put not your face nor body
To such a forc'd expression of fear :
I am Bosola, your friend.

*Ant.* Bosola !
This mole does undermine me—Heard you not
A noise even now?

*Bos.* From whence ?

*Ant.* From the duchess' lodging.

*Bos.* Not I : did you ?

*Ant.* I did, or else I dream'd.

*Bos.* Let's walk towards it.

*Ant.* No : it may be 'twas
But the rising of the wind.

*Bos.* Very likely :
Methinks 'tis very cold, and yet you sweat.
You look wildly.

*Ant.* I have been setting a figure
For the duchess' jewels.

*Bos.* Ah, and how falls your question ?
Do you find it radical ?

*Ant.* What's that to you ?
'Tis rather to be question'd what design,
When all men were commanded to their lodgings,
Makes you a night-walker.

*Bos.* In sooth I'll tell you :
Now all the court's asleep, I thought the devil
Had least to do here ; I came to say my prayers,
And if it do offend you I do so,
You are a fine courtier.

*Ant.* This fellow will undo me.
You gave the duchess apricocks to-day :
Pray heaven they were not poison'd.

*Bos.* Poison'd ! a Spanish fig[1]

---

[1] Figs were a common medium for poison.

For the imputation.

    *Ant.* Traitors are ever confident,
Till they are discover'd.   There were jewels stol'n too:
In my conceit, none are to be suspected
More than yourself.

    *Bos.* You are a false steward.

    *Ant.* Saucy slave, I'll pull thee up by the roots.

    *Bos.* Maybe the ruin will crush you to pieces.

    *Ant.* You are an impudent snake indeed, sir.
Are you scarce warm, and do you show your sting?
You libel well, sir.

    *Bos.* No, sir : copy it out,
And I will set my hand to't.

    *Ant.* My nose bleeds.
One that were superstitious would count
This ominous, when it merely comes by chance :
Two letters, that are wrote here for my name,
Are drown'd in blood !
Mere accident.—For you, sir, I'll take order
I'th' morn you shall be safe—'tis that must colour
Her lying in—sir, this door you pass not :
I do not hold it fit that you come near
The duchess' lodgings, till you have quit yourself.—
The great are like the base, nay, they are the same,
When they seek shameful ways to avoid shame.  [*Exit.*

    *Bos.* Antonio hereabout did drop a paper.
Some of your help, false friend.[1]   O, here it is :
What's here? a child's nativity calculated !

    *The Duchess was delivered of a son, 'tween the hours*
*twelve and one in the night, Anno Dom.* 1504, (that's this

---

[1] (To his lantern.)

year) *decimo nono Decembris,* (that's this night,) *taken
according to the meridian of Malfi* (that's our Duchess :
happy discovery !) *The lord of the first house being com-
bust in the ascendant, signifies short life ; and Mars being in a human sign, joined to the tail of the Dragon, in
the eighth house, doth threaten a violent death.* Cætera
non scrutantur.

Why, now 'tis most apparent : this precise fellow
Is the duchess' bawd—I have it to my wish !
This is a parcel of intelligency
Our courtiers were cas'd up for : it needs must follow,
That I must be committed, on pretence
Of poisoning her ; which I'll endure, and laugh at.
If one could find the father now ! but that
Time will discover.    Old Castruccio
I'th' morning posts to Rome : by him I'll send
A letter, that shall make her brothers' galls
O'erflow their livers.    This was a thrifty way.
Though lust do mask in ne'er so strange disguise,
She's oft found witty, but is never wise.        [*Exit.*


## SCENE IV.

*Enter* CARDINAL, *and* JULIA.

*Card.* Sit : thou art my best of wishes.    Prithee tell
      me,
What trick didst thou invent to come to Rome
Without thy husband?
    *Julia.* Why, my lord, I told him
I came to visit an old anchorite
Here, for devotion.

*Card.* Thou art a witty false one ;
I mean, to him.

*Julia.* You have prevail'd with me
Beyond my strongest thoughts : I would not now
Find you inconstant.

*Card.* Do not put thyself
To such a voluntary torture, which proceeds
Out of your own guilt.

*Julia.* How, my lord ?

*Card.* You fear my constancy, because you have approv'd
Those giddy and wild turnings in yourself.

*Julia.* Did you e'er find them ?

*Card.* Sooth, generally ; for women,
A man might strive to make glass malleable,
Ere he should make them fixed.

*Julia.* So, my lord.

*Card.* We had need go borrow that fantastic glass,
Invented by Galileo the Florentine,
To view another spacious world i'th' moon,
And look to find a constant woman there.

*Julia.* This is very well, my lord.

*Card.* Why do you weep ?
Are tears your justification ? the self-same tears
Will fall into your husband's bosom, lady,
With a loud protestation that you love him
Above the world.   Come, I'll love you wisely :
That's jealousy ; since I am very certain
You cannot make me cuckold.

*Julia.* I'll go home
To my husband.

*Card.* You may thank me, lady :

I have taken you off your melancholy perch,
Bore you upon my fist, and shew'd you game,
And let you fly at it.—I pray thee kiss me.—
When thou was't with thy husband, thou was't watch'd
Like a tame elephant :—(still you are to thank me:)—
Thou hadst only kisses from him, and high feeding ;
But what delight was that? 'twas just like one
That hath a little fingering on the lute,
Yet cannot tune it :—still you are to thank me.
   *Julia.* You told me of a piteous wound i'th' heart,
And a sick liver, when you woo'd me first,
And spake like one in physic.
   *Card.* Who's that?—

*Enter* SERVANT.[1]

Rest firm, for my affection to thee,
Lightning moves slow to't.
   *Serv.* Madam, a gentleman,
That's come post from Malfi, desires to see you.
   *Card.* Let him enter : I'll withdraw.    [*Exit.*
   *Serv.* He says,
Your husband, old Castruccio, is come to Rome.
Most pitifully tired with riding post.    [*Exit.*

*Enter* DELIO.

   *Julia.* Signior Delio ! 'tis one of my old suitors.
   *Delio.* I was bold to come and see you.
   *Julia.* Sir, you are welcome.
   *Delio.* Do you lie here?
   *Julia.* Sure, your own experience

[1] Supplied by Mr. Dyce.

Will satisfy you, no : our Roman prelates
Do not keep lodging for ladies.

    *Delio.* Very well :
I have brought you no commendations from your hus-
      band,
For I know none by him.

    *Julia.* I hear he's come to Rome.

    *Delio.* I never knew man and beast, of a horse and
      a knight,
So weary of each other ; if he had had a good back,
He would have undertook to have borne his horse,
His breech was so pitifully sore.

    *Julia.* Your laughter
Is my pity.[1]

    *Delio.* Lady, I know not whether
You want money, but I have brought you some.

    *Julia.* From my husband ?

    *Delio.* No, from mine own allowance.

    *Julia.* I must hear the condition, ere I be bound to
      take it.

    *Delio.* Look on't, 'tis gold ; hath it not a fine colour?

    *Julia.* I have a bird more beautiful.

    *Delio.* Try the sound on't.

    *Julia.* A lute-string far exceeds it :
It hath no smell, like cassia, or civet ;
Nor is it physical, though some fond doctors
Persuade us seeth't in cullises.[2]   I'll tell you,
This is a creature bred by——

---

   [1] I pity that which moves your laughter.
   [2] A cullis was a strong and savoury broth of boiled meat,
strained, for debilitated persons : the old receipt books recommend " pieces of gold " among its ingredients.—DYCE.

*Enter* SERVANT.

*Serv.* Your husband's come,
Hath deliver'd a letter to the Duke of Calabria,
That to my thinking, hath put him out of his wits. [*Exit.*
  *Julia.* Sir, you hear :
Pray let me know your business, and your suit,
As briefly as can be.
  *Delio.* With good speed, I would wish you,
At such time as you are non-resident
With your husband, my mistress.
  *Julia.* Sir, I'll go ask my husband if I shall,
And straight return your answer.          [*Exit.*
  *Delio.* Very fine.
Is this her wit, or honesty, that speaks thus ?
I heard one say the duke was highly mov'd
With a letter sent from Malfi.   I do fear
Antonio is betray'd : how fearfully
Shews his ambition now ! unfortunate fortune !
They pass through whirlpools, and deep woes do shun,
Who the event weigh, ere the action's done.     [*Exit.*


## SCENE V.

*Enter* CARDINAL, *and* FERDINAND *with a letter.*

*Ferd.* I have this night digg'd up a mandrake.
*Card.* Say you ?
*Ferd.* And I am grown mad with't.
*Card.* What's the prodigy ?
*Ferd.* Read there, a sister damn'd : she's loose i'th'
  hilts ;

Grown a notorious strumpet.

*Card.* Speak lower.

*Ferd.* Lower!

Rogues do not whisper't now, but seek to publish't
(As servants do the bounty of their lords)
Aloud; and with a covetous searching eye,
To mark who note them.   O, confusion seize her!
She hath had most cunning bawds to serve her turn,
And more secure conveyances for lust,
Than towns of garrison for service.

*Card.* Is't possible?
Can this be certain?

*Ferd.* Rhubarb, O, for rhubarb,
To purge this choler! here's the cursed day
To prompt my memory; and here't shall stick
Till of her bleeding heart I make a sponge
To wipe it out.   .

*Card.* Why do you make yourself
So wild a tempest?

*Ferd.* Would I could be one,
That I might toss her palace 'bout her ears,
Root up her goodly forests, blast her meads,
And lay her general territory as waste,
As she hath done her honours.

*Card.* Shall our blood,
The royal blood of Arragon and Castile,
Be thus attainted?

*Ferd.* Apply desperate physic:
We must not now use balsamum, but fire,
The smarting cupping-glass, for that's the mean
To purge infected blood, such blood as hers.

There is a kind of pity in mine eye,
I'll give it to my handkerchief; and now 'tis here
I'll bequeath this to her bastard.
    *Card.* What to do?
    *Ferd.* Why, to make soft lint for his mother's wounds,
When I have hewed her to pieces.
    *Card.* Curs'd creature!
Unequal nature, to place women's hearts
So far upon the left side!
    *Ferd.* Foolish men,
That e'er will trust their honour in a bark
Made of so slight weak bulrush as is woman,
Apt every minute to sink it!
    *Card.* Thus
Ignorance, when it hath purchas'd honour,
It cannot wield it.
    *Ferd.* Methinks I see her laughing:—
Excellent hyena! Talk to me somewhat, quickly,
Or my imagination will carry me
To see her in the shameful act of sin.
    *Card.* With whom?
    *Ferd.* Happily with some strong-thigh'd bargeman,
Or one o'th' wood-yard, that can quoit the sledge,
Or toss the bar, or else some lovely squire
That carries coals up to her privy lodgings.
    *Card.* You fly beyond your reason.
    *Ferd.* Go to, mistress!
Tis not your whore's milk that shall quench my wild-fire,
But your whore's blood.
    *Card.* How idly shews this rage, which carries you,
As men convey'd by witches through the air,

On violent whirlwinds ! this intemperate noise
Fitly resembles deaf men's shrill discourse,
Who talk aloud, thinking all other men
To have their imperfection.

    *Ferd.* Have not you
My palsy ?

    *Card.* Yes ; I can be angry
Without this rupture : there is not in nature
A thing that makes man so deform'd, so beastly,
As doth intemperate anger.   Chide yourself.
You have divers men, who never yet express'd
Their strong desire of rest, but by unrest,
By vexing of themselves.   Come, put yourself
In tune.

    *Ferd.* So : I will only study to seem
The thing I am not.   I could kill her now,
In you, or in myself ; for I do think
It is some sin in us, heaven doth revenge
By her.

    *Card.* Are you stark mad ?

    *Ferd.* I would have their bodies
Burnt in a coal-pit with the ventage stopp'd,
That their curs'd smoke might not ascend to heaven ;
Or dip the sheets they lie in in pitch or sulphur,
Wrap them in't, and then light them like a match ;
Or else to boil their bastard to a cullis
And give't his lecherous father, to renew
The sin of his back.

    *Card.* I'll leave you.

    *Ferd.* Nay, I have done.
I am confident, had I been damn'd in hell,

And should have heard of this, it would have put me
Into a cold sweat.  In, in, I'll go sleep.
Till I know who leaps my sister, I'll not stir :
That known, I'll find scorpions to string my whips,
And fix her in a general eclipse.  [*Exeunt.*

## ACT III.—Scene I.

*Enter* Antonio *and* Delio.

### Antonio.

UR noble friend, my most beloved Delio !
O, you have been a stranger long at court :
Came you along with the Lord Ferdinand?
*Delio.* I did, sir: and how fares your noble duchess?
*Ant.* Right fortunately well : she's an excellent
Feeder of pedigrees ; since you last saw her,
She hath had two children more, a son and daughter.
*Delio.* Methinks 'twas yesterday ; let me but wink,
And not behold your face—which to mine eye
Is somewhat leaner—verily I should dream
It were within this half hour.
*Ant.* You have not been in law, friend Delio,
Nor in prison, nor a suitor at the court,
Nor begg'd the reversion of some great man's place,
Nor troubled with an old wife, which doth make
Your time so insensibly hasten.
*Delio.* Pray, sir, tell me,
Hath not this news arriv'd yet to the ear
Of the lord Cardinal ?
*Ant.* I fear it hath :

The Lord Ferdinand, that's newly come to court,
Doth bear himself right dangerously.

*Delio.* Pray, why?

*Ant.* He is so quiet, that he seems to sleep
The tempest out, as dormice do in winter:
Those houses that are haunted, are most still
Till the devil be up.

*Delio.* What say the common people?

*Ant.* The common rabble do directly say
She is a strumpet.

*Delio.* And your graver heads,
Which would be politic, what censure [1] they?

*Ant.* They do observe, I grow to infinite purchase, [2]
The left hand way; and all suppose the duchess
Would amend it, if she could: for, say they,
Great princes, though they grudge their officers
Should have such large and unconfined means
To get wealth under them, will not complain,
Lest thereby they should make them odious
Unto the people; for other obligation
Of love or marriage, between her and me,
They never dream of.

*Delio.* The Lord Ferdinand
Is going to bed.

*Enter* DUCHESS, FERDINAND, BOSOLA.

*Ferd.* I'll instantly to bed,
For I am weary.   I am to bespeak

---

[1] Think.
[2] *Purchase*—great gains, ordinarily understood, in our author's time, as having been acquired by unjust and dishonest means.

A husband for you.

 *Duch.* For me, sir ! pray who is't ?

 *Ferd.* The great Count Malateste.

 *Duch.* Fie upon him :

A count ! he's a mere stick of sugar-candy ;

You may look quite thorough him.   When I choose

A husband, I will marry for your honour.

 *Ferd.* You shall do well in't.   How is't, worthy

  Antonio ?

 *Duch.* But, sir, I am to have private conference with

  you

About a scandalous report is spread

Touching mine honour.

 *Ferd.* Let me be ever deaf to't :

One of Pasquil's paper-bullets, court-calumny,

A pestilent air, which princes' palaces

Are seldom purg'd of.   Yet, say that it were true,

I pour it in your bosom : my fix'd love

Would strongly excuse, extenuate, nay, deny

Faults, were they apparent in you.   Go, be safe

In your own innocency.

 *Duch.* O bless'd comfort !

This deadly air is purg'd.

    [*Exeunt all but Ferdinand and Bosola.*

 *Ferd.* Her guilt treads on

Hot burning culters.   Now, Bosola,

How thrives our intelligence ?

 *Bos.* Sir, uncertainly :

'Tis rumour'd she hath had three bastards, but

By whom, we may go read i'th' stars.

 *Ferd.* Why some

Hold opinion, all things are written there.

*Bos.* Yes, if we could find spectacles to read them.
I do suspect, there hath been some sorcery
Us'd on the duchess.

*Ferd.* Sorcery! to what purpose?

*Bos.* To make her dote on some desertless fellow,
She shames to acknowledge.

*Ferd.* Can your faith give way
To think there's power in potions, or in charms,
To make us love whether we will or no?

*Bos.* Most certainly.

*Ferd.* Away, these are mere gulleries, horrid things,
Invented by some cheating mountebanks,
To abuse us.   Do you think that herbs, or charms,
Can force the will?   Some trials have been made
In this foolish practice, but the ingredients
Were lenitive poisons, such as are of force
To make the patient mad; and straight the witch
Swears by equivocation they are in love.
The witch-craft lies in her rank blood.   This night
I will force confession from her.   You told me
You had got, within these two days, a false key
Into her bed-chamber.

*Bos.* I have.

*Ferd.* As I would wish.

*Bos.* What do you intend to do?

*Ferd.* Can you guess?

*Bos.* No.

*Ferd.* Do not ask then:
He that can compass me, and know my drifts,
May say he hath put a girdle 'bout the world,
And sounded all her quicksands.

*Bos.* I do not think so.

*Ferd.* What do you think, then, pray ?

*Bos.* That you are

Your own chronicle too much, and grossly
Flatter yourself.

*Ferd.* Give me thy hand ; I thank thee :
I never gave pension but to flatterers,
Till I entertained thee.   Farewell.
That friend a great man's ruin strongly checks,
Who rails into his belief all his defects.        [*Exeunt.*


## SCENE II.

*Enter* DUCHESS, ANTONIO, *and* CARIOLA.

*Duch.* Bring me the casket hither, and the glass.
You get no lodging here to night, my lord.

*Ant.* Indeed, I must persuade one.

*Duch.* Very good :
I hope in time 'twill grow into a custom,
That noblemen shall come with cap and knee,
To purchase a night's lodging of their wives.

*Ant.* I must lie here.

*Duch.* Must ! you are a lord of misrule.

*Ant.* Indeed, my rule is only in the night.

*Duch.* To what use will you put me ?

*Ant.* We'll sleep together.

*Duch.* Alas,
What pleasure can two lovers find in sleep !

*Cari.* My lord, I lie with her often ; and I know
She'll much disquiet you.

*Ant.* See, you are complain'd of.

*Cari.* For she's the sprawlingest bedfellow.

*Ant.* I shall like her the better for that.

*Cari.* Sir, shall I ask you a question?

*Ant.* Ay, pray thee, Cariola.

*Cari.* Wherefore still, when you lie with my lady,
Do you rise so early?

*Ant.* Labouring men
Count the clock oftenest, Cariola;
Are glad when their task's ended.

*Duch.* I'll stop your mouth.

*Ant.* Nay, that's but one; Venus had two soft doves
To draw her chariot; I must have another.
When wilt thou marry, Cariola?

*Cari.* Never, my lord.

*Ant.* O, fie upon this single life! forego it.
We read how Daphne, for her peevish [1] flight,
Became a fruitless bay-tree; Syrinx turn'd
To the pale empty reed; Anaxarete
Was frozen into marble: whereas those
Which married, or prov'd kind unto their friends,
Were, by a gracious influence, transhap'd
Into the olive, pomegranate, mulberry,
Became flowers, precious stones, or eminent stars.

*Cari.* This is a vain poetry; but I pray you tell me,
If there were propos'd me, wisdom, riches, and beauty,
In three several young men, which should I choose.

*Ant.* 'Tis a hard question: this was Paris' case,
And he was blind in't, and there was great cause;
For how was't possible he could judge right,
Having three amorous goddesses in view,

---

[1] *Peevish*—foolish.

And they stark naked? 'twas a motion
Were able to benight the apprehension
Of the severest counsellor of Europe.
Now I look on both your faces so well form'd,
It puts me in mind of a question I would ask.

   *Cari.* What is't?

   *Ant.* I do wonder why hard-favour'd ladies,
For the most part, keep worse-favour'd waiting-women,
To attend them, and cannot endure fair ones.

   *Duch.* O, that's soon answer'd.
Did you ever in your life know an ill painter
Desire to have his dwelling next door to the shop
Of an excellent picture-maker? 'twould disgrace
His face-making, and undo him.   I prithee,
When were we so merry?   My hair tangles.

   *Ant.* Pray thee, Cariola, let's steal forth the room,
And let her talk to herself: I have divers times
Serv'd her the like, when she hath chaf'd extremely.
I love to see her angry.   Softly, Cariola.      [*Exeunt.*

   *Duch.* Doth not the colour of my hair 'gin to change?
When I wax gray, I shall have all the court
Powder their hair with arras[1] to be like me.
You have cause to love me; I enter'd you into my heart
Before you would vouchsafe to call for the keys.

*Enter* FERDINAND *unseen.*

We shall one day have my brothers take you napping:
Methinks his presence, being now at court,
Should make you keep your own bed; but you'll say
Love mixt with fear is sweetest.   I'll assure you,

---

[1] *Arras.*—See note, ante p. 116.

You shall get no more children till my brothers
Consent to be your gossips.   Have you lost your tongue?
      'Tis welcome :[1]
For know, whether I am doom'd to live or die,
I can do both like a prince.
      *Ferd.* Die then quickly.

            [*Ferdinand gives her a poniard.*
Virtue, where art thou hid? what hideous thing
Is it that doth eclipse thee?
      *Duch.* Pray, sir, hear me.
      *Ferd.* Or is it true thou art but a bare name,
And no essential thing?
      *Duch.* Sir——
      *Ferd.* Do not speak.
      *Duch.* No, sir :
I will plant my soul in mine ears, to hear you.
      *Ferd.* O, most imperfect light of human reason,
That mak'st us[2] so unhappy to foresee
What we can least prevent!   Pursue thy wishes,
And glory in them : there's in shame no comfort,
But to be past all bounds and sense of shame.
      *Duch.* I pray, sir, hear me : I am married.
      *Ferd.* So.
      *Duch.* Happily,[3] not to your liking : but for that,
Alas, your shears do come untimely now
To clip the bird's wings, that's already flown !
Will you see my husband?
      *Ferd.* Yes,

      [1] So in the original; but there are evidently some words
missing.
      [2] *Us,*—supplied by Mr. Dyce.
      [3] Perchance.

If I could change eyes with a basilisk.

    *Duch.* Sure, you came hither
By his confederacy.

    *Ferd.* The howling of a wolf
Is music to thee, screech-owl : prithee, peace.
Whate'er thou art that hast enjoy'd my sister,
For I am sure thou hears't me, for thine own sake
Let me not know thee.   I come hither prepar'd
To work thy discovery ; yet am now persuaded
It would beget such violent effects
As would damn us both.   I would not for ten millions
I had beheld thee: therefore use all means
I never may have knowledge of thy name ;
Enjoy thy lust still, and a wretched life,
On that condition.   And for thee, vile woman,
If thou do wish thy lecher may grow old
In thy embracements, I would have thee build
Such a room for him as our anchorites
To holier use inhabit.   Let not the sun
Shine on him, till he's dead ; let dogs and monkies
Only converse with him, and such dumb things
To whom nature denies use to sound his name ;
Do not keep a paraquito,[1] lest she learn it ;
If thou do love him, cut out thine own tongue
Lest it bewray him.

    *Duch.* Why might not I marry ?
I have not gone about in this to create
Any new world or custom.

    *Ferd.* Thou art undone ;
And thou hast ta'en that massy sheet of lead

---

[1] Paroquet.

That hid thy husband's bones, and folded it
About my heart.

*Duch.* Mine bleeds for't!

*Ferd.* Thine! thy heart!
What should I name't, unless a hollow bullet
Fill'd with unquenchable wild-fire?

*Duch.* You are in this
Too strict; and were you not my princely brother,
I would say, too wilful: my reputation
Is safe.

*Ferd.* Dost thou know what reputation is?
I'll tell thee,—to small purpose, since th' instruction
Comes now too late.
Upon a time Reputation, Love, and Death
Would travel o'er the world; and it was concluded
That they should part, and take three several ways.
Death told them, they should find him in great battles,
Or cities plagu'd with plagues: Love gives them counsel
To enquire for him 'mongst unambitious shepherds,
Where dowries were not talk'd of, and sometimes
'Mongst quiet kindred, that had nothing left
By their dead parents: stay, quoth Reputation,
Do not forsake me; for it is my nature
If once I part from any man I meet,
I am never found again.   And so, for you;
You have shook hands with Reputation,
And made him invisible.   So fare you well:
I will never see you more.

*Duch.* Why should only I,
Of all the other princes of the world,
Be cas'd up, like a holy relic? I have youth,

And a little beauty.

*Ferd.* So you have some virgins,
That are witches.   I will never see thee more.   [*Exit.*

*Enter* ANTONIO *with a pistol.*

*Duch.* You saw this apparition?

*Ant.* Yes : we are
Betray'd.   How came he hither? I should turn
This to thee, for that.[1]

*Cari.* Pray, sir, do ; and when
That you have cleft my heart, you shall read there
Mine innocence.

*Duch.* That gallery gave him entrance.

*Ant.* I would this terrible thing would come again,
That, standing on my guard, I might relate
My warrantable love ! Ha ! what means this?
                              [*She shews the poniard.*

*Duch.* He left this with me.

*Ant.* And it seems, did wish
You would use it on yourself.

*Duch.* His action
Seem'd to intend so much.

*Ant.* This hath a handle to't,
As well as a point : turn it towards him,
And so fasten the keen edge in his rank gall.
How now ! who knocks? more earthquakes !

*Duch* I stand
As if a mine beneath my feet were ready
To be blown up.

*Cari.* 'Tis Bosola.

---

[1] To Cariola.

*Duch.* Away.
O misery ! methinks unjust actions
Should wear these masks and curtains, and not we.
You must instantly part[1] hence: I have fashion'd it
  already.                     [*Exit Antonio.*

        *Enter* BOSOLA.

*Bos.* The duke your brother is ta'en up in a whirlwind;
Hath took horse, and's rid post to Rome.
*Duch.* So late !
*Bos.* He told me, as he mounted into th' saddle,
You were undone.
*Duch.* Indeed, I am very near it.
*Bos.* What's the matter ?
*Duch.* Antonio, the master of our household,
Hath dealt so falsely with me in's accounts :
My brother stood engag'd with me for money
Ta'en up of certain Neapolitan Jews,
And Antonio lets the bonds be forfeit.
*Bos.* Strange !—this is cunning !
*Duch.* And hereupon
My brother's bills at Naples are protested
Against.   Call up our officers.
*Bos.* I shall.                   [*Exit.*

        *Enter* ANTONIO.

*Duch.* The place that you must fly to, is Ancona :
Hire a house there ; I'll send after you
My treasure, and my jewels.   Our weak safety
Runs upon enginous[2] wheels : short syllables,
Must stand for periods.   I must now accuse you

---

[1] Depart.       [2] Ingenious ; or, perhaps, complicated.

Of such a feigned crime, as Tasso calls
*Magnanima menzogna,* a noble lie,
'Cause it must shield our honours :—hark, they are
    coming !

*Enter* Bosola *and Gentlemen.*

*Ant.* Will your grace hear me ?
*Duch.* I have got well by you ; you have yielded me
A million of loss : I am like to inherit
The people's curses for your stewardship.
You had the trick in audit-time to be sick,
Till I had signed your *Quietus ;* and that cur'd you
Without help of a doctor.   Gentlemen,
I would have this man be an example to you all,
So shall you hold my favour ; I pray, let him ;
For h'as done that, alas ! you would not think of,
And, because I intend to be rid of him,
I mean not to publish.   Use your fortune elsewhere.
*Ant.* I am strongly arm'd to brook my overthrow :
As commonly men bear with a hard year,
I will not blame the cause on't ; but do think
The necessity of my malevolent star
Procures this, not her humour.   O, the inconstant
And rotten ground of service ! you may see,
'Tis even like him, that in a winter night,
Takes a long slumber o'er a dying fire,
A-loath to part from't ; yet parts thence as cold,
As when he first sat down.
*Duch.* We do confiscate
Towards the satisfying of your accounts,
All that you have.
*Ant.* I am all yours ; and 'tis very fit

All mine should be so.

*Duch.* So, sir, you have your pass.

*Ant.* You may see, gentlemen, what it is to serve
A prince with body and soul.                    [*Exit.*

*Bos.* Here's an example for extortion : what moisture
Is drawn out of the sea, when foul weather comes
Pours down, and runs into the sea again.

*Duch.* I would know what are your opinions
Of this Antonio.

*Second Off.* He could not abide to see a pig's head
gaping : I thought your grace would find him a Jew.

*Third Off.* I would you had been his officer, for your
own sake.

*Fourth Off.* You would have had more money.

*First Off.* He stopped his ears with black wool, and to
those came to him for money, said he was thick of hearing.

*Second Off.* Some said he was an hermaphrodite, for
he could not abide a woman.

*Fourth Off.* How scurvy proud he would look, when
the treasury was full ! well, let him go.

*First Off.* Yes, and the chippings of the buttery fly
after him, to scour his gold chain.

*Duch.* Leave us.                              [*Exeunt.*
What do you think of these ?

*Bos.* That these are rogues, that in's prosperity,
But to have waited on his fortune, could have wish'd
His dirty stirrup rivetted through their noses ;
And follow'd after's mule, like a bear in a ring.
Would have prostituted their daughters to his lust ;
Made their first-born intelligencers;[1] thought none happy

---

[1] Informers.

But such as were born under his blest planet,
And wore his livery: and do these lice drop off now?
Well, never look to have the like again:
He hath left a sort[1] of flattering rogues behind him;
Their doom must follow.   Princes pay flatterers
In their own money: flatterers dissemble their vices,
And they dissemble their lies; that's justice.
Alas, poor gentleman!

   *Duch.* Poor! he hath amply fill'd his coffers.

   *Bos.* Sure he was too honest.   Plutus, the god of riches,
When he's sent by Jupiter to any man,
He goes limping, to signify that wealth
That comes on god's name, comes slowly; but when he's
      sent
On the devil's errand, he rides post and comes in by
      scuttles.[2]
Let me shew you, what a most unvalued jewel
You have in a wanton humour thrown away,
To bless the man shall find him.   He was an excellent
Courtier, and most faithful; a soldier, that thought it
As beastly to know his own value too little,
As devilish to acknowledge it too much.
Both his virtue and form deserv'd a far better fortune.
His discourse rather delighted to judge itself, than shew
      itself:
His breast was fill'd with all perfection,
And yet it seemed a private whispering-room,
It made so little noise of't.

   *Duch.* But he was basely descended.

   *Bos.* Will you make yourself a mercenary herald,
Rather to examine men's pedigrees, than virtues?

---

   [1] Company.      [2] Scuttle, "to walk fast."—HALLIWELL.

You shall want him :
For know an honest statesman to a prince,
Is like a cedar planted by a spring :
The spring bathes the tree's root, the grateful tree
Rewards it with his shadow—you have not done so.
I would sooner swim to the Bermoothles[1] on
Two politicians' rotten bladders, tied
Together with an intelligencer's heart-string,
Than depend on so changeable a prince's favour.
Fare thee well, Antonio ! since the malice of the world
Would needs down with thee, it cannot be said yet
That any ill happened unto thee, considering thy fall
Was accompanied with virtue.

    *Duch.* O, you render me excellent music !

    *Bos.* Say you ?

    *Duch.* This good one that you speak of, is my husband.

    *Bos.* Do I not dream ? can this ambitious age
Have so much goodness in't, as to prefer
A man merely for worth, without these shadows
Of wealth and painted honours ? possible ?

    *Duch.* I have had three children by him.

    *Bos.* Fortunate lady !
For you have made your private nuptial bed
The humble and fair seminary of peace.
No question but many an unbenefic'd scholar
Shall pray for you for this deed, and rejoice
That some preferment in the world can yet
Arise from merit.   The virgins of your land
That have no dowries, shall hope your example
Will raise them to rich husbands.   Should you want

---

[1] The Bermudas.

Soldiers, 'twould make the very Turks and Moors
Turn Christians, and serve you for this act.
Last, the neglected poets of your time,
In honour of this trophy of a man,
Rais'd by that curious engine, your white hand,
Shall thank you, in your grave, for't; and make that
More reverend than all the cabinets
Of living princes.   For Antonio,
His fame shall likewise flow from many a pen,
When heralds shall want coats to sell to men.

*Duch.* As I taste comfort in this friendly speech,
So would I find concealment.

*Bos.* O, the secret of my prince,
Which I will wear on th' inside of my heart!

*Duch.* You shall take charge of all my coin and jewels,
And follow him; for he retires himself
To Ancona.

*Bos.* So.

*Duch.* Whither, within few days,
I mean to follow thee.

*Bos.* Let me think :
I would wish your grace to feign a pilgrimage
To our lady of Loretto, scarce seven leagues
From fair Ancona; so may you depart
Your country with more honour, and your flight
Will seem a princely progress, retaining
Your usual train about you.

*Duch.* Sir, your direction
Shall lead me by the hand.

*Cari.* In my opinion,
She were better progress to the baths at Lucca,

Or go visit the Spa
In Germany; for, if you will believe me,
I do not like this jesting with religion,
This feigned pilgrimage.

    *Duch.* Thou art a superstitious fool!
Prepare us instantly for our departure.
Past sorrows, let us moderately lament them,
For those to come, seek wisely to prevent them.

                    *[Exeunt Duchess and Cariola.*

    *Bos.* A politician is the devil's quilted anvil;
He fashions all sins·on him, and the blows
Are never heard : he may work in a lady's chamber,
As here for proof.   What rests but I reveal
All to my lord?   O, this base quality
Of intelligencer! why, every quality i'th' world
Prefers but gain or commendation.
Now, for this act I am certain to be rais'd,
And men that paint weeds to the life, are prais'd.

                              *[Exit.*

## SCENE III.

*Enter* CARDINAL, FERDINAND, MALATESTE, PESCARA,
DELIO, *and* SILVIO.

    *Card.* Must we turn soldier then?
    *Mal.* The emperor,
Hearing your worth that way, ere you attain'd
This reverend garment, joins you in commission
With the right fortunate soldier, the Marquess of Pescara,
And the famous Lannoy.

    *Card.* He that had the honour
Of taking the French king prisoner?

*Mal.* The same.
Here's a plot[1] drawn for a new fortification
At Naples.

*Ferd.* This great Count Malateste, I perceive,
Hath got employment ?[2]

*Delio.* No employment, my lord ;
A marginal note in the muster-book, that he is
A voluntary lord.

*Ferd.* He's no soldier.

*Delio.* He has worn gunpowder in's hollow tooth, for
the tooth-ache.

*Sil.* He comes to the leaguer with a full intent
To eat fresh beef and garlic, means to stay
Till the scent be gone, and straight return to court.

*Delio.* He hath read all the late service,
As the City Chronicle relates it :
And keeps two pewterers[3] going, only to express
Battles in model.

*Sil.* Then he'll fight by the book.

*Delio.* By the almanack, I think,
To choose good days, and shun the critical ;
That's his mistress' scarf.

*Sil.* Yes, he protests
He would do much for that taffata.

*Delio.* I think he would run away from a battle,
To save it from taking prisoner.

---

[1] Plan
[2] The friendly comments upon Malateste which follow are,
of course, spoken apart from their subject.
[3] i. e. to make models in pewter of the events.  Pewter, it
may be observed, was formerly considered costly furniture.
The Northumberland Household Book shows that pewter was
hired by the year, even in noble families.—NARES.

*Sil.* He is horribly afraid
Gunpowder will spoil the perfume on't.
    *Delio.* I saw a Dutchman break his pate once
For calling him pot-gun ; he made his head
Have a bore in't like a musket.
    *Sil.* I would he had made a touchhole to't.
He is indeed a guarded sumpter-cloth,
Only for the remove of the court.

*Enter* BOSOLA.

    *Pes.* Bosola arriv'd ! what should be the business ?
Some falling out amongst the cardinals.
These factions amongst great men, they are like
Foxes, when their heads are divided,
They carry fire in their tails, and all the country
About them goes to wrack for't.
    *Sil.* What's that Bosola ?
    *Delio.* I knew him in Padua,—a fantastical scholar,
Like such, who study how many knots was in
Hercules' club, of what colour Achilles' beard was,
Or whether Hector were not troubled
With the tooth-ache.
He hath studied himself half blear-eyed to know
The true symmetry of Cæsar's nose by a shoeing-horn ;
      and this
He did to gain the name of a speculative man.
    *Pes.* Mark Prince Ferdinand :
A very salamander lives in's eye,
To mock the eager violence of fire.
    *Sil.* That Cardinal hath made more bad faces with his

oppression than ever Michael Angelo made good ones :
he lifts up's nose, like a foul porpoise before a storm.

*Pes.* The Lord Ferdinand laughs.

*Delio.* Like a deadly cannon,
That lightens ere it smokes.

*Pes.* These are your true pangs of death,
The pangs of life, that struggle with great statesmen.

*Delio.* In such a deformed silence, witches whisper
    their charms.

*Card.* Doth she make religion her ridinghood
To keep her from the sun and tempest?

*Ferd.* That, that damns her.
Methinks her fault and beauty,
Blended together, shew like leprosy,
The whiter, the fouler.   I make it a question
Whether her beggarly brats were ever christen'd.

*Card.* I will instantly solicit the state of Ancona
To have them banish'd.

*Ferd.* You are for Loretto :
I shall not be at your ceremony ; fare you well.
Write to the Duke of Malfi, my young nephew
She had by her first husband, and acquaint him
With's mother's honesty.

*Bos.* I will.

*Ferd.* Antonio !
A slave that only smell'd of ink and counters,
And never in's life look'd like a gentleman,
But in the audit-time.   Go, go presently,
Draw me out an hundred and fifty of our horse,
And meet me at the fort-bridge.            [*Exeunt.*

## SCENE IV.

*Enter* TWO PILGRIMS *to the Shrine of our Lady of Loretto.*

*First Pil.* I have not seen a goodlier shrine than this,
Yet I have visited many.
*Second Pil.* The cardinal of Arragon
Is this day to resign his cardinal's hat:
His sister duchess likewise is arriv'd
To pay her vow of pilgrimage.    I expect
A noble ceremony.
*First Pil.* No question.   They come.

[*Here the ceremony of the Cardinal's instalment, in
the habit of a soldier, performed in delivering up
his cross, hat, robes, and ring, at the shrine, and in-
vesting him with sword, helmet, shield, and spurs:
then Antonio, the Duchess, and their children, having presented themselves at the shrine, are, by a form
of banishment in dumb-shew expressed towards
them by the Cardinal and the state of Ancona,
banished.   During all which ceremony, this ditty
is sung, to very solemn music, by divers churchmen,
and then exeunt :*

Arms, and honours deck thy story,[1]
To thy fame's eternal glory :
Adverse fortune ever fly thee ;
No disastrous fate come nigh thee.

_____

[1] The 4to. of 1623 has this marginal note : " The author
disclaims this ditty to be his."

I alone will sing thy praises,
Whom to honour virtue raises ;
And thy study, that divine is,
Bent to martial discipline is.
Lay aside all those robes lie by thee ;
Crown thy arts with arms, they'll beautify thee.
O, worthy of worthiest name, adorn'd in this manner,
Lead bravely thy forces on, under war's warlike
     banner !
O, may'st thou prove fortunate in all martial courses !
Guide thou still by skill in arts and forces :
Victory attend thee nigh, whilst fame sings loud thy
     powers ;
Triumphant conquest crown thy head, and blessings
     pour down showers !

  *First Pil.* Here's a strange turn of state ! who would
     have thought
So great a lady would have match'd herself
Unto so mean a person ? yet the cardinal
Bears him much too cruel.
  *Second Pil.* They are banish'd.
  *First Pil.* But I would ask what power hath this state
Of Ancona, to determine of a free prince ?
  *Second Pil.* They are a free state, sir, and her brother
     shew'd
How that the Pope fore-hearing of her looseness,
Hath seiz'd into the protection of the church
The dukedom, which she held as dowager.
  *First Pil.* But by what justice ?
  *Second Pil.* Sure I think by none,
Only her brother's instigation.

*First Pil.* What was it with such violence he took
Off from her finger?

*Second Pil.* 'Twas her wedding ring,
Which he vow'd shortly he would sacrifice
To his revenge.

*First Pil.* Alas, Antonio!
If that a man be thrust into a well,
No matter who sets hand to't, his own weight
Will bring him sooner to th' bottom.  Come, let's hence.
Fortune makes this conclusion general,
All things do help th' unhappy man to fall.    [*Exeunt.*

## SCENE V.

*Enter* DUCHESS, ANTONIO, CHILDREN, CARIOLA, *and*
SERVANTS.

*Duch.* Banish'd Ancona!

*Ant.* Yes, you see what power
Lightens in great men's breath.

*Duch.* Is all our train
Shrunk to this poor remainder?

*Ant.* These poor men,
Which have got little in your service, vow
To take your fortune : but your wiser buntings,[1]
Now they are fledg'd, are gone.

*Duch.* They have done wisely.
This puts me in mind of death : physicians thus,
With their hands full of money, use to give o'er
Their patients.

---

[1] *Bunting,*—a woodlark.—HALLIWELL.

*Ant.* Right the fashion of the world :
From decay'd fortunes every flatterer shrinks ;
Men cease to build where the foundation sinks.
   *Duch.* I had a very strange dream to night.
   *Ant.* What was't ?
   *Duch.* Methought I wore my coronet of state,
And on a sudden all the diamonds
Were chang'd to pearls.
   *Ant.* My interpretation
Is, you'll weep shortly ; for to me the pearls
Do signify your tears.
   *Duch.* The birds that live i'th' field
On the wild benefit of nature, live
Happier than we ; for they may choose their mates,
And carol their sweet pleasures to the spring.

*Enter* BOSOLA *with a letter.*

   *Bos.* You are happily o'erta'en.
   *Duch.* From my brother ?
   *Bos.* Yes, from the Lord Ferdinand, your brother,
All love and safety.
   *Duch.* Thou dost blanch mischief,
Would'st make it white.   See, see, like to calm weather
At sea before a tempest, false hearts speak fair
To those they intend most mischief.
*Send Antonio to me ; I want his head in a business.*
                            [*Reads the letter.*
A politic equivocation !
He doth not want your counsel, but your head ;
That is, he cannot sleep till you be dead.
And here's another pitfall that's strew'd o'er

With roses ; mark it, 'tis a cunning one ;
*I stand engaged for your husband, for several debts at*
*Naples: let not that trouble him ; I had rather have his*
*heart than his money :*
And I believe so too.

*Bos.* What do you believe ?

*Duch.* That he so much distrusts my husband's love,
He will by no means believe his heart is with him,
Until he see it : the devil is not cunning enough
To circumvent us in riddles.

*Bos.* Will you reject that noble and free league
Of amity and love, which I present you ?

*Duch.* Their league is like that of some politic kings,
Only to make themselves of strength and power
To be our after-ruin : tell them so.

*Bos.* And what from you ?

*Ant.* Thus tell him ; I will not come.

*Bos.* And what of this ?

*Ant.* My brothers have dispers'd
Blood-hounds abroad ; which till I hear are muzzled,
No truce, though hatch'd with ne'er such politic skill,
Is safe, that hangs upon our enemies' will.
I'll not come at them.

*Bos.* This proclaims your breeding :
Every small thing draws a base mind to fear,
As the adamant draws iron.   Fare you well, sir :
You shall shortly hear from 's.                    [*Exit.*

*Duch.* I suspect some ambush :
Therefore by all my love I do conjure you
To take your eldest son, and fly towards Milan.
Let us not venture all this poor remainder,

In one unlucky bottom.

*Ant.* You counsel safely.
Best of my life, farewell, since we must part :
Heaven hath a hand in't : but no otherwise,
Than as some curious artist takes in sunder
A clock, or watch, when it is out of frame,
To bring't in better order.

*Duch.* I know not which is best,
To see you dead, or part with you.   Farewell, boy :
Thou art happy, that thou hast not understanding
To know thy misery ; for all our wit
And reading brings us to a truer sense
Of sorrow.   In the eternal church, sir,
I do hope we shall not part thus.

*Ant.* O, be of comfort !
Make patience a noble fortitude,
And think not how unkindly we are us'd :
Man, like to cassia, is prov'd best, being bruis'd.

*Duch.* Must I, like to a slave-born Russian,
Account it praise to suffer tyranny ?
And yet, O heaven, thy heavy hand is in't !
I have seen my little boy oft scourge his top,
And compar'd myself to't : nought made me e'er go
     right
But heaven's scourge-stick.

*Ant.* Do not weep :
Heaven fashion'd us of nothing ; and we strive
To bring ourselves to nothing.   Farewell, Cariola,
And thy sweet armful.   If I do never see thee more,
Be a good mother to your little ones,
And save them from the tiger : fare you well.

*Duch.* Let me look upon you once more, for that speech
Came from a dying father: your kiss is colder
Than that I have seen an holy anchorite
Give to a dead man's skull.

*Ant.* My heart is turn'd to a heavy lump of lead,
With which I sound my danger: fare you well. [*Exit.*

*Duch.* My laurel is all wither'd.

*Cari.* Look, madam, what a troop of armed men
Make toward us.

Enter BOSOLA *and* SOLDIERS, *with vizards.*

*Duch.* O, they are very welcome !
When fortune's wheel is over-charg'd with princes,
The weight makes it move swift: I would have my ruin
Be sudden.   I am your adventure, am I not ?

*Bos.* You are : you must see your husband no more.

*Duch.* What devil art thou, that counterfeits heaven's
        thunder ?

*Bos.* Is that terrible ?   I would have you tell me
Whether is that note worse that frights the silly birds
Out of the corn, or that which doth allure them
To the nets? you have hearken'd to the last too much.

*Duch.* O misery! like to a rusty o'er-charg'd cannon.
Shall I ne'er fly in pieces ?   Come, to what prison ?

*Bos.* To none.

*Duch.* Whither, then ?

*Bos.* To your palace.

*Duch.* I have heard that Charon's boat serves to convey
All o'er the dismal lake, but brings none back again.

*Bos.* Your brothers mean you safety and pity.

*Duch.* Pity !   With such a pity men preserve alive
Pheasants and quails, when they are not fat enough

To be eaten.

    *Bos.* These are your children ?

    *Duch.* Yes.

    *Bos.* Can they prattle ?

    *Duch.* No :

But I intend, since they were born accurs'd,

Curses shall be their first language.

    *Bos.* Fie, madam,

Forget this base, low fellow.

    *Duch.* Were I a man,

I'd beat that counterfeit face into thy other.

    *Bos.* One of no birth.

    *Duch.* Say that he was born mean,

Man is most happy when's own actions

Be arguments and examples of his virtue.

    *Bos.* A barren, beggarly virtue.

    *Duch.* I prithee who is greatest ? can you tell ?

Sad tales befit my woe : I'll tell you one.

A salmon, as she swam unto the sea,

Met with a dog-fish, who encounters her

With this rough language : Why art thou so bold

To mix thyself with our high state of floods,

Being no eminent courtier, but one

That for the calmest, and fresh time o'th' year

Dost live in shallow rivers, rank'st thyself

With silly smelts and shrimps ? and darest thou

Pass by our dog-ship without reverence?

O, quoth the salmon, sister, be at peace :

Thank Jupiter, we both have past the net !

Our value never can be truly known,

Till in the fisher's basket we be shown :

I' th' market then my price may be the higher,
Even when I am nearest to the cook and fire.
So to great men the moral may be stretched ;
Men oft are valu'd high, when th' are most wretched.
But come, whither you please.   I am arm'd 'gainst
        misery ;
Bent to all sways of the oppressor's will :
There's no deep valley but near some great hill.

[*Exeunt.*

### ACT IV.—Scene I.

*Enter* Ferdinand *and* Bosola.

*Ferdinand.*

OW doth our sister duchess bear herself
        In her imprisonment?
        *Bos.* Nobly : I'll describe her.
She's sad, as one long us'd to't, and she seems
Rather to welcome the end of misery,
Than shun it ; a behaviour so noble,
As gives a majesty to adversity :
You may discern the shape of loveliness
More perfect in her tears than in her smiles :
She will muse for hours together ; and her silence,
Methinks, expresseth more than if she spake.
    *Ferd.* Her melancholy seems to be fortified
With a strange disdain.
    *Bos.* 'Tis so ; and this restraint,
Like English mastiffs that grow fierce with tying,    .
Makes her too passionately apprehend
Those pleasures she's kept from.

*Ferd.* Curse upon her !
I will no longer study in the book
Of another's heart.  Inform her what I told you. [*Exit.*

*Enter* DUCHESS.

*Bos.* All comfort to your grace.
*Duch.* I will have none.
Pray thee, why dost thou wrap thy poison'd pills
In gold and sugar ?
*Bos.* Your elder brother, the Lord Ferdinand,
Is come to visit you, and sends you word,
'Cause once he rashly made a solemn vow
Never to see you more, he comes i'th' night ;
And prays you gently neither torch nor taper
Shine in your chamber: he will kiss your hand,
And reconcile himself ; but, for his vow,
He dares not see you.
*Duch.* At his pleasure.
Take hence the lights ; he's come.

*Enter* FERDINAND.

*Ferd.* Where are you ?
*Duch.* Here, sir.
*Ferd.* This darkness suits you well.
*Duch.* I would ask you pardon.
*Ferd.* You have it ;
For I account it the honorabl'st revenge,
Where I may kill, to pardon.  Where are your cubs ?
*Duch.* Whom ?
*Ferd.* Call them your children,
For though our national law distinguish bastards

From true legitimate issue, compassionate nature
Makes them all equal.

*Duch.* Do you visit me for this?
You violate a sacrament o'th' church
Shall make you howl in hell for't.

*Ferd.* It had been well,
Could you have liv'd thus always; for indeed,
You were too much i'th' light—but no more;
I come to seal my peace with you.   Here's a hand,
     [*Gives her a dead man's hand.*
To which you have vow'd much love; the ring upon't
You gave.

*Duch.* I affectionately kiss it.

*Ferd.* Pray do, and bury the print of it in your heart.
I will leave this ring with you, for a love-token;
And the hand, as sure as the ring; and do not doubt
But you shall have the heart too: when you need a friend,
Send it to him that ow'd[1] it; you shall see
Whether he can aid you.

*Duch.* You are very cold :
I fear you are not well after your travel.
Ha! lights!   O, horrible!

*Ferd.* Let her have lights enough.    [*Exit.*

*Duch.* What witchcraft doth he practise, that he
  hath left
A dead man's hand here?
  [*Here is discovered, behind a traverse, the artificial
   figures of Antonio and his children, appear-
   ing as if they were dead.*

*Bos.* Look you, here's the piece, from which 'twas
  ta'en.
He doth present you this sad spectacle,

     [1] Owned, possessed.

That, now you know directly they are dead,
Hereafter you may wisely cease to grieve
For that which cannot be recovered.

*Duch.* There is not between heaven and earth one wish
I stay for after this : it wastes me more
Than were't my picture, fashion'd out of wax,
Stuck with a magical needle, and then buried
In some foul dunghill;[1] and yond's an excellent property
For a tyrant, which I would account mercy.

*Bos.* What's that?

*Duch.* If they would bind me to that lifeless trunk,
And let me freeze to death.

*Bos.* Come, you must live.

*Duch.* That's the greatest torture souls feel in hell,
In hell that they must live, and cannot die.
Portia, I'll new kindle thy coals again,
And revive the rare and almost dead example
Of a loving wife.

*Bos.* O fie ! despair? remember
You are a Christian.

*Duch.* The church enjoins fasting:
I'll starve myself to death.

*Bos.* Leave this vain sorrow.
Things being at the worst, begin to mend : the bee
When he hath shot his sting into your hand,
May then play with your eyelid.

*Duch.* Good comfortable fellow !
Persuade a wretch that's broke upon the wheel
To have all his bones new set ; entreat him live

---

[1] In allusion to the mode by which witches were supposed
gradually to destroy those whom they were incited to kill.

To be executed again.   Who must dispatch me?
I account this world a tedious theatre,
For I do play a part in't 'gainst my will.

    *Bos.* Come, be of comfort ; I will save your life.

    *Duch.* Indeed I have not leisure to tend so small
       a business.

    *Bos.* Now, by my life, I pity you.

    *Duch.* Thou art a fool then,
To waste thy pity on a thing so wretched
As cannot pity itself.   I am full of daggers.
Puff, let me blow these vipers from me.

*Enter* SERVANT.

What are you?

    *Serv.* One that wishes you long life.

    *Duch.* I would thou wert hang'd for the horrible
       curse
Thou hast given me : I shall shortly grow one
Of the miracles of pity.   I'll go pray ; no,
I'll go curse.

    *Bos.* O, fie !

    *Duch.* I could curse the stars.

    *Bos.* O, fearful !

    *Duch.* And those three smiling seasons of the year
Into a Russian winter : nay, the world
To its first chaos.

    *Bos.* Look you, the stars shine still.

    *Duch.* O, but you must remember,
My curse hath a great way to go :—
Plagues, that make lanes through largest families,
Consume them !

    *Bos.* Fie, lady.

*Duch.* Let them like tyrants
Never be remember'd, but for the ill they have done ;
Let all the zealous prayers of mortified
Churchmen forget them !

*Bos.* O, uncharitable !

*Duch.* Let heaven, a little while, cease crowning
     martyrs,
To punish them !   Go, howl them this, and say, I long
     to bleed :
It is some mercy when men kill with speed.     [*Exit.*

*Enter* FERDINAND.

*Ferd.* Excellent, as I would wish ; she's plagu'd in art :
These presentations are but fram'd in wax,
By the curious master in that quality,
Vincentio Lauriola, and she takes them
For true substantial bodies.

*Bos.* Why do you do this ?

*Ferd.* To bring her to despair.

*Bos.* 'Faith, end here,
And go no farther in your cruelty ;
Send her a penitential garment to put on
Next to her delicate skin, and furnish her
With beads, and prayer-books.

*Ferd.* Damn her ! that body of hers,
While that my blood ran pure in't, was more worth
Than that which thou wouldst comfort, called a soul.
I will send her masks of common courtesans,
Have her meat serv'd up by bawds and ruffians,
And, 'cause she'll needs be mad, I am resolv'd
To remove forth the common hospital
All the mad-folk, and place them near her lodging ;

There let them practise together, sing and dance,
And act their gambols to the full o'th' moon :
If she can sleep the better for it, let her.
Your work is almost ended.

    *Bos.* Must I see her again ?

    *Ferd.* Yes.

    *Bos.* Never.

    *Ferd.* You must.

    *Bos.* Never in mine own shape ;
That's forfeited by my intelligence,[1]
And this last cruel lie : when you send me next,
The business shall be comfort.

    *Ferd.* Very likely ;
Thy pity is nothing of kin to thee.   Antonio
Lurks about Milan : thou shalt shortly thither,
To feed a fire as great as my revenge,
Which never will slack till it have spent his fuel :
Intemperate agues make physicians cruel.      [*Exeunt.*

## SCENE II.

### *Enter* DUCHESS *and* CARIOLA.

    *Duch.* What hideous noise was that ?

    *Cari.* 'Tis the wild consort[2]
Of madmen, lady, which your tyrant brother
Hath plac'd about your lodging : this tyranny,
I think, was never practis'd till this hour.

    *Duch.* Indeed, I thank him : nothing but noise and
        folly

---

[1] My having turned informer.
[2] An old form of *concert.*

Can keep me in my right wits ; whereas reason
And silence make me stark mad.　Sit down ;
Discourse to me some dismal tragedy.

　*Cari.* O, 'twill increase your melancholy.

　*Duch.* Thou art deceiv'd :
To hear of greater grief would lessen mine.
This is a prison.

　*Cari.* Yes, but you shall live
To shake this durance off.

　*Duch.* Thou art a fool :
The robin-red-breast and the nightingale
Never live long in cages.

　*Cari.* Pray, dry your eyes :
What think you of, madam ?

　*Duch.* Of nothing ;
When I muse thus, I sleep.

　*Cari.* Like a madman, with your eyes open ?

　*Duch.* Dost thou think we shall know one another
In th' other world ?

　*Cari.* Yes, out of question.

　*Duch.* O, that it were possible we might
But hold some two days' conference with the dead !
From them I should learn somewhat, I am sure,
I never shall know here.　I'll tell thee a miracle ;
I am not mad yet, to my cause of sorrow :
Th' heaven o'er my head seems made of molten brass,
The earth of flaming sulphur, yet I am not mad.
I am acquainted with sad misery,
As the tann'd galley-slave is with his oar ;
Necessity makes me suffer constantly,
And custom makes it easy.　Whom do I look like now ?

*Cari.* Like to your picture in the gallery,
A deal of life in show, but none in practice ;
Or rather like some reverend monument
Whose ruins are even pitied.
　*Duch.* Very proper ;
And fortune seems only to have her eyesight,
To behold my tragedy.　How now !
What noise is that ?

### *Enter* SERVANT.

*Serv.* I am come to tell you,
Your brother hath intended you some sport.
A great physician, when the pope was sick
Of a deep melancholy, presented him
With several sorts of madmen, which wild object
Being full of change and sport, forc'd him to laugh,
And so th' imposthume broke : the selfsame cure
The duke intends on you.
　*Duch.* Let them come in.

### *Enter* MADMEN.

*Serv.* There's a mad lawyer ; and a secular priest ;
A doctor, that hath forfeited his wits
By jealousy ; an astrologian
That in his works said, such a day o'th' month
Should be the day of doom, and failing of't,
Ran mad ; an English tailor, craz'd i'th' brain
With the study of new fashions ; a gentleman usher,
Quite beside himself with care to keep in mind
The number of his lady's salutations,
Or "how do you," she employ'd him in each morning ;

A·farmer too, an excellent knave in grain,
Mad 'cause he was hinder'd transportation ;[1]
And let one broker that's mad loose to these,
You'd think the devil were among them.

   *Duch.* Sit, Cariola.    Let them loose when you please,
For I am chain'd to endure all your tyranny.

*Here by a madman this Song is sung, to a dismal kind
of music.*

   O, let us howl some heavy note,
     Some deadly dogged howl,
  Sounding, as from the threatening throat
     Of beasts and fatal fowl !
  As ravens, screech-owls, bulls, and bears,
     We'll bell, and bawl our parts,
  Till irksome noise have cloy'd your ears,
     And corrasiv'd[2] your hearts.
  At last, whenas our quire wants breath,
     Our bodies being blest,
  We'll sing, like swans, to welcome death,
     And die in love and rest.

   *First Madman.* Doom's-day not come yet! I'll draw
it nearer by a perspective, or make a glass that shall set
all the world on fire upon an instant.    I cannot sleep;
my pillow is stuffed with a litter of porcupines.
   *Second Madman.* Hell is a mere glass-house, where
the devils are continually blowing up women's souls on
hollow irons, and the fire never goes out.

----

[1] Prohibited from exporting his corn.
[2] *Corrasiv'd*, i. e. corrosiv'd, corroded.

*Third Madman.* I will lie with every woman in my parish the tenth night; I will tythe them over like hay-cocks.

*Forth Madman.* Shall my 'pothecary outgo me, because I am a cuckold? I have found out his roguery; he makes alum of his wife's urine, and sells it to Puritans that have sore throats with overstraining.

*First Madman.* I have skill in heraldry.

*Second Madman.* Hast?

*First Madman.* You do give for your crest a woodcock's head, with the brains picked out on't; you are a very ancient gentleman.

*Third Madman.* Greek is turned Turk: we are only to be saved by the Helvetian translation.[1]

*First Madman.* Come on, sir, I will lay the law to you.

*Second Madman.* O, rather lay a corrasive; the law will eat to the bone.

*Third Madman.* He that drinks but to satisfy nature, is damned.

*Fourth Madman.* If I had my glass here, I would shew a sight should make all the women here call me mad doctor.

*First Madman.* What's he, a rope-maker?

*Second Madman.* No, no, no, a snuffling knave, that while he shews the tombs, will have his hand in a wench's placket.[2]

*Third Madman.* Woe to the caroch,[3] that brought home my wife from the mask at three a'clock in the morning! it had a large featherbed in it.

[1] i. e. presumably, the translation of the New Testament into English, at Geneva, in 1557.

[2] Under-petticoat.     [3] Great coach.

*Fourth Madman.* I have pared the devil's nails forty times, roasted them in ravens' eggs, and cured agues with them.

*Third Madman.* Get me three hundred milch bats, to make possets to procure sleep.

*Fourth Madman.* All the college may throw their caps at me ; I have made a soapboiler costive : it was my masterpiece.

[*Here the dance, consisting of eight madmen, with music answerable thereunto ; after which, Bosola, like an old man, enters.*

*Duch.* Is he mad too ?

*Serv.* Pray question him. I'll leave you.

[*Exeunt all but the Duchess and Bosola.*

*Bos.* I am come to make thy tomb.

*Duch.* Ha ! my tomb !
Thou speak'st, as if I lay upon my death-bed,
Gasping for breath : dost thou perceive me sick ?

*Bos.* Yes, and the more dangerously, since thy sickness
Is insensible.

*Duch.* Thou art not mad sure : dost know me ?

*Bos.* Yes.

*Duch.* Who am I ?

*Bos.* Thou art a box of worm-seed, at best but a salvatory[1]
Of green mummy.[2] What's this flesh? a little cruded milk
Fantastical puff-paste. Our bodies are weaker than those
Paper-prisons boys use to keep flies in; more contemptible,
Since ours is to preserve earth-worms. Didst thou ever see
A lark in a cage? such is the soul in the body: this world

---

[1] French, *salvatoire :* a place where anything is preserved.
[2] See note, ante, page 12.

Is like her little turf of grass, and the heaven˙ o'er our
    heads,
Like her looking-glass, only gives us a miserable know-
    ledge
Of the small compass of our prison.
   *Duch.* Am not I thy duchess?
   *Bos.* Thou art some great woman sure, for riot
Begins to sit on thy forehead (clad in gray hairs)
Twenty years sooner
Than on a merry milkmaid's.
Thou sleepest worse than if a mouse
Should be forced to take up her lodging in a cat's ear:
A little infant that breeds its teeth, should it lie with thee,
Would cry out, as if thou wert
The more unquiet bedfellow.
   *Duch.* I am Duchess of Malfi still.
   *Bos.* That makes thy sleep so broken :
Glories, like glowworms, afar off shine bright,
But look'd to near, have neither heat nor light.
   *Duch.* Thou art very plain.
   *Bos.* My trade is to flatter the dead, not the living ;
I am a tomb-maker.
   *Duch.* And thou com'st to make my tomb?
   *Bos.* Yes.
   *Duch.* Let me be a little merry :
Of what stuff wilt thou make it?
   *Bos.* Nay, resolve me first, of what fashion ?
   *Duch.* Why, do we grow fantastical in our death-bed?
Do we affect fashion in the grave ?
   *Bos.* Most ambitiously.  Princes' images on their
    tombs
Do not lie, as they were wont, seeming to pray

Up to heaven; but with their hands under their cheeks,
As if they died of the tooth-ache : they are not carved
With their eyes fixt upon the stars ; but
As their minds were wholly bent upon the world,
The selfsame way they seem to turn their faces.

*Duch.* Let me know fully, therefore, the effect
Of this thy dismal preparation,
This talk, fit for a charnel.

*Bos.* Now I shall :

[*A coffin, cords, and a bell brought in.*

Here is a present from your princely brothers,
And may it arrive welcome, for it brings
Last benefit, last sorrow.

*Duch.* Let me see it :
I have so much obedience in my blood,
I wish it in their veins to do them good.

*Bos.* This is your last presence-chamber.

*Cari.* O, my sweet lady !

*Duch.* Peace ; it affrights not me.

*Bos.* I am the common bellman,
That usually is sent to condemn'd persons
The night before they suffer.

*Duch.* Even now thou said'st
Thou wast a tomb-maker.

*Bos.* 'Twas to bring you
By degrees to mortification.    Listen : [*dirge.*

> Hark, now everything is still,
> The screech-owl, and the whistler shrill,
> Call upon our dame aloud,
> And bid her quickly don her shroud !
> Much you had of land and rent ;

Your length in clay's now competent :
A long war disturb'd your mind ;
Here your perfect peace is sign'd.
Of what is't fools make such vain keeping ?
Sin their conception, their birth weeping ;
Their life a general mist of error,
Their death a hideous storm of terror.
Strew your hair with powders sweet,
Don clean linen, bathe your feet,
And (the foul fiend more to check)
A crucifix let bless your neck :
'Tis now full tide 'tween night and day ;
End your groan, and come away.

*Cari.* Hence, villains, tyrants, murderers ! alas !
What will you do with my lady ?—Call for help.
　*Duch.* To whom, to our next neighbours ? they are
　　mad-folks.
　*Bos.* Remove that noise.
　*Duch.* Farewell, Cariola.
In my last will, I have not much to give :
A many hungry guests have fed upon me ;
Thine will be a poor reversion.
　*Cari.* I will die with her.
　*Duch.* I pray thee, look thou giv'st my little boy
Some syrup for his cold, and let the girl
Say her prayers ere she sleep.—Now what you please :
　　　　　　　　[*Cariola is forced out.*
What death ?
　*Bos.* Strangling ; here are your executioners.
　*Duch.* I forgive them :

The apoplexy, catarrh, or cough o'th' lungs,
Would do as much as they do.

*Bos.* Doth not death fright you?

*Duch.* Who would be afraid on't,
Knowing to meet such excellent company
In th' other world?

*Bos.* Yet, methinks,
The manner of your death should much afflict you;
This cord should terrify you.

*Duch.* Not a whit:
What would it pleasure me to have my throat cut
With diamonds? or to be smothered
With cassia? or to be shot to death with pearls?
I know death hath ten thousand several doors
For men to take their exits; and 'tis found
They go on such strange geometrical hinges,
You may open them both ways: any way, for heaven
        sake,
So I were out of your whispering.   Tell my brothers,
That I perceive death, now I am well awake,
Best gift is they can give, or I can take.
I would fain put off my last woman's fault,
I'd not be tedious to you.

*Execut.* We are ready.

*Duch.* Dispose my breath how please you, but my body
Bestow upon my women, will you?

*Execut.* Yes.

*Duch.* Pull, and pull strongly, for your able strength,
Must pull down heaven upon me:
Yet stay, heaven-gates are not so highly arch'd
As princes' palaces; they that enter there,
Must go upon their knees.   Come, violent death,

Serve for mandragora, to make me sleep :
Go, tell my brothers, when I am laid out,
They then may feed in quiet.    [*They strangle her.*[1]

*Bos.* Where's the waiting-woman ?
Fetch her : some other strangle the children.

*Enter* CARIOLA.

Look you, there sleeps your mistress.

*Cari.* O, you are damn'd
Perpetually for this ! My turn is next ;
Is't not so order'd ?

*Bos.* Yes, and I am glad
You are so well prepar'd for't.

*Cari.* You are deceiv'd, sir,
I am not prepared for't ; I will not die :
I will first come to my answer, and know

---

[1] "All the several parts of the dreadful apparatus with which the duchess's death is ushered in are not more remote from the conceptions of ordinary vengeance than the strange character of suffering which they seem to bring upon their victim is beyond the imagination of ordinary poets. As they are not like inflictions *of this life*, so her language seems *not of this world*. She has lived among horrors till she is become ' native and endowed unto that element.' She speaks the dialect of despair ; her tongue has a smatch of Tartarus and the souls in bale. What are ' Luke's iron crown,' the brazen bull of Perillus, Procrustes' bed, to the waxen images which counterfeit death, to the wild masque of madmen, the tomb-maker, the bellman, the living person's dirge, the mortification by degrees ! To move a horror skilfully, to touch a soul to the quick, to lay upon fear as much as it can bear, to wean and weary a life till it is ready to drop, and then step in with mortal instruments to take its last forfeit ; this only a Webster can do. Writers of an inferior genius may ' upon horror's head horrors accumulate,' but they cannot do this. They mistake quantity for quality, they ' terrify babes with painted devils,' but they know not how a soul is capable of being moved ; their terrors want dignity, their affrightments are without decorum."—C. LAMB, *Spec. of Eng. Dram. Poets.*

How I have offended.

- *Bos.* Come, dispatch her.
You kept her counsel, now you shall keep ours.

   *Cari.* I will not die, I must not; I am contracted
To a young gentleman.

   *Execut.* Here's your wedding-ring.

   *Cari.* Let me but speak with the duke; I'll discover
Treason to his person.

   *Bos.* Delays :—throttle her.

   *Execut.* She bites and scratches.

   *Cari.* If you kill me now,
I am damn'd ; I have not been at confession
This two years.

   *Bos.* When ?[1]

   *Cari.* I am quick with child.

   *Bos.* Why then,
Your credit's sav'd.—Bear her into the next room ;
Let this[2] lie still.

Enter FERDINAND.

   *Ferd.* Is she dead ?

   *Bos.* She is what
You'd have her.   But here begin your pity :
[Shews the children strangled.

Alas ! how have these offended ?

   *Ferd.* The death
Of young wolves is never to be pitied

   *Bos.* Fix your eye here.

   *Ferd.* Constantly.

---

[1] *When,*—an exclamation of impatience addressed to the executioners.
[2] i. e. the duchess' body.

*Bos.* Do you not weep?
Other sins only speak ; murder shrieks out :
The element of water moistens the earth,
But blood flies upwards and bedews the heavens.

   *Ferd.* Cover her face; mine eyes dazzle: she died
      young.

   *Bos.* I think not so ; her infelicity
Seem'd to have years too many.

   *Ferd.* She and I were twins ;
And should I die this instant, I had liv'd
Her time to a minute.

   *Bos.* It seems she was born first :
You have bloodily approv'd the ancient truth,
That kindred commonly do worse agree
Than remote strangers. .

   *Ferd.* Let me see her face again.
Why didst not thou pity her? what an excellent
Honest man might'st thou have been
If thou hadst borne her to some sanctuary ;
Or, bold in a good cause, oppos'd thyself,
With thy advanced sword above thy head,
Between her innocence and my revenge.
I bad thee, when I was distracted of my wits,
Go kill my dearest friend, and thou hast done't.
For let me but examine well the cause :
What was the meanness of her match to me?
Only I must confess I had a hope,
Had she continu'd widow, to have gain'd
An infinite mass of treasure by her death ;
And that was the main cause, her marriage,
That drew a stream of gall quite through my heart.
For thee, as we observe in tragedies

That a good actor many times is curs'd
For playing a villain's part, I hate thee for't,
And for my sake say thou hast done much ill, well.

*Bos.* Let me quicken your memory, for I perceive
You are falling into ingratitude ; I challenge
The reward due to my service.

*Ferd.* I'll tell thee
What I'll give thee.

*Bos.* Do.

*Ferd.* I'll give thee a pardon
For this murder.

*Bos.* Ha !

*Ferd.* Yes, and 'tis
The largest bounty I can study to do thee.
By what authority didst thou execute
This bloody sentence ?

*Bos.* By yours.

*Ferd.* Mine ! was I her judge ?
Did any ceremonial form of law,
Doom her to not being ? did a complete jury
Deliver her conviction up i'th' court ?
Where shalt thou find this judgment register'd,
Unless in hell ?  See, like a bloody fool,
Th' hast forfeited thy life, and thou shalt die for't.

*Bos.* The office of justice is perverted quite,
When one thief hangs another.  Who shall dare
To reveal this ?

*Ferd.* O, I'll tell thee ;
The wolf shall find her grave, and scrape it up,
Not to devour the corpse, but to discover
The horrid murder.

*Bos.* You, not I, shall quake for't.

*Ferd.* Leave me.

*Bos.* I will first receive my pension.

*Ferd.* You are a villain.

*Bos.* When your ingratitude
Is judge, I am so.

*Ferd.* O horror,
That not the fear of him, which binds the devils,
Can prescribe man obedience!
Never look upon me more.

*Bos.* Why, fare thee well:
Your brother and yourself are worthy men:
You have a pair of hearts are hollow graves,
Rotten, and rotting others; and your vengeance,
Like two chain'd bullets, still goes arm in arm.
You may be brothers; for treason, like the plague,
Doth take much in a blood. I stand like one
That long hath ta'en a sweet and golden dream:
I am angry with myself, now that I wake.

*Ferd.* Get thee into some unknown part o'th' world,
That I may never see thee.

*Bos.* Let me know
Wherefore I should be thus neglected? Sir,
I serv'd your tyranny, and rather strove,
To satisfy yourself, than all the world:
And though I loath'd the evil, yet I lov'd
You that did counsel it; and rather sought
To appear a true servant, than an honest man.

*Ferd.* I'll go hunt the badger by owl-light:
'Tis a deed of darkness. [*Exit.*

*Bos.* He's much distracted. Off, my painted honour!

While with vain hopes our faculties we tire,
We seem to sweat in ice and freeze in fire.
What would I do, were this to do again?
I would not change my peace of conscience
For all the wealth of Europe.   She stirs; here's life:—
Return, fair soul, from darkness, and lead mine
Out of this sensible hell:—she's warm, she breathes:—
Upon thy pale lips I will melt my heart,
To store them with fresh colour.—Who's there!
Some cordial drink!   Alas! I dare not call:
So pity would destroy pity.   Her eye opes,
And heaven in it seems to ope, that late was shut,
To take me up to mercy.

    *Duch.* Antonio!

    *Bos.* Yes, madam, he is living;
The dead bodies you saw, were but feign'd statues;
He's reconcil'd to your brothers; the Pope hath wrought
The atonement.

    *Duch.* Mercy!            *[She dies.*

    *Bos.* O, she's gone again! there the cords of life
        broke.
O, sacred innocence, that sweetly sleeps
On turtles' feathers, whilst a guilty conscience
Is a black register, wherein is writ
All our good deeds and bad, a perspective
That shews us hell!   That we cannot be suffer'd
To do good when we have a mind to it!
This is manly sorrow;
These tears, I am very certain, never grew
In my mother's milk: my estate is sunk
Below the degree of fear: where were
These penitent fountains, while she was living?

O, they were frozen up !   Here is a sight
As direful to my soul, as is the sword
Unto a wretch hath slain his father.   Come,
I'll bear thee hence,
And execute thy last will ; that's deliver
Thy body to the reverend dispose
Of some good women : that, the cruel tyrant
Shall not deny me.   Then I'll post to Milan,
Where somewhat I will speedily enact
Worth my dejection.                              [*Exit.*

## ACT V.—Scene I.

*Enter* Antonio *and* Delio.

*Antonio.*

HAT think you of my hope of reconcilement
To the Arragonian brethren ?
    *Delio.* I misdoubt it ;
For though they have sent their letters of safe conduct
For your repair to Milan, they appear
But nets to entrap you.   The Marquis of Pescara,
Under whom you hold certain land in cheat,[1]
Much 'gainst his noble nature hath been mov'd
To seize those lands, and some of his dependents
Are at this instant making it their suit
To be invested in your revenues.
I cannot think they mean well to your life,
That do deprive you of your means of life,

----

[1] i.e. in escheat.

Your living.

*Ant.* You are still an heretic
To any safety I can shape myself.

*Delio.* Here comes the marquis : I will make myself
Petitioner for some part of your land,
To know whither it is flying.

*Ant.* I pray do.

### *Enter* PESCARA.

*Delio.* Sir, I have a suit to you.

*Pes.* To me?

*Delio.* An easy one :
There is the citadel of St. Bennet,
With some demesnes, of late in the possession
Of Antonio Bologna,—please you bestow them on me.

*Pes.* You are my friend ; but this is such a suit,
Nor fit for me to give, nor you to take.

*Delio.* No, sir?

*Pes.* I will give you ample reason for't,
Soon in private : here's the cardinal's mistress.

### *Enter* JULIA.

*Julia.* My lord, I am grown your poor petitioner,
And should be an ill beggar, had I not
A great man's letter here, the cardinal's,
To court you in my favour.

*Pes.* He entreats for you
The citadel of St. Bennet, that belong'd
To the banish'd Bologna.

*Julia.* Yes.

*Pes.* I could not have thought of a friend I could
　　rather

Pleasure with it : 'tis yours.

*Julia.* Sir, I thank you ;
And he shall know how doubly I am engag'd
Both in your gift, and speediness of giving,
Which makes your grant the greater.          [*Exit.*

*Ant.* How they fortify
Themselves with my ruin !

*Delio.* Sir, I am
Little bound to you.

*Pes.* Why ?

*Delio.* Because you denied this suit to me, and gave't
To such a creature.

*Pes.* Do you know what it was ?
It was Antonio's land ; not forfeited
By course of law, but ravish'd from his throat
By the cardinal's entreaty : it were not fit
I should bestow so main a piece of wrong
Upon my friend ; 'tis a gratification
Only due to a strumpet, for it is injustice.
Shall I sprinkle the pure blood of innocents
To make those followers I call my friends
Look ruddier upon me ?   I am glad
This land, ta'en from the owner by such wrong,
Returns again unto so foul an use,
As salary for his lust.   Learn, good Delio,
To ask noble things of me, and you shall find
I'll be a noble giver.

*Delio.* You instruct me well.

*Ant.* Why, here's a man now, would fright impudence
From sauciest beggars.

*Pes.* Prince Ferdinand's come to Milan,

Sick, as they give out, of an apoplexy;
But some say, 'tis a frenzy: I am going
To visit him.                                         [*Exit.*

 *Ant.* 'Tis a noble old fellow.

 *Delio.* What course do you mean to take, Antonio?

 *Ant.* This night I mean to venture all my fortune,
Which is no more than a poor lingering life,
To the cardinal's worst of malice: I have got
Private access to his chamber; and intend
To visit him about the mid of night,
As once his brother did our noble duchess.
It may be that the sudden apprehension
Of danger, for I'll go in mine own shape,
When he shall see it fraight[1] with love and duty,
May draw the poison out of him, and work
A friendly reconcilement: if it fail,
Yet it shall rid me of this infamous calling;
For better fall once, than be ever falling.

 *Delio.* I'll second you in all danger, and, howe'er;[2]
My life keeps rank with yours.

 *Ant.* You are still my lov'd and best friend.

            [*Exeunt.*


## SCENE II.

*Enter* PESCARA *and* DOCTOR.

 *Pes.* Now, doctor, may I visit your patient?

 *Doc.* If't please your lordship: but he's instantly
To take the air here in the gallery
By my direction.

---

 [1] Fraught.      [2] In whatever manner.

*Pes.* Pray thee, what's his disease?

*Doc.* A very pestilent disease, my lord,
They call lycanthropia.

*Pes.* What's that?
I need a dictionary to't?

*Doc.* I'll tell you.
In those that are possess'd with't there o'erflows
Such melancholy humour, they imagine
Themselves to be transformed into wolves;
Steal forth to church-yards in the dead of night,
And dig dead bodies up: as two nights since
One met the duke 'bout midnight in a lane
Behind St. Mark's Church, with the leg of a man
Upon his shoulder, and he howl'd fearfully;
Said he was a wolf, only the difference
Was, a wolf's skin was hairy on the outside,
His on the inside; bade them take their swords,
Rip up his flesh, and try: straight, I was sent for,
And having minister'd unto him, found his grace
Very well recover'd.

*Pes.* I am glad on't.

*Doc.* Yet not without some fear
Of a relapse.   If he grow to his fit again,
I'll go a nearer way to work with him
Than ever Paracelsus dream'd of; if
They'll give me leave, I'll buffet his madness out of him.
Stand aside; he comes.


*Enter* FERDINAND, MALATESTE, CARDINAL,
*and* BOSOLA.


*Ferd.* Leave me.

*Mal.* Why doth your lordship love this solitariness?

*Ferd.* Eagles commonly fly alone : they are crows,
Daws, and starlings that flock together.   Look,
What's that follows me?

*Mal.* Nothing, my lord.

*Ferd.* Yes.

*Mal.* 'Tis your shadow.

*Ferd.* Stay it ; let it not haunt me.

*Mal.* Impossible, if you move, and the sun shine.

*Ferd.* I will throttle it.[1]

*Mal.* O, my lord, you are angry with nothing.

*Ferd.* You are a fool :
How is't possible I should catch my shadow,
Unless I fall upon't? When I go to hell,
I mean to carry a bribe ; for, look you,
Good gifts evermore make way for the worst persons.

*Pes.* Rise, good my lord.

*Ferd.* I am studying the art of patience.

*Pes.* 'Tis a noble virtue.

*Ferd.* To drive six snails before me from this town
To Moscow ; neither use goad nor whip to them,
But let them take their own time;—(the patient'st man
        i'th' world
Match me for an experiment)—and I'll crawl
After like a sheep-biter.

*Card.* Force him up.

*Ferd.* Use me well, you were best.
What I have done, I have done : I'll confess nothing.

*Doc.* Now let me come to him.—Are you mad,

---

[1] *Throws himself on the ground.—Stage Direction,* in the
4to. of 1708.

My lord? are you out of your princely wits?

*Ferd.* What's he?

*Pes.* Your doctor.

*Ferd.* Let me have his beard sawed off,
And his eye-brows filed more civil.

   *Doc.* I must do mad tricks with him, for that's the
       only way on't.—I have brought
Your grace a salamander's skin, to keep you
From sun-burning.

   *Ferd.* I have cruel sore eyes.

   *Doc.* The white of a cockatrix's egg is present remedy.

   *Ferd.* Let it be a new-laid one, you were best.
Hide me from him : physicians are like kings,
They brook no contradiction.

   *Doc.* Now he begins to fear me:
Now let me alone with him.

   *Card.* How now? put off your gown!¹

   *Doc.* Let me have
Some forty urinals filled with rose-water :
He and I'll go pelt one another with them.—
Now he begins to fear me.—Can you fetch a frisk, sir?
Let him go, let him go upon my peril :
I find by his eye he stands in awe of me ;
I'll make him as tame as a dormouse.

   *Ferd.* Can you fetch your frisks, sir! I will stamp him
Into a cullis,
Flay off his skin, to cover one of the anatomies
This rogue hath set i'th' cold yonder
In Barber-Chirurgeon's-hall.

---

¹ *Puts off his four cloaks, one after another.—Stage Direction*
Ed. of 1708.

Hence, hence! you are all of you like beasts for sacrifice:
There's nothing left of you, but tongue and belly,
Flattery and lechery.[1]                                    [*Exit.*

    *Pes.* Doctor, he did not fear you throughly.

    *Doc.* True; I was somewhat too forward.

    *Bos.* Mercy upon me, what a fatal judgment
Hath fall'n upon this Ferdinand!

    *Pes.* Knows your grace
What accident hath brought unto the prince
This strange distraction?

    *Card.* I must feign somewhat:[2]—Thus they say it grew.
You have heard it rumour'd for these many years,
None of our family dies but there is seen
The shape of an old woman, which is given
By tradition to us to have been murder'd
By her nephews, for her riches.   Such a figure
One night, as the prince sat up late at's book,
Appear'd to him: when, crying out for help,
The gentleman of's chamber, found his grace
All on a cold sweat, alter'd much in face
And language: since which apparition,
He hath grown worse and worse, and I much fear
He cannot live.

    *Bos.* Sir, I would speak with you.

    *Pes.* We'll leave your grace,
Wishing to the sick prince, our noble lord,
All health of mind and body.

    *Card.* You are most welcome.

            [*Exeunt all but Cardinal and Bosola.*

---

[1] *Throws the Doctor down and beats him.—Stage Direction,*
Ed. of 1708.

[2] (Aside.)

Are you come? so.—This fellow must not know
By any means I had intelligence
In our duchess' death; for though I counsell'd it,
The full of all th' engagement seem'd to grow
From Ferdinand.—Now, sir, how fares our sister?
I do not think but sorrow makes her look
Like to an oft-dy'd garment: she shall now
Taste comfort from me.   Why do you look so wildly?
O, the fortune of your master here, the prince,
Dejects you; but be you of happy comfort:
If you'll do one thing for me, I'll entreat,
Though he had a cold tombstone o'er his bones,
I'd make you what you would be
   *Bos.* Anything,
Give it me in a breath, and let me fly to't:
They that think long, small expedition win,
For musing much o'th' end, cannot begin.

*Enter* JULIA.

   *Julia.* Sir, will you come in to supper?
   *Card.* I am busy; leave me.
   *Julia.* What an excellent shape hath that fellow!
                                    *[Exit.*
   *Card.* 'Tis thus.   Antonio lurks here in Milan:
Enquire him out, and kill him.   While he lives,
Our sister cannot marry, and I have thought
Of an excellent match for her.   Do this, and style me
Thy advancement
   *Bos.* But by what means shall I find him out?
   *Card.* There is a gentleman call'd Delio,
Here in the camp, that hath been long approv'd

His loyal friend.  Set eye upon that fellow;
Follow him to mass : maybe Antonio,
Although he do account religion
But a school-name, for fashion of the world
May accompany him ; or else go enquire out
Delio's confessor, and see if you can bribe
Him to reveal it.  There are a thousand ways
A man might find to trace him ; as to know
What fellows haunt the Jews, for taking up
Great sums of money, for sure he's in want ;
Or else to go to th' picture-makers, and learn
Who bought her picture lately : some of these
Happily[1] may take.

 *Bos.* Well, I'll not freeze i'th' business :
I would see that wretched thing, Antonio,
Above all sights i'th' world.

 *Card.* Do, and be happy.     *[Exit.*

 *Bos.* This fellow doth breed basilisks in's eyes,
He's nothing else but murder ; yet he seems
Not to have notice of the duchess' death.
'Tis his cunning : I must follow his example ;
There cannot be a surer way to trace
Than that of an old fox.

*Enter* Julia.

 *Julia.* So, sir, you are well met.
 *Bos.* How now ?
 *Julia.* Nay, the doors are fast enough :
Now, sir, I will make you confess your treachery.
 *Bos.* Treachery !

<hr>

[1] Perchance.

*Julia.* Yes, confess to me
Which of my women 'twas you hired to put
Love-powder into my drink ?
    *Bos.* Love-powder !
*Julia.* Yes, when I was at Malfi.
Why should I fall in love with such a face else ?
I have already suffer'd for thee so much pain,
The only remedy to do me good,
Is to kill my longing.
    *Bos.* Sure your pistol holds
Nothing but perfumes, or kissing-comfits. Excellent lady !
You have a pretty way on't to discover
Your longing.    Come, come, I'll disarm you,
And arm you thus : yet this is wondrous strange.
    *Julia.* Compare thy form and my eyes together,
You'll find my love no such great miracle. Now you'll say
I am wanton : this nice modesty in ladies
Is but a troublesome familiar
That haunts them.
    *Bos.* Know you me, I am a blunt soldier.
    *Julia.* The better ;
Sure, there wants fire, where there are no lively sparks
Of roughness.
    *Bos.* And I want compliment.
    *Julia.* Why, ignorance in courtship cannot make you
        do amiss,
If you have a heart to do well.
    *Bos.* You are very fair.
    *Julia.* Nay, if you lay beauty to my charge,
I must plead unguilty.
    *Bos.* Your bright eyes

Carry a quiver of darts in them, sharper
Than sun-beams.

 *Julia.* You will mar me with commendation,
Put yourself to the charge of courting me,
Whereas now I woo you.

 *Bos.* I have it ; I will work upon this creature.—
Let us grow most amorously familiar :
If the great cardinal should see me thus,
Would he not count me a villain ?

 *Julia.* No, he might count me a wanton,
Not lay a scruple of offence on you ;
For if I see, and steal a diamond,
The fault is not i'th' stone, but in me the thief
That purloins it.  I am sudden with you :
We that are great women of pleasure, use to cut off
These uncertain wishes and unquiet longings,
And in an instant join the sweet delight
And the pretty excuse together.  Had you been i'th'
  street,
Under my chamber window, even there
I should have courted you.

 *Bos.* O, you are an excellent lady !

 *Julia.* Bid me do somewhat for you presently,
To express I love you.

 *Bos.* I will, and if you love me,
Fail not to effect it.  The cardinal is grown wondrous
  melancholy :
Demand the cause, let him not put you off
With feign'd excuse ; discover the main ground on't.

 *Julia.* Why would you know this ?

 *Bos.* I have depended on him,

And I hear that he is fall'n in some disgrace
With the emperor; if he be, like the mice
That forsake falling houses, I would shift
To other dependance.

    *Julia.* You shall not need follow the wars:
I'll be your maintenance.

    *Bos.* And I your loyal servant;
But I cannot leave my calling.

    *Julia.* Not leave
An ungrateful general, for the love of a sweet lady!
You are like some cannot sleep in feather-beds,
But must have blocks for their pillows.

    *Bos.* Will you do this?

    *Julia.* Cunningly.

    *Bos.* To-morrow, I'll expect th' intelligence.

    *Julia.* To-morrow! get you into my cabinet;
You shall have it with you.  Do not delay me,
No more than I do you: I am like one
That is condemn'd; I have my pardon promis'd,
But I would see it seal'd.  Go, get you in:
You shall see me wind my tongue about his heart,
Like a skein of silk.          [*Exit Bosola.*


          *Enter* CARDINAL *and* SERVANTS.


    *Card.* Where are you?

    *Serv.* Here.

    *Card.* Let none, upon your lives
Have conference with the prince Ferdinand,
Unless I know it:—         [*Exeunt Servants.*[1]

      [1] An *exeunt* supplied by Mr. Dyce.

In this distraction, he may reveal the murder.
Yond's my lingering consumption :
I am weary of her, and by any means
Would be quit of.

 *Julia.* How now, my lord, what ails you?

 *Card.* Nothing.

 *Julia.* O, you are much alter'd !
Come, I must be your secretary, and remove
This lead from off your bosom: what's the matter?

 *Card.* I may not tell you.

 *Julia.* Are you so far in love with sorrow,
You cannot part with part of it? or think you
I cannot love your grace when you are sad
As well as merry? or do you suspect
I, that have been a secret to your heart
These many winters, cannot be the same
Unto your tongue?

 *Card.* Satisfy thy longing ;
The only way to make thee keep my counsel
Is, not to tell thee.

 *Julia.* Tell your echo this,
Or flatterers, that like echoes still report
What they hear though most imperfect, and not me ;
For, if that you be true unto yourself,
I'll know.

 *Card.* Will you rack me?

 *Julia.* No, judgment shall
Draw it from you : it is an equal fault,
To tell one's secrets unto all or none.

 *Card.* The first argues folly.

 *Julia.* But the last tyranny.

*Card.* Very well; why, imagine I have committed
Some secret deed, which I desire the world
May never hear of.

*Julia.* Therefore may not I know it?
You have conceal'd for me as great a sin
As adultery.   Sir, never was occasion
For perfect trial of my constancy
Till now : sir, I beseech you—

*Card.* You'll repent it.

*Julia.* Never.

*Card.* It hurries thee to ruin : I'll not tell thee.
Be well advis'd, and think what danger 'tis
To receive a prince's secrets : they that do,
Had need have their breasts hoop'd with adamant
To contain them.   I pray thee yet be satisfied;
Examine thine own frailty; 'tis more easy
To tie knots, than unloose them: 'tis a secret
That, like a lingering poison, may chance lie
Spread in thy veins, and kill thee seven year hence.

*Julia.* Now you dally with me.

*Card.* No more, thou shalt know it.
By my appointment, the great Duchess of Malfi,
And two of her young children, four nights since,
Were strangl'd.

*Julia.* O heaven ! sir, what have you done?

*Card.* How now ! how settles this? think you
Your bosom will be a grave dark and obscure enough
For such a secret?

*Julia.* You have undone yourself, sir.

*Card.* Why?

*Julia.* It lies not in me to conceal it.

*Card.* No! Come, I will swear you to't upon this
    book.
*Julia.* Most religiously.
*Card.* Kiss it.
Now you shall never utter it; thy curiosity
Hath undone thee: thou art poison'd with that book;
Because I knew thou couldst not keep my counsel,
I have bound thee to't by death.

*Enter* BOSOLA.

*Bos.* For pity sake, hold.
*Card.* Ha, Bosola!
*Julia.* I forgive you
This equal piece of justice you have done;
For I betray'd your counsel to that fellow:
He overheard it; that was the cause I said
It lay not in me to conceal it.
    *Bos.* O, foolish woman,
Couldst not thou have poison'd him?
    *Julia.* 'Tis weakness,
Too much to think what should have been done.
I go, I know not whither.         [*Dies.*
    *Card.* Wherefore com'st thou hither?
    *Bos.* That I might find a great man, like yourself,
Not out of his wits, as the Lord Ferdinand,
To remember my service.
    *Card.* I'll have thee hew'd in pieces.
    *Bos.* Make not yourself such a promise of that life,
Which is not yours to dispose of.
    *Card.* Who plac'd thee here?
    *Bos.* Her lust, as she intended.

*Card.* Very well: now you know me
For your fellow-murderer.

*Bos.* And wherefore should you lay fair marble colours
Upon your rotten purposes to me?
Unless you imitate some that do plot great treasons,
And when they have done, go hide themselves i'th
      graves
Of those were actors in't?

*Card.* No more;
There is a fortune attends thee.

*Bos.* Shall I go sue to fortune any longer?
'Tis the fool's pilgrimage.

*Card.* I have honours in store for thee.

*Bos.* There are a many ways that conduct to seeming
Honour, and some of them very dirty ones.

*Card.* Throw to the devil
Thy melancholy.  The fire burns well;
What need we keep a stirring of't, and make
A greater smother? thou wilt kill Antonio?

*Bos.* Yes.

*Card.* Take up that body.

*Bos.* I think I shall
Shortly grow the common bier for church-yards.

*Card.* I will allow thee some dozen of attendants,
To aid thee in the murder.

*Bos.* O, by no means.
Physicians that apply horseleeches to any rank swelling,
Use to cut off their tails, that the blood may run through
      them
The faster: let me have no train when I go to shed blood,
Lest it make me have a greater when I ride to the gal-
      lows.

*Card.* Come to me after midnight, to help to remove
that body
To her own lodging: I'll give out she died o'th' plague;
'Twill breed the less enquiry after her death.

*Bos.* Where's Castruccio, her husband?

*Card.* He's rode to Naples, to take possession
Of Antonio's citadel.

*Bos.* Believe me, you have done a very happy turn.

*Card.* Fail not to come: there is the master-key
Of our lodgings; and by that you may conceive
What trust I plant in you.

*Bos.* You shall find me ready.  [*Exit Cardinal.*
O, poor Antonio, though nothing be so needful
To thy estate, as pity, yet I find
Nothing so dangerous!  I must look to my footing:
In such slippery ice-pavements, men had need
To be frost-nail'd well, they may break their necks else;
The precedent's here afore me.  How this man
Bears up in blood! seems fearless! why, 'tis well:
Security some men call the suburbs of hell,
Only a dead wall between.  Well, good Antonio,
I'll seek thee out; and all my care shall be
To put thee into safety from the reach
Of these most cruel biters, that have got
Some of thy blood already.  It may be,
I'll join with thee, in a most just revenge:
The weakest arm is strong enough, that strikes
With the sword of justice.  Still methinks the duchess
Haunts me: there, there!—'tis nothing but my melan-
choly.
O Penitence, let me truly taste thy cup,
That throws men down, only to raise them up!  [*Exit.*

## SCENE III.

*Enter* ANTONIO *and* DELIO.

*Delio.* Yond's the cardinal's window.  This fortifica-
   tion
Grew from the ruins of an ancient abbey ;
And to yond' side o'th' river lies a wall,
Piece of a cloister, which in my opinion
Gives the best echo that you ever heard,
So hollow and so dismal, and withal
So plain in the distinction of our words,
That many have suppos'd it is a spirit
That answers.
   *Ant.* I do love these ancient ruins.
We never tread upon them, but we set
Our foot upon some reverend history :
And, questionless, here in this open court,
Which now lies naked to the injuries
Of stormy weather, some men lie interr'd
Lov'd the church so well, and gave so largely to't,
They thought it should have canopied their bones
Till doom's-day ; but all things have their end :
Churches and cities, which have diseases like to men,
Must have like death that we have.
   *Echo (from the Duchess' grave). Like death that we
      have.*
   *Delio.* Now the echo hath caught you.
   *Ant.* It groan'd, methought, and gave
A very deadly accent.
   *Echo. Deadly accent.*

*Delio.* I told you 'twas a pretty one : you may make it

A huntsman, or a falconer, a musician,
Or a thing of sorrow.

*Echo. A thing of sorrow.*

*Ant.* Ay sure, that suits it best.

*Echo. That suits it best.*

*Ant.* 'Tis very like my wife's voice.

*Echo. Ay, wife's voice.*

*Delio.* Come, let us walk farther from't.
I would not have you go to th' cardinal's to-night :
Do not.

*Echo. Do not.*

*Delio.* Wisdom doth not more moderate wasting sorrow,

Than time : take time for't ; be mindful of thy safety.

*Echo. Be mindful of thy safety.*

*Ant.* Necessity compels me :
Make scrutiny throughout the passes
Of your own life, you'll find it impossible
To fly your fate.

*Echo. O fly your fate !*

*Delio.* Hark ! the dead stones seem to have pity on you,
And give you good counsel.

*Ant.* Echo, I will not talk with thee,
For thou art a dead thing.

*Echo. Thou art a dead thing.*

*Ant.* My duchess is a-sleep now,
And her little ones, I hope sweetly : O heaven,
Shall I never see her more ?

*Echo. Never see her more.*

*Ant.* I mark'd not one repetition of the echo
But that ; and on the sudden, a clear light

Presented me a face folded in sorrow.

*Delio.* Your fancy merely.

*Ant.* Come, I'll be out of this ague,
For to live thus, is not indeed to live;
It is a mockery and abuse of life:
I will not henceforth save myself by halves;
Lose all, or nothing.

*Delio.* Your own virtue save you!
I'll fetch your eldest son, and second you:
It may be that the sight of his own blood
Spread in so sweet a figure, may beget
The more compassion.
However, fare you well.
Though in our miseries fortune have a part,
Yet in our noble sufferings she hath none;
Contempt of pain, that we may call our own. [*Exeunt.*

## SCENE IV.

*Enter* CARDINAL, PESCARA, MALATESTE,
RODERIGO, GRISOLAN.

*Card.* You shall not watch to-night by the sick prince;
His grace is very well recover'd.

*Mal.* Good, my lord, suffer us.

*Card.* O, by no means:
The noise and change of object in his eye
Doth more distract him: I pray, all to bed;
And though you hear him in his violent fit,
Do not rise, I entreat you.

*Pes.* So, sir; we shall not.

*Card.* Nay, I must have you promise
Upon your honours, for I was enjoin'd to't
By himself; and he seem'd to urge it sensibly.
   *Pes.* Let our honours bind this trifle.
   *Card.* Nor any of your followers.
   *Mal.* Neither.
   *Card.* It may be, to make trial of your promise,
When he's asleep, myself will rise and feign
Some of his mad tricks, and cry out for help,
And feign myself in danger.
   *Mal.* If your throat were cutting, .-
I'd not come at you, now I have protested against it.
   *Card.* Why, I thank you.
   *Gris.* 'Twas a foul storm to-night.
   *Rod.* The Lord Ferdinand's chamber shook like an
      osier.
   *Mal.* 'Twas nothing but pure kindness in the devil,
To rock his own child.   [*Exeunt all but the Cardinal.*
   *Card.* The reason why I would not suffer these
About my brother, is, because at midnight
I may with better privacy convey
Julia's body to her own lodging.  O, my conscience!
I would pray now; but the devil takes away my heart
For having any confidence in prayer.
About this hour I appointed Bosola
To fetch the body: when he hath served my turn,
He dies.                        [*Exit.*

*Enter* BOSOLA.

   *Bos.* Ha! 'twas the cardinal's voice; I heard him name
Bosola, and my death: listen, I hear one's footing.

*Enter* FERDINAND.

*Ferd.* Strangling is a very quiet death.

*Bos.* Nay then, I see I must stand upon my guard.

*Ferd.* What say to that? whisper softly; do you
   agree to't?
So, it must be done i'th' dark; the cardinal
Would not for a thousand pounds the doctor should see
   it.                                    [*Exit.*

*Bos.* My death is plotted; here's the consequence of
   murder.
We value not desert nor Christian breath,
When we know black deeds must be cur'd with death.

*Enter* SERVANT *and* ANTONIO.

*Serv.* Here stay, sir, and be confident, I pray:
I'll fetch you a dark lantern.                  [*Exit.*

*Ant.* Could I take him at his prayers,
There were hope of pardon.

*Bos.* Fall right my sword:
I'll not give thee so much leisure as to pray.[1]

*Ant.* O, I am gone! Thou hast ended a long suit
In a minute.

*Bos.* What art thou?

*Ant.* A most wretched thing,
That only have the benefit in death,
To appear myself.

*Enter* SERVANT *with a light.*

*Serv.* Where are you, sir?

-----
[1] Stabs Antonio, supposing him to be the Cardinal.

*Ant.* Very near my home.—Bosola !

*Serv.* O, misfortune !

*Bos.* Smother thy pity, thou art dead else.—Antonio!
The man I would have sav'd 'bove mine own life !
We are merely the stars' tennis-balls, struck and banded
Which way please them.   O good Antonio,
I'll whisper one thing in thy dying ear,
Shall make thy heart break quickly ! thy fair duchess
And two sweet children——

*Ant.* Their very names
Kindle a little life in me.

*Bos.* Are murder'd.

*Ant.* Some men have wish'd to die
At the hearing of sad tidings ; I am glad
That I shall do't in sadness : I would not now
Wish my wounds balm'd nor heal'd, for I have no use
To put my life to.   In all our quest of greatness,
Like wanton boys, whose pastime is their care,
We follow after bubbles blown in th' air.
Pleasure of life, what is't ? only the good hours
Of an ague ; merely a preparative to rest,
To endure vexation.   I do not ask
The process of my death ; only commend me
To Delio.

*Bos.* Break, heart !

*Ant.* And let my son fly the courts of princes. [*Dies.*

*Bos.* Thou seem'st to have lov'd Antonio ?

*Serv.* I brought him hither,
To have reconcil'd him to the Cardinal.

*Bos.* I do not ask thee that :
Take him up, if thou tender thy own life,

And bear him where the lady Julia
Was wont to lodge.—O my fate moves swift!
I have this cardinal in the forge already,
Now I'll bring him to th' hammer.   O direful mis-
      prision ! [1]
I will not imitate things glorious,
No more than base ; I'll be mine own example.—
On, on, and look thou represent, for silence,
The thing thou bear'st.[2]         *[Exeunt.*

## SCENE V.

*Enter* CARDINAL, *with a book.*

*Card.* I am puzzled in a question about hell :
He says, in hell there's one material fire,
And yet it shall not burn all men alike.
Lay him by.   How tedious is a guilty conscience !
When I look into the fish-ponds in my garden,
Methinks I see a thing arm'd with a rake,
That seems to strike at me.—Now, art thou come ?
      thou look'st ghastly ;
There sits in thy face some great determination,
Mix'd with some fear.

*Enter* BOSOLA *and the* SERVANT.

*Bos.* Thus it lightens into action :
I am come to kill thee.
    *Card.* Ha ! help ! our guard !

---

[1] Mistake from the French *méprise.*
[2] Be as silent as the dead body thou bearest.

*Bos.* Thou art deceiv'd ;
They are out of thy howling.
   *Card.* Hold ; and I will faithfully divide
Revenues with thee.
   *Bos.* Thy prayers and proffers
Are both unseasonable.
   *Card.* Raise the watch ! we are betray'd.
   *Bos.* I have confin'd your flight :
I'll suffer your retreat to Julia's chamber,
But no further.
   *Card.* Help ! we are betray'd.

      *Enter* MALATESTE, PESCARA, RODERIGO,
        *and* GRISOLAN, *above.*[1]

   *Mal.* Listen.
   *Card.* My dukedom for rescue !
   *Rod.* Fie upon his counterfeiting.
   *Mal.* Why, 'tis not the Cardinal.
   *Rod.* Yes, yes, 'tis he :
But I'll see him hang'd ere I'll go down to him.
   *Card.* Here's a plot upon me ; I am assaulted ! I am
      lost
Unless some rescue !
   *Gris.* He doth this pretty well ;
But it will not serve to laugh me out of mine honour.
   *Card.* The sword's at my throat !
   *Rod.* You would not bawl so loud then.
   *Mal.* Come, come, let's go to bed : he told us thus
      much aforehand.

   [1] *Above,* i. e. on the upper stage ; the raised platform towards the back of the stage.—DYCE.

*Pes.* He wish'd you should not come at him ; but believe't,
The accent of the voice sounds not in jest :
I'll down to him, howsoever, and with engines
Force ope the doors.    *[Exit.*

*Rod.* Let's follow him aloof,
And note how the Cardinal will laugh at him.

> *[Exeunt, above, Malateste, Roderigo, and Grisolan.*

*Bos.* There's for you first,
'Cause you shall not unbarricade the door
To let in rescue.    *[He kills the Servant.*

*Card.* What cause hast thou to pursue my life ?

*Bos.* Look there.

*Card.* Antonio !

*Bos.* Slain by my hand unwittingly :
Pray, and be sudden : when thou kill'd'st thy sister,
Thou took'st from justice her most equal balance,
And left her nought but her sword.

*Card.* O mercy !

*Bos.* Now it seems thy greatness was only outward ;
For thou fall'st faster of thyself, than calamity
Can drive thee : I'll not waste longer time ; there.

> *[Stabs him.*

*Card.* Thou hast hurt me.

*Bos.* Again.

*Card.* Shall I die like a leveret,
Without any resistance ?   Help, help, help !
I am slain.

*Enter* FERDINAND.

*Ferd.* Th' alarum ! give me a fresh horse ;
Rally the vaunt-guard,[1] or the day is lost.
Yield, yield : I give you the honours of arms,
Shake my sword over you ; will you yield ?
    *Card.* Help me, I am your brother !
    *Ferd.* The devil ! my brother fight upon the adverse
      party ! [*He wounds the Cardinal, and (in the scuffle)*
                   *gives Bosola his death wound.*
There flies your ransom.
    *Card.* O justice !
I suffer now for what hath former bin :[2]
Sorrow is held the eldest child of sin.
    *Ferd.* Now you're brave fellows.
Cæsar's fortune was harder than Pompey's ;
Cæsar died in the arms of prosperity,
Pompey at the feet of disgrace.
You both died in the field.
The pain's nothing : pain many times is taken away with
The apprehension of greater, as the tooth-ache with the
      sight
Of a barber that comes to pull it out : there's philosophy
      for you.
    *Bos.* Now my revenge is perfect.  Sink, thou main
      cause               [*He stabs Ferdinand.*
Of my undoing.  The last part of my life
Hath done me best service.

---

[1] The vanguard.
[2] So in the original, and retained for the sake of the rhyme.

*Ferd.* Give me some wet hay, I am broken-winded.
I do account this world but a dog-kennel :
I will vault credit and affect high pleasures,
Beyond death.

    *Bos.* He seems to come to himself, now he's so near
        the bottom.

    *Ferd.* My sister, O my sister ! there's the cause on't.
Whether we fall by ambition, blood, or lust,
Like diamonds, we are cut with our own dust. [*Dies.*

    *Card.* Thou hast thy payment too.

    *Bos.* Yes, I hold my weary soul in my teeth ;
'Tis ready to part from me.   I do glory
That thou, which stood'st like a huge pyramid
Begun upon a large and ample base,
Shalt end in a little point, a kind of nothing.

*Enter* PESCARA *and the others.*

    *Pes.* How now, my lord !

    *Mal.* O, sad disaster !

    *Rod.* How comes this ?

    *Bos.* Revenge for the Duchess of Malfi, murder'd
By the Arragonian brethren ; for Antonio,
Slain by this hand ; for lustful Julia,
Poison'd by this man ; and lastly for myself,
That was an actor in the main of all
Much 'gainst mine own good nature, yet i'th' end
Neglected.

    *Pes.* How now, my lord !

    *Card.* Look to my brother :
He gave us these large wounds, as we were struggling

Here i'th' rushes.[1]   And now, I pray, let me
Be laid by and never thought of.                    [*Dies.*

   *Pes.* How fatally, it seems, he did withstand
His own rescue !

   *Mal.* Thou wretched thing of blood,
How came Antonio by his death ?

   *Bos.* In a mist : I know not how :
Such a mistake as I have often seen
In a play.   O, I am gone !
We are only like dead walls, or vaulted graves,
That ruin'd, yield no echo.   Fare you well.
It may be pain, but no harm to me to die,
In so good a quarrel.   O, this gloomy world !
In what a shadow, or deep pit of darkness,
Doth womanish and fearful mankind live !
Let worthy minds ne'er stagger in distrust
To suffer death or shame for what is just :
Mine is another voyage.                    [*Dies.*

   *Pes.* The noble Delio, as I came to th' palace,
Told me of Antonio's being here, and shew'd me
A pretty gentleman, his son and heir.


*Enter* DELIO, *and Antonio's* SON.


   *Mal.* O sir, you come too late !
   *Delio.* I heard so, and
Was arm'd for't, ere I came.   Let us make noble use
Of this great ruin ; and join all our force
To establish this young hopeful gentleman

---

[1] i. e. on the rushes that then covered the floor, in lieu of
a carpet.

In's mother's right.   These wretched eminent things
Leave no more fame behind 'em, than should one
Fall in a frost, and leave his print in snow :
As soon as the sun shines, it ever melts,
Both form and matter.   I have ever thought
Nature doth nothing so great for great men,
As when she's pleas'd to make them lords of truth :
Integrity of life is fame's best friend,
Which nobly, beyond death, shall crown the end.

END OF VOL. II.

PRIORY PRESS :

PRINTED BY JAMES BELL, ST. JOHN SQUARE, LONDON, E.C.